Stealing From Bandits

A Novel
By

Al W. Moe

Puget Sound Books

Also by Al W. Moe
&
Puget Sound Books

Nevada's Golden Age of Gambling

Stealing From Bandits

Published by Puget Sound Books

This is a work of fiction. Names, characters, places, and incidents either are products of the author's imagination, or are used fictitiously. Any resemblance to actual events or locales or persons, living or dead, is entirely coincidental.

Copyright ©2002 by Al W. Moe

All rights reserved under International and Pan-American Copyright Conventions. Portions may be reproduced for review purposes only. For more information: Puget Sound Books; P. O. Box 2018; Angel Fire, NM 87710

Visit our website at:
www.pugetsoundbooks.com

Library of Congress Catalog Card Number: 2002190015

ISBN: 0-9715019-1-2

Manufactured In Canada

Cover Design by Lin Shih at Stonepatch Design
www.stonepatch.com

To my wife
Shannon
Who can not be described
By even my most Tender Words

&

To the Daughters III
Brienne Carly Lauren

Inspiration Intuition Individualism

Stealing From Bandits

Chapter One

There was a brief chirp from the brakes before three-thousand pounds of lumbering steel entered the crosswalk being used slowly, ever so slowly with rum-n-coke legs by Teddy Ryan, who found his 200-pound frame launched into a circus-act of tumbling, turning and twisting that ended when his body came into abrupt contact with a high concrete curb, his head wrenched backwards and face contorted with pain. He had looked better.

A moment before, it had been an easy walk across Virginia Street from the Pioneer Casino. He and his date left the club holding hands as Teddy stared across the street at the columns of neon-light that surrounded each casino, leaving rainbows in his liquored eyes and the never-ending promise of gold in a pot at the journey's end.

Teddy never imagined the cool morning air would unleash a stalking, steel animal capable of taking his life, but as the car's driver released the brake and the vehicle moved slowly forward, Teddy's face took-on a final, slack-jawed look of confusion before his breath turned milky-white and covered him in a shroud of death.

Inside the car, insulated from Teddy's final, moist breath, the driver leaned towards the dash and viewed the crumpled body sprawled along the dry gutter. He shook his head, then drove away visibly upset. He had lost a headlight.

Slowly shrinking down to insignificant proportions in his rearview mirror, the driver watched the young lady who had accompanied Teddy in the crosswalk. He couldn't hear the blood racing through her veins as it acquired adrenalin and surged back to her heart.

Her breath came in gasps of the now frigid air, and tears welled-up in her young eyes. Into the Reno night those very eyes searched in vain for a witness. Shimmering-up from the crosswalk was a sea of nickels and her now empty slot machine coin cup.

Plucking the cup from the asphalt, she turned on her heel and sent her long legs into motion away from the downtown casino area. There was no need to look back, the night was over.

Chapter Two

      Kevin Webb looked intently at the typed page in his hand. Each key had crushed its weight against the snowy canvas leaving a bold impression surrounded by a tiny splash of ink. Every letter was a necessary part of a word, and each word part of a group. Together they had meaning. For a moment, he too was part of a group, and he wondered about his role in the story while waiting for the paragraph to end.
      The Royal Casino's motivational speaker was being quietly ignored by several dozen people and Kevin generously returned his focus to Stan's words that spewed-out into the crowd before collapsing under their own weight like so many lumps of wet clay.
      "Fran here has done a terrific job, and I'm as proud of her as I am of all of you. I know that if something happens down on the casino floor you will see it, and take appropriate action. Crossroaders beware! We have the finest surveillance team in town, and that is why we pay you more than any other club. That is also why we expect the most from you, and you, and you," Stan said. As he finished his diatribe, a fat finger somehow escaped the sleeve of his pea-green sports coat and pointed menacingly at the semi-conscience group.
      Kevin folded his one-page manuscript and replaced it in the pocket of his battered leather jacket. His hand haunted the pocket once more, long fingers lingering, then thrusting forward and capturing a small, frayed paper with well-worn creases. Betraying his quarry to the harsh light he cursed its bluntness.
      There was a whimper, not a bang, and the meeting succumbed to the inevitable. The din of footsteps reverberated off the walls as the attendees quickly turned the room into an empty shell, leaving Kevin behind. He held his paper, starring at the final lines and wondering how he would pay Tolan the nearly twenty-thousand dollars his account had swelled to, then folded the paper yet again and placed it gently into his jacket. His knee's creaked as he stood and joined the stragglers in the group as they made their way to the door with their scuffling, thumping shoes sounding like an army. And so they were.
      A casino hires an army of spies to maintain their cameras. Every performance of

the day or night is swallowed-up through the lenses of these invisible demons and viewed by their captives in small, dim rooms. The larger the casino, the larger the army, because casinos are voracious eaters, and only proper feeding can keep them alive. They live, eat and breath money, and still their hunger burns.

Owners constantly worry that those they have standing the long vigil over their money might fail, so the list is long. Dealers do their best, and are watched by floor supervisors. The supervisors are watched by pit bosses who in turn are questioned by shift supervisors. The casino manager tries to oversee the whole affair, and if all else fails, there is always the eye-in-the-sky.

The sky' carries no weapon but the common phone, and divulges only the secrets that the ear on the other end needs to hear. They answer only to the owner. They are an electric wire, energy running from their humble catwalk to every corner of the casino. They are not omnipotent, just omnipresent.

Kevin felt nothing grand about his job as he emerged from the portals of work and pushed himself past the casino's glass doors. A small groan escaped his lips as his size twelve shoes attacked the last few stairs towards the parking lot. The late afternoon sun played tag with the clouds, leaving him in shadow and causing the search for his car to become a game of mouse and memory.

At this time of day, the wind delighted in twisting along the inside of the hotel grounds, gaining speed and enthusiasm as it swept along the employee area of the parking lot. A fast moving candy-wrapper passed Kevin twice, and beyond the Royal casino, Mount Rose showed movement of its own.

The clouds swept-in, tripping over the high mountains and spilling themselves out above Reno. Along the foothills, shadows danced between the tall pines and houses. Searching his mind, as well as the lot, Kevin looked for the small MG buried somewhere amongst the *real* cars. There was a strange thought rattling around the recesses of his mind. He tried as always to keep it repressed, but it banged away and gave him no peace. In the instant it took to recognize his car, the thought made its way to the forefront; a simple notion of life taking a back seat to sanity. His backseat was empty, and a trip from sanity would be a short one indeed. Somewhere there had been a wrong turn. Surely *his* life merited more than a "nine to five", and a microwave dinner alone.

As time passed, the line between Kevin's success and failure drew-out like a bad dream. Often just a razor's edge, the blade was sharp, and cut both ways. Those who have success get bloody along the way too, but their wounds heal quickly. For those on Kevin's side, healing was a slow process, if it came at all.

The car was unlocked, and the short ride home uneventful. Pulling into his apartment complex he waved at the guard, Bob.

"All right, my job sucks, but that guy really has it tough! At least I work in a real building, not some tiny shack," Kevin thought.

He drove-on past the gray buildings, one looking like another. People from all walks of life, thrown together, but still so far apart. Each home had a connecting wall, and neighbors that were close enough to hear at the most inopportune times, but the chances of ever knowing those people was slight. Walls. Put 'em up, keep everybody apart. It was a great name. *Apartments*.

The "battleship-gray" color reminding Kevin of the "moth-ball" fleet below the Benicia bridge where his father once took him to fish. They went to the steel-blue waters of the Suisun Bay for excitement, but often landed only anxiety. Still, Northern California and the cool, deep waters of the sloughs had a pull on him.

There was something mysterious and scary about the tides that rippled around those dying ships and their moaning sounds set against the quiet of the early morning as waves drummed against the steel hulls. The US Navy moored dozens of the hulking dinosaurs along the inlet to Sacramento, and from those waters came the prehistoric sturgeon, often in the hundred-pound range. Landing one in your small craft was tough, and the fear of being capsized in those dark, teeming waters weighed heavily upon Kevin's young mind. Sometimes the fish escaped, but the fight was what it was all about.

He missed the time alone with his father. They didn't talk much anymore, being so many miles away. When they fished, they had talked lightly of inconsequential things, but they were together. Wasn't that what mattered? Didn't that count, even if he had seen that disappointed look in his father's eyes slip out while the smile remained?

Kevin remembered in anguish a single event, or not so much the event as his father's face after one of the ancient fish had snapped Kevin's line. At the age of fourteen, he took it as the end of the fight, the loss of the fish. But as he grew older and the look came again, he knew it was based on what his father perceived as weakness. Kevin had been shouting in both fear and excitement as he tried to land the huge fish, but fear won-out. He was never as strong as his father.

Approaching his building, Kevin cursed the small, blue Honda Civic in his space. "She probably can't even read the numbers," he thought.

The accursed owner happened to walk out of her apartment as Kevin stepped from his car.

"Hi, Kelvin," she cooed.

"Hi, Melanie," he forced from his constricting throat. She waved a tan arm and leapt into her car.

"I guess that explains why she can't get my name right, she's a bird brain."

He managed a small chuckle while ascending the eleven concrete steps to his porch, then stopped and looked back at the hard and menacing sky. It would be hours before the sun walked down the other side of the mountains, but darkness was coming quickly.

It was all a prank of Mother Nature's doing, for not a drop of rain would fall on the parched town tonight. It was only May, and the rains that came this time of year were disappointing. Reno lives on the run-off of winter snow, not the illusive mist of the summer season with its choking smell and the dusty film it leaves on the cars.

Inside the apartment, heavy drapes kept the lowering rays of the sun out, but eyes and memory worked together to sort-out the picture of the sparsely furnished room. A red glow foretold the arrival of a phone message. Pressing the play-button, Kevin heard the canned voice announce, "You have one message".

"No kidding, how 'bout letting me know what it is?" Kevin asked of the air while affecting a country drawl.

He flipped the light switch in the kitchen, announcing his arrival to the emptiness.

"Good morning, this message is for Kevin Webb. Please call Detective Paul Kozar at the Reno Police Department." The message continued as the woman messenger delivered the request in a dispassionate monotone. The words hung in the air, but Kevin missed the number and had to run the tape a second time.

Chapter Three

Kevin cradled his phone and dutifully called the number of the RPD detectives unit, but Paul Kozar had gone home for the day. He dialed him at home, then checked the number in his address book while the phone rang and rang.

"Hi, Becky, it's Kevin. Is your no-good husband home, or is he off with his secretary?"

For some reason Kevin could not fathom, she didn't seem to like him.

"Sure," she said with a slight heave in her voice, "Paul is home, hold on."

When Paul got on the line he was out of breath. Probably not the best time to make a joke about his secretary.

"What's up buddy?"

"Hey, I'm returning your call, remember?"

"Right, right. I thought we could get in at least nine-holes. I made a tee time for six o'clock. You want to meet me at Reno muni. in about a half-hour?"

"Sounds good, see you then."

Paul would be running out of the house soon. No wonder Becky was always mad at Kevin. The phone was his friend, and her foe. He had to be available at all hours to his job, and therefore he wasn't available at all hours for her. Never marry a cop.

Kevin hung up the phone and smiled. Overtime from today's meeting would pay for golf, and that would help. The course was usually full in the afternoon, but a late start like tonight would be easy to walk-on without a tee time.

There was time for a snack of turkey and ham on dry toast, no Mayo, and crumbs everywhere. His customary "Seven-Up" helped wash it down. There was still pride to be taken in his appearance. Not that he could sprint up and down the tennis court like he used to, but he kept in shape. Golf was no great workout, but still better than sitting around the house. The house, the house, the house. All axioms are not true. His house was no longer actually his, and his apartment was not a home.

Heading out to the course, a few notes from the meeting invaded his thoughts. Drifting in and out, maybe there *were* a few good points that Stan had brought up. Sometimes, the casino just seemed to miss the obvious. Gaming is a social interaction for most players, but they also want instant gratification. That even applied to the people that Kevin was paid to watch-out for.

Cheats enjoy the old game of cat and mouse. They weren't just there to make a few bucks. It was fun to "take-off" the club. Well, maybe the slot cheats *were* there just to make money. The days of a slot cheat drilling the side of the machine and manipulating the reels with a coat hanger have passed. The crooks and scam artists are a lot more sophisticated today.

It was no more than five minutes after arriving at the putting green that Paul walked up with his clubs, housed inside his "MGM" logo'ed bag.

He strutted over and his six-foot four frame blocked-out Kevin's line of sight to the practice hole.

"Hey, I thought you were getting rid of your old bag."

"What, and be single, like you?"

"Not your wife, bone-head. Your golf bag."

"Yeah-yeah, I know, oldest bag on the course. How are ya, Kevin?" Paul asked while giving him that "steely-eyed" look of his.

"Great, just great. Any better, and you'd have to arrest me for having a life."

"Hey, I'm the cop with the deep-seated Freudian problems, okay?"

Kevin nodded in agreement and closed an eye as the sun peeked-out from behind a cloud. "Ah, sorry about calling at a bad time and joking about your secretary. Becky really doesn't like me anymore, does she?"

"She may be coming around," Paul stated in a confident tone while brushing some blond hairs from his forehead. "Even suggested setting you up with a friend of hers, Karen Cannon."

"Forget it! I seem to remember a Karen from a couple years ago, and she looked like my uncle Ray."

"Not *that* Karen, this one owns Grayson's Jewelers. Remember a few months back when they had a robbery?"

"No, I don't keep up on the latest robberies and murders. I have a safe job. You know, in my little box."

"Right. Anyway, Becky's known her for years, and after the robbery she found a good group for her at the clinic. Nice lady," Paul stated, while tilting his head forward and giving Kevin that furled-brow look as only a cop can. "She's a good cook, and even has some money. Not like those ex-wives of yours."

"Bull-shit, both my ex-wives have money. I know, it used to be mine! Enough small talk, how much are we betting?"

"I'll give you two strokes on the front nine, and five on the round if we can get in the whole eighteen," said Paul.

"Fair enough, it's tee time, no puns intended. We usually play at four, tee time, *fair* enough, oh never mind. I already paid for us."

Paul raised an eyebrow and said, "Great."

"Shall we say $5 per bet, or will that put you over-budget with the little lady when I beat you?"

"Gee, I sure don't know why Becky would have any feelings of hostility towards you, Kevin."

Paul had been a good student, and star athlete at Reno High, and still looked like a football player with his wide chest and shoulders, but he had no interest in pursuing any more sports in college. Only interested in police work, he was riding around in cop cars at eighteen and became a detective when he got out of the University of Nevada at Reno.

Kevin remembered the first time he had seen him in a uniform after they were at the university. Before going to work in plain clothes he looked like a poster boy for the police academy with his boyish grin and straight hair. Well, he wasn't going to be working undercover in narcotics, that was for sure.

Before Paul blasted his first shot into the sagebrush, their two-some became a four-some as Paul's Captain, Ron Packard, waddled up to the tee. He was talking, but Kevin could barely tell where the sound was coming from. His mustache was so long, you couldn't see his lips move. He would have fit right into a Zane Gray novel, the gruff old sheriff that nobody ever messed with. The last thing Kevin wanted was to play golf with him. He was always suspicious, but at the same time, seemed to be working an angle of his own. And, he never had anything nice to say to Kevin. The other officer, Cory, had even less to say than Packard. Just a guy with one big eyebrow across his forehead.

After three holes the Captain had spent more time in the sand than a family at the beach, and the sun was racing from the moon. At the next tee-box, Packard's mustache twitched next to Paul's ear, "I know you're working hard, but I'm going to add the Vellardi file to your cases. Meyer is aware that Richardson can't handle it, so it's yours."

Kevin turned and looked away from their conversation, unsure whether Packard had intended for him to hear or not. Vellardi's picture had been in the newspaper a few months back during an investigation into questionable campaign financing in New York.

Packard knew what Kevin did for a living, and that made him a lower form of life. Less than a police officer, less than a security officer. Less. Kevin didn't tell many people about his job. Big deal, what difference did it make. The police didn't have a lot to do with the casinos. The Gaming Control Board was the boss in Nevada, but even they could tell people what they did for a living. That old feeling of being a "non-person" crept back into Kevin's mind. He fought it, pushing it back to the recesses of his consciousness where it hung-on like the final leaf on a tree, swaying and defying nature.

"What the hell are you waiting for, a personal invitation?" cried Packard.

"Sorry guys, I was just thinking."

"Well, don't go trying to work without any tools."

"Thanks for your input, Buick. ..."

"Come-on Kevin," said Paul. "Put that little ball in flight and let's get on with the hole before it gets dark."

"Okay, I predict that I reach the green on this par five in just two strokes!"

Laughter immediately followed Kevin's statement. The putter he still held in his hand from the last green just wasn't going to do the job. "Where the hell is my mind today?" Kevin wondered. He tipped his hat to the peanut gallery and let his straight black hair wave in the breeze. It felt good, and he didn't even mind seeing a few gray hairs on the brim as he stuffed the cap into his bag and played without it the rest of the evening.

After a less than stellar round of golf, Kevin headed home.

"That was a quick sixty-bucks. What the hell am I doing picking up the green fees for Paul and myself anyway? I'm not rich anymore," he said, slightly disgusted.

Kevin thought about his last statement as it echoed in his head. He'd never been rich, but having the things he wanted did make him *feel* that way once. Now it was a fight just to keep ahead of the bill collectors. Child support and old bills were eating up most of his cash. Fortunately, his "friends" had been nice about carrying him on the money he owed. They wouldn't wait forever. Friends in Reno like Tolan don't like to wait for their money.

Kevin waved again at Bob, then turned towards his building. "Wow, my space is even available," he intoned, refusing to acknowledge the color of the buildings. Heading up to his one-bedroom apartment, he decided to spend the rest of the evening doing some electronics work.

A little soldering and he could get another "ears-three" going. It was a good way to pass the time. For twenty bucks, he could buy a ready-made receiver that worked almost as well, but there was no challenge in that. His work was good, and it made the night go by.

Before settling in, he made the phone call.

"Hey, Tolan, it's Kevin." The other end was silent, and Kevin twisted in his chair. "Listen, I know I'm getting really overdue, but things have been slow. I haven't been able to make any extra money."

There was a long pause before a voice finally slithered into Kevin's ear.

"No problem, just pay me before anything else next week. I don't want to have to send any friends over, and you're approaching twenty-large. We go back, but don't make me wait too long." The voice was calm and disarming. Cold.

"I'm gon'na have something for you next week."

The conversation was over, and Kevin was once again able to let the tightly compressed air out of his lungs. It whistled past his teeth and into the kitchen. The next breath he drew-in was deep, and he let it go more easily, but his peripheral vision caught the room growing smaller as he contemplated where he would get next week's thousand-dollars.

He knew instinctively to get his mind on other things. At the end of the table in the dining area his typewriter sat in lonely despair. He had spent months trying to write a story, but you have to be vibrant and alive to write, and he was emotionally barren. He liked what he had read at the meeting earlier in the day, but the story was stalled. In the typewriter was to be found but two lines:

> Sometimes I think we are all Poets and Prose
> Those who just Listen, and those who Compose

"It must be nice writing poetry and lyrics," Kevin thought, "because the end is always within sight." He had started a story, but had no idea where it was going. It was easier to work on his electronics. The "ears-three" was his latest modification, and its ability to pick-up the faintest of conversations was really extraordinary. He had even put together a black and white surveillance camera with old bits and pieces from work. The Royal had only the best, and when things got old, they got trashed. Kevin often took broken components home and reconstructed them. The camera he made was very tiny, and the wires were fitted with just a few strands of filament that were almost unnoticeable. How else could he know that Melanie downstairs was not a true blond?

A few months back, close to Christmas, Kevin had knocked on her door. Just because she wasn't in his parking spot didn't mean she wasn't home. Silence. He pulled a string of colorful lights from the closet and began stringing them outside, along his porch, then dropped the end down in front of her apartment.

From there he drilled a small hole above her door, near the right corner. It took a special drill-bit with a four-inch length, but it worked perfectly. The hole outside was enlarged enough to get the postage-stamp size camera lens into the frame of the apartment, but the actual hole inside was tiny. Next, Kevin strung the cable back to his apartment along the Christmas lights.

Running inside, he attached the cable to the waiting transfer box on his TV and took a look. The lens had picked up some dust, but that would drift away when the door of her apartment was opened a few times. After seeing how good the view was, Kevin patched the outside hole and turned-on his lights. Christmas cheer.

When the lights came down in January he couldn't muster the initiative to take the camera down also. He spent some time getting the wiring under the slats of the siding along the wall to his apartment and decided that nobody would find the line unless the managers suddenly decided to paint. He was safe, and the video interesting.

Kevin worked into the night on his current project as the shape and texture of Antonia filled his thoughts. Her voice was soft and pure, not filled with pretentious, idle chatter. When she came to the surveillance room, Kevin was always thrilled. She was a secretary in the computer department, just down the hall from the surveillance team and with a full view of who was heading up towards the cave.

Reno is a not a *cosmopolitan* area, but it still boasts a good number of educated people, and Antonia was one of them. Still young, she seemed to be worldly at the same time, and Kevin found it to be an exciting and appealing combination.

When she did visit him, the small quarters would fill instantly with the smell of Calvin Klein's "Escape". It was soft and playful, but at the same time it took-over the atmosphere and enveloped him. When he smelled it on another woman, he immediately thought of her. Still, on the many occasions he had asked her to go to Lake Tahoe she always had a reason not to.

"Shit! Burned myself again," Kevin cried. He replaced the soldering iron on the table and worked more skillfully now, forcing Antonia from his mind. Turning his attention to the final stages of production, he knew the device would be as good as the other dozen he had produced, and soon he could add it to the others hooked-up to the console on his table. The group of twelve audio monitors easily picked-up conversations from the listening devices even at a distance of five or six miles. Some nights Kevin tuned into a full range of conversations down at the Royal.

Standing up, his lower back ached and the muscles on the sides of his neck did some screaming of their own. Twisting his head from side to side his bleary eyes caught the time: 12:30 a.m., much later than he thought. "Geez, I've got that meeting at eight, what a rotten way to start the day!"

Crawling into bed, he felt the neatly folded sheets crinkle against his body, cold and stiff. Kevin kept to a schedule, and Wednesday meant clean sheets. Changed in the hope of entertaining on his days off, Kevin rolled onto them alone, more often than not. His thoughts drifted back to Antonia, and sleep came easily.

Chapter Four

The phone's convulsions brought Kevin's senses back from the bliss of sleep, where there were no expectations.

"Howdy Kev', it's Billy, ya know mahn, from the Royal. I know ya got to come in for dah meeting at eight, and I thought maybe, ah, could ya come in at six, ya know, so I could get outta here for a while? Mahn, my live-in thinks I'm having an affair as it is, so, ya know, I could like, head home and then I could..."

"Sure, sure, no problem. I'll be there. I'm about a half-hour out, good enough?"

"Yeah, thanks dude! See ya soon."

Billy was all right. He probably *was* having an affair. Heaven forbid he should go 24-hours without getting-off.

Kevin didn't stifle his yawn while struggling into the little MG Roadster, coffee lapping against the door jam. "See, I don't even *have* a real back seat," he chuckled.

The Reno skyline came into view with a huge orange sun rising over the mountains. "Nothing more beautiful than that. Almost as pretty as if I was up at Tahoe looking this way." Kevin mused.

The ride was too short for any real thinking, just a quick brush with his dreams from college and he found himself at work. On the way to the surveillance room he passed through three employee lounges, each painted a depressing green color. They were dank and musty, oppressive, like a work camp. And the rugs, God, the rugs were *years* old, and they just kept steam-cleaning 'em, even with absolutely no way of getting that smell of cigarettes and "tired-bodies" out of those worn, vile pieces of interwoven history holders.

"Tahoe-one to dispatch, we have a code-seven at the sports bar." The voice coming into the surveillance room was a serious monotone.

"Hey, Billy, don't worry, I'll take it. If you don't get out before he calls you'll have to do the report."

"Thanks Kev', and don't worry, I'll make it up to ya. Oh, Fran called, ah, never mind. See ya, later."

The action at the sports bar radiated back at Kevin from the console as the bartender shook his head into a thirsty-faced guest who's own face was distorted into something you might see on a first-grader getting their first homework assignment.

Turning down the squawk box, Kevin logged the call, switched to an additional VCR, and pressed "copy". Making an additional notation on the log of the security officer who made the call was unnecessary, it was the shift supervisor, Leonard Curtis. As far as security went, the guy knew his business. Thirteen years as a police officer in San Diego had sharpened his skills while an endless assault on every bottle of "Jack Daniel's" in the vicinity had dulled his senses. It helped him forget the events of the day, and it also helped him get removed from the force. Now he ran his security shift with a pompous air of superiority; an all-around pain in the ass. The fact he did his job well was irrelevant to Kevin.

Kevin logged the monitor number and waited for the call that came from dispatch a mere twenty-seconds later, "Do you have the sports bar up on a monitor?"

"Yes, I've got it, and I'll have a 'hard' copy for you." Leonard would want a photo of the guest in question to put with the report. The drunk was escorted off the floor and Leonard was immediately on the phone.

"Do you have a photo for me? Can I come by and pick it up?"

"Yes, Leonard, you can come by the cave and pick it up whenever you want." Looking up, Kevin re-read for the 100th time a little statement he had semi-stolen from Albert Einstein, and taped to the wall.

> Regimentation
> no matter how subtle
> can not produce the standards desired in a free land
> Remember
> the value of pure thought
> objective and dissociated from external or exterior circumstances
> while nearly impossible in these troubled times
> should still be cherished
> Even
> if it inspires ideas and ideals
> that conflict with current precepts

"There is nothing wrong with lightening-up a little," Kevin said to nobody in the room with him. He could answer the questions before Leonard even arrived... "Yes, the officers were professional. Yes, they responded within thirty seconds, and yes, I'll save the tape. That's right, we save every fucking tape, every fucking day, from every fucking event, and you know it, so stop asking me the same fucking questions." Kevin toned it down a bit, capitulating during their conversation. The only thing worse than spending eight hours a day in the cave alone, was spending it with someone in your way. With company it was like working in a phone booth, and the air was close. Of course if it had been Antonia... but she worked later in the day, so...........

Kevin watched a high-roller playing one of the $25 slot machines, two coins at a time. He went through $1,000 in less than three minutes and turned his change-light on to get more ammunition. More bullets, more bullets!

Panning a camera around the casino, Kevin could see the action was fairly slow at this time of the morning. Kevin spent some time watching the bartender and off-duty dealers hanging out at the sports bar.

The bartender was serving drinks, but she wasn't making any trips to the cash register, the money for the cocktails staying on the bar. Kevin waited, then saw the bartender reach for some drink-tokes from the back of the bar. She rang-up a few drinks on the cash register, plopped the coupons in the till and smiled, then took the bills on the counter and tapped them briefly before dropping them in her toke bucket.

Kevin massaged the phone pad and reached the beverage supervisor. "Hey, Cathy, this is Kevin in surveillance. Your bartender at the sports bar is selling drink tokes and keeping the cash for herself. You wan'na come look at the film?"

"Who's over there now, Mary?"

"Yup."

"Damn. I'll get the CSM."

When Cathy arrived at the casino shift manager's office she gave Kevin a callback, and he played the tape for them on Dave Baker's monitor. Ten minutes later the bartender had been replaced, and she was in the detention room trying to explain what had happened. It wasn't her first offense, and her ass was on the street just as soon as she emptied her locker. Really, she gave it a good try, and a good cry, but gave-up her name badge with her time-clock code imbedded in it without any more fuss.

Another forty-five minutes crept by like a funeral procession. Kevin's life made its way past. There went his youth, to the gravesite. Then his hope went slipping away, and his dreams. He had one foot in the grave and the other on a banana peel when the door buzzed and opened, stopping the mourning. It was Dan Ness, hair still wet and sticking to his forehead.

"Whoa, where's Billy? Talked that cocktail server from section six into a date, didn't he?"

"No, he wanted to run home for a while before the meeting, and he knew you wouldn't come in early for him again so he called me."

"We've got a guy counting on table 12. The one in the ugly Hawaiian shirt. I already called down to pit one with a confirmation, but Mr. Cautious down there wants to be sure. He's using a Revere plus minus with a side-count of aces, and his spread is 7 to 1, going from $25 to $175, so he'll probably win another couple thousand before the pit boss gets up the nerve to throw him out. Mind if I run down to the computer room for a coffee?"

"No, not if you bring me one," Dan mumbled with a smirk.

Kevin headed out the door and down the maze of hallways that led back to the surveillance entrance. His watch whispered that he still had a few minutes, and he took the hint. A good time to get some air.

Fran had set up quite a security system for her crew. Each member came in a regular casino door, unlike the other employees that had to use a security-monitored entrance. After going up the hotel elevator to the third floor they entered the employee break area. Everyone else filtered in here too, but the surveillance staff continued-on past the lounge towards one of the computer rooms.

There were other plain-clothes people who used the door at the end of the hall too. The "hacks" went down the stairs, and the "peekers" went up. One short flight of uncarpeted stairs and then the never-ending maze of halls back to the "eye-in-the-sky". It kept most employees from knowing any of the people who were doing the watching.

Paychecks came in the mail, as not a single front-line employee was to have any contact with surveillance. Kevin thought it was a lot more precaution than it was worth. After all, the security supervisors were allowed up to the attic, as they liked to call the surveillance room. So too, were the casino managers, and the games manager, who called it the "tower". Everyone else could use the employee cafeteria and the break rooms, but not the surveillance crew. As Kevin unlocked his car door he turned back towards the casino and shouted, "I am not a ghost".

He pulled himself into the front seat for a five-minute rest and closed his eyes, the sun radiating through the windshield. There was a pleasant smell of leather working its way to his brain from the worn seats when a knock on his window snapped his eyes open.

"Hi, what are you doing here? The meeting was changed to tomorrow morning. Didn't Billy call and let you know?" Fran asked.

"No, Billy called me to come in early for him. If you're serious about the change, I may have to kill him!"

Sorry, Kevin. We just couldn't get everybody together today. See you tomorrow at 8 a.m., all right?"

Kevin thought about making a screeching exit from his parking place, but the keys were still in his pocket. They jangled as he took them out and slowly started the engine. "Well, what the hell, I'll go back and get some more sleep. Good thing I didn't get another cup of coffee."

Chapter Five

Kevin pulled off his coat as he ran up to his apartment while stray pieces of concrete flew from the pitted stairs. The door swung open and his coat went to its customary spot in the rocking chair. He headed straight to the bedroom, slipping off his loafers before he arrived. Pants were next, and they took a spot on the floor. Sliding beneath the covers the sheets felt cool against his legs and they were momentarily covered with goose bumps. It didn't take long for him to drift into more pleasant surroundings.

The morning sun filtered lazily between the palms overhead, providing a cool shade, and there was the steady rhythm of the waves as they broke on the beach. Kevin buried his feet in the hot sand and wiggled his toes. In the surf was a familiar, shapely blond. Tan and smiling, she waved at Kevin as he popped open a Corona. Condensation ran down the sides of the bottle and onto his bare leg. He took a sip, then slid the bottle safely into the grainy earth and looked back toward the ocean. As he waved, there was a thunderous crash. He was awake.

Kevin reached across the bed and slammed his closet door into the wall, *"thud"*. "OOPS, sorry," he screamed into the wall. The noises next door stopped for a moment, then returned to fever pitch.

It was only 10 a.m., but the noise continued and convinced him he was rested. Along the way to the bathroom his mirror reflected the truth about his current condition. Kevin remembered when his muscles used to ripple across his chest. Now they didn't ripple so much as "lap" at his belt.

He patted his belly like a drum and jumped in the shower. An audible sigh escaped from his chest as the thought of going to the gym entered his mind, but it was just too much like being at work with the close quarters and people he didn't really care about, plus the stale-air and groaning. Every person who called the cave moaned that they wanted something, but more often than not they didn't know what it was. "Just keep an eye on the guy," was their favorite saying.

The cool water in the shower took Kevin back to his dream and the sweet vision of a bikini-clad Antonia in the surf. She was his only lifeline to the world of sensitive women, having alienated Becky to such an extent that she was trying to set him up again. Thinking back, he remembered the first time he and Becky had been introduced.

She looked so tiny when he offered his hand, and she turned ever so slightly, just enough for a wisp of wind to kick her wild bangs down in front of those hazel eyes. Searing, smoldering eyes, but they held a fire for someone else.

She was a psychologist, so she would be setting him up again with a dowdy, pear-shaped spinster harboring lingering mental problems. The thought sent a shiver down his spine, and the cool water continued the effect. It was always a few minutes before the temperature got to a reasonable level, but Kevin jumped out before it got there.

His pants were fine, once they climbed up his legs from the floor, but the shirt he had been napping in would have to go. Grabbing a new one from the closet, he spied his old robe in the corner. It looked lonely. He stared at the brown-on-tan design, and the smell of smoke preyed on his mind.

He could see his ex-wife clearly now, sitting in their living room, face distorted with disgust, the smoke buzzing a ring around her. A thin arm across her chest kept him at bay, while the other arm was propped-up for easy access to the nicotine. Their business had collapsed, and he was no longer "promising". He moved out the next week.

Kevin settled into a bowl of Honey Comb cereal and laughed at his life. He ate most of the bowl-full, then pushed it away. The force was just enough for the remaining milk to rise above the far rim and trickle down to the table. He considered getting up for a paper towel, but only momentarily.

There was a faint smell of resin and burnt diodes lingering in the apartment. Looking up past his bowl, he realized that the Weller soldering station had been left on all night. Reaching under the table he pulled on the extension cord. It popped from the wall socket with a resounding "thunk".

"Does anybody really get up and pull on just the plug, like the packaging always shows?" Kevin wondered aloud.

He slipped into the kitchen and reached up to the cupboard above the microwave. "Thank God for the microwave! I'd probably have starved to death without it," Kevin continued. Inside the cabinet was a quagmire of small boxes, each with their own assortment of bits and pieces. Memory served, and he came out with enough pieces to put together a color hook-up for his camera system.

Plowing through the boxes, he spread components across the dining room table and contemplated his next step. *"Dining room,"* what a joke, he thought. "Half the living room is more like it." He trudged back to the kitchen for a pencil, stopping to answer the phone. It was Fran, asking if he could make a meeting later in the day instead of tomorrow.

"Yes, mom, I'm up."

"Listen Kevin, there's a lot going on right now, and we need to pull-together, so no sarcasm today."

"Well that cuts my speech pattern and vocabulary in-half. Why don't you call George? He's the one that keeps missing our meetings. It's my day-off you know."

"Yes, and next meeting I'll try to schedule on a day you are working, okay?"

"Yeah, that would be nice. See you in a while." The phone was silent, but he hesitated before hanging up.

Kevin walked back to the table and slumped into the chair. He stared at the typewriter. It stared back. The pencil he had gone for had eluded him and he trudged back in the kitchen as the phone rang, again. This time it was the friendly folks at Mountain City Bank.

"Gee, we hope everything is all right," they said, but they really meant something else, like: "We sure hope you aren't dead, because we want our money." The bank was so nice, they also wanted to let him know that he was hurting his credit. How thoughtful. Once they were assured a check would be on the way that day they allowed Kevin to head back to the table, with a pencil.

The pencil flew across the pad of paper as he checked each component carefully and completed a list of working pieces. Some items he knew were good because occasionally a perfectly good piece made its way into the trash. Of course those pieces never made it to the dumpster outside.

The work at home was fulfilling, unlike his paying job. He saw the same players, the same dealers every day. He saw the same pit supervisors, each desperate to do the right thing, trying to make a decision. Kevin would call them and confirm a blackjack player was counting cards, but twenty-minutes later they would still be playing. The supervisor would be strutting about, hands behind their back and head bobbing like a chicken, too afraid to get beat for any substantial money, but also too afraid the player would make a scene if they threw them out.

The alarm rang shrill from across the table and Kevin grabbed his jacket and headed back downstairs to his trusty steed. The roadster was a faithful friend, one he kept promising a new coat of paint, but the offer had been put-off several times.

The guardhouse was empty as the mostly blue MG made its way back to the Royal. After so many trips, it knew the way itself. Kevin just put it in gear and let it go, his mind running elsewhere.

His thoughts nearly had an accident when he caught Antonia in a new BMW behind him. As the light turned red, so did he. In the car beside her was Steven Lester, and the sight of him left Kevin muttering to himself. What a choice of company. Lester was a skinny, boring, little computer nerd. Plus, he made a lot more money than Kevin.

When the light turned green, Kevin shifted quickly into first-gear and floored the gas, taking the roadster into full gallop. He didn't want to look back and see Antonia and what's-his-name anymore. In the distance the casino loomed as a tall, brooding monster.

Threading his way through the back parking lot, a space opened-up right by the back door. He struggled getting out of the small car as his right foot got hooked-up on the petals as he swung his long legs out the door and his left foot thumped against the pavement.

Regaining his composure, Kevin took the back stairs two at a time while thrusting his wrist to his face. Seven minutes from home, not bad. It would take him longer to go from the parking lot to the surveillance room, but he would be on time for the meeting. Yanking open the heavy door he was startled to look straight into the face of Robert Weston.

"Good morning," each man said to the other with no show of emotion.

Weston was a tough boss, and looked the part with his perfectly tailored

"Armani" suits. The blue pin stripe he had on today was less intimidating than an all black one he sometimes wore. That was a scary outfit. His brown eyes bordered on black, and they were set deep into his chiseled face, looking lifeless, dead. Kevin could just those eyes rolling-back in Weston's head as he chomped down on some poor middle-executive.

Young for his position, Weston made all the right moves in his climb up the ladder of success. His shrewdest move was being born the son of a major partner in the Royal. Yes, that was a brilliant stroke by the thirty-seven year old. Now a Senior Vice President of "City Casinos", he had control over a company with six casinos, a bank and real estate interests. The company went-public three years back, making all the family members even bigger millionaires without relinquishing any of their power. The stock market is a wonderful thing. Initial public offerings allow businessmen to sell a part of their company without selling a part of their company. America at work.

As Kevin walked towards the elevators, he wondered if he was still on Weston's shit list. The surveillance personnel were not a well-known group, but Weston knew Kevin from a recent meeting. Kevin hoped he also remembered him from some good work he had done earlier in the year. Weston dropped by the surveillance room once in a while, and had done so after a group of "dice sliders" were arrested in the casino.

The group of four players had gone to work on a craps game, each with cash in hand and ready to play. They positioned themselves strategically around the game, two on either side of the stick-man, who controls the dice. While each man had a job of getting change and making large cash bets, the most important member needed to slide the dice down the table without letting them tumble off the pair of sixes he had set them on.

While he was about to shoot from the right, a partner on the left side of the stickman was bending over the table and asking for several different bets, including a two-way on twelve. That two-way bet is half for the player, half for the dealers, and always a good incentive.

Kevin and Mitch were working in the cave that night, and the action was strong. If either had been jabbering on the phone or reading Playboy they would have missed the set-up. Tonight they were lucky.

These guys at the table were good, but they missed the obvious. It just wasn't that often that four players suddenly bought-in for two or three thousand dollars on the craps game. Most big players took a marker, or credit at the table, and for there to be four guys at one time, well…by the time the team had their four players all set-up, Kevin had three cameras on the game. Mitch was calling security at the same time Kevin was calling the craps pit.

The shooter began whooping and hollering, shaking his fist as though the dice were loose in his hand, not wedged neatly between his pinky and thumb. To his right, a team member was throwing a stack of $100's onto the table in the field-bet area, and anticipating a three-to-one payoff, and on the left side of the stick-man, two team members were bending over the layout and asking for bets. The dice left the shooter's hand and came out the other side of the tunnel created by the bent-over members showing boxcars. The supervisor watching the game was quick enough to see what was happening and grabbed at the money in the field, scuffling with the player's trying to get their money, and get out.

Two cheats were apprehended on the spot. The other two headed into the crowded casino. As they ran, Kevin and Mitch switched from camera to camera by punching numbers into a keypad and moving the tiny joystick to operate the pan-and-tilt cameras.

One suspect ended up in the men's room, security close behind. In handcuffs the next time he came into view, his eyes were black, and his gray tee shirt torn and splattered with blood from a broken nose. Bathroom floors can be slippery.

The last team member was lost in the crowd. He was the moneyman, and better prepared than the others. Kevin quickly backed-up the film from camera eight, searching for how the disappearing act was deployed.

Ducking behind a pillar in the Keno area the moneyman dropped his sweatshirt and pulled-off his baseball cap and glasses. His now red shirt allowed him to calmly walk into the Joker's Lounge and head out the back towards the poker room.

As he struggled through the poker room to the "up" escalator, Kevin informed security as to his new attire. He was imprisoned by three officers at the top of the escalator, and went quietly, after being introduced to the carpet.

For security and surveillance, it was a job well done. The craps supervisor was commended for quick thinking in grabbing the money along the green felt, and the stickman who had happily called-out "twelve" was fired. The following day, Weston had personally thanked both Kevin, and Mitch.

Kevin felt his emotions turning, the rush he felt during the action on the craps game coming back to him, and the feeling of being a rat in a maze didn't bother him as he wound his way back to the surveillance room.

Dorothy was keying-in her code number as he arrived at the door to the cave. Wearing the same jacket as always, she gave Kevin a short smile. Not bad to work with, she knew her job and was efficient. And, she smelled better than Mitch or George ever did. A glance around the room and Kevin realized they were the last to arrive. Nope, George wasn't in yet. He felt a twinge of pain for George. The guy tried hard, but the weight of his life's daily events bogged him down.

"Don't worry, George will be here in a few minutes, he was just having a little trouble with the "stop" sign at 4th and Wells."

His joke was greeted with pained looks. The others knew they would have to wait for George to show up, and the air was already close, but then to the surprise of everybody, Fran started the meeting without him.

"First off, we have at least one player on the floor right now with a light-wand." Mitch looked at Kevin, his eyebrows crunched together, while Fran continued. "This is a new problem for us. You can actually buy all the parts on the internet, and put one of these suckers together for about twenty-bucks. It is a simple optical device that sends out a beam of light at different pulses. You shove this wand up into the drop-slot on a slot machine and get its light to hit the optical sensor on the hopper."

Fran's arms were spinning, her shoulder's hunched over. "Once the light hits the hopper, it starts paying-off coins until the light is stopped or the hopper runs dry. We need to be looking at anybody standing or sitting real close to their machines, and any group of more than two people around a machine."

Her right arm shot across the room towards monitor four, which showed what looked like a husband and wife having a fine time, but the wife was continually looking around, and the man had a hand in the coin tray. Fran used the zoom lens to intensify the view on the man's hand. He was pushing dollar tokens out of the coin-tray and into a bucket, but with only three fingers. His index finger was stationary, and Fran pointed-out the metal cord going into the coin chute.

"Gaming is on this guy from down by the gift shop, but we are going to get more like him. I need everybody to keep an extra eye-out for this stuff." Her face brightened with pride at being able to impart this new knowledge on her charges. She only continued after looking every one of them directly in the eyes.

"Overall, you guys are doing a good job, but Dave wants to put in a few more cameras this month. There are only a few weak spots in our defense, and we're going to go after them. If everybody hustles, with a little overtime, we can really take it to them." Kevin wondered who "them" was.

As she outlined the new locations there was a beep at the door. It sounded again after the code was input incorrectly and Mitch graciously turned the doorknob.

"Sorry, Fran, I got stuck on the way over. Lots of traffic, you know?" Her face took-on a weak smile to compliment his weak excuse.

The meeting went on for another half-hour before Fran gave Kevin a nod. "We need to get these done by the end of the month, and I want you to handle the set-up and wiring."

"Should I get started today?" he asked.

Her lip quivered as though in a tiny smile of approval, but it was gone quickly. "Yes, that would be great. I've already had the new cameras brought-up from receiving."

It was better this way. Kevin wouldn't be making a call to Antonia hoping for a date anymore, so he might as well get started making some overtime pay immediately. The surveillance group faded away and left Dan alone, happy to have some space to himself again. The monitors were all in action, and with so many bodies in the room it was impossible to keep track of the action downstairs.

Kevin headed down the hall to the storage room. His passkey slipped silently into the slot and he opened the door to reveal the many wonderful toys of surveillance work. The eyes may be the windows to the soul, but there is plenty to be seen with a new color camera!

He placed calls to security and engineering, begging for some help on graveyard, but it was blindly optimistic. He would work alone for a month.

The next closet in the hall housed a cart with a rainbow of colored wire. Kevin spent time deciding what needed to be put into place first, and doing a few sketches. He was happy Fran was giving him so much space to do his own thing this time. It was refreshing to be allowed to work his own hours for a change, and be trusted. He immediately went home for lunch.

Kevin could hear the phone ringing while walking up the stairs. "Wow, she caught me already!" But no, it was Paul's wife, Becky, of all people. "Hi Becky, Paul's not here. I just walked in the door, myself."

"Kevin, I called to talk to you. I have this friend that wants to meet you. She's really terrific, and before you say anything, think about it for a minute. Her name is Karen, and she is just a really super lady, has her own business and is about your age. Listen, I thought you guys might hit-it-off, but if you don't, you can always leave early. It's not a date or anything, just come by the house on Friday at about seven and we'll barbecue some steaks."

Kevin stared at his empty kitchen and Becky added a nice long, "Please". Kevin knew he could duck-out of this one by claiming to be busy at work, but what the hell. He could always do like Becky said; show up, and then say he had to leave early to finish a job. After Becky promised a wonderful dessert, he took the high road and told her "yes". There was a thud on the other end of the line and he thought perhaps Becky had fainted, but her voice gave nothing away, she just reminded him to be there at seven.

"Well, at least I'll have some company this Friday," he mumbled to himself as he searched the kitchen for snacks. There weren't enough varieties of foods he shouldn't eat, and a trip to the store was necessary.

After picking up plenty of high-caloric, cardio-vascular delights, Kevin fixed himself enough to last through the night. Wrapping up part of the meal, he headed back to the club. And, just in case he ran into anymore of the casino's big bosses, he brought along some coveralls. Topped-off by an old baseball cap, he looked like he was from an outside agency that had been hired to do some rewiring.

He parked on the street this time and grabbed his toolbox out of the tiny trunk. The night went quickly. Much of the construction was concrete and necessitated actual crawling through the ceilings. Ventilation was great in the casino, but the air ducts did not point in Kevin's direction. His cover-all's snagged on twisted bolts, his own rancid sweat cascaded from his hair and into his eyes, and his skin crawled as each bead of sweat slid down his back. A few wildly spun spider webs convinced him to tape shut the cover-all's at his wrists and ankles. He felt safer, but was immediately drenched from the heat. When he could pull himself up his ladder no more, it was time to head home.

A final trip to the surveillance room allowed him to use the time clock. Walking out after he did the dirty deed he wondered why he couldn't be trusted to just write down his hours.

Walking away, he remembered that he really needed to think of a trick to play on Billy. "Yup, I need a real good one for his latest transgression."

Lying in bed later his mind whirled with plots of revenge, but nothing was really interesting, and when he closed his eyes, there was only Antonia on his mind. It had been a long day, and he hadn't seen her since viewing that beautiful, laughing face in his rear-view mirror. Something within him urged his thoughts on. The swelling of her breasts under a soft sweater as she drew each breath, the wise yet naive way she smiled at him when they talked. Her attraction was more than physical; he longed to hear her thoughts. No, it wasn't just the thought of running his hands up the back of her legs, or the feel of her lips as they squeezed into a kiss. It wasn't even the moist, steamy way she would draw those lips against his neck as he pulled her body next to his. He was in and out of sleep for a couple hours before taking a good glance around the half-lit room.

He leaned back against the soft pillow and stared at the ceiling. There was an ever-so light tickle on his neck from between the pillows. He twisted in the bed and shook the pillow, then got up and turned on the light, but that was just so he could straighten the sheets. He straightened until the bed was made, knowing he would not be able to resume sleep.

After a quick shave and shower, he padded into the kitchen. It wasn't a ritual, this inability to recapture the nocturnal bliss of sleep, but there was a pattern. His brain was set for multiple tasks, but when it overloaded in the blank rays of a moon-less night, that dark room was more prison than playground.

He missed playing poker for a living, with its excitement and pure aggression. He recalled the many hours of Texas hold-em and seven-card stud he had played over the years. They had been filled with a strange loneliness. There he was, sitting with a table of other players, but still his own island. Alone with his thoughts, and his plots for the chips in the center of the table.

Never the star player he had dreamed of being, there was still enough money to be made across the green felt to keep him happy, at least until a recent run of bad-beats. His ability to stay focused and sharp for hours was an asset that could not be taught, but it made him mechanical in his play, and easy to read. After making a large bet when bluffing, he could feel his heart pounding. He was certain the other players could see the blood forcing its way through the veins in his neck. After fifteen or twenty seconds, he wanted to scream "All right, I don't have anything - take the money".

He wasn't bluffing this morning, this was real life, stiff and dull. Not like the roller-coaster ride of gambling for a living. A regular paycheck had a lot of calming effects, but not the thrill that came with a real gamble. Kevin looked at his calendar, then finished getting ready for work.

"Overtime, overtime for me," he thought. His monthly child support was set by the court, but overtime became his as soon as the check arrived in the mail. That extra cash was all his, and it was going to be a big help this month.

There was a rap at the door and Kevin walked back from the bedroom. Not bothering with the peep-hole, he opened the door to the smell of "Poison". It rushed past him and into the living room. All around the kitchen it settled-in like the morning dew. Starring back from outside was Melanie, and she had less on than when lounging around the pool. The tiny top was puckered in front, and he tried not to stare at her cleavage. Its white border was in contrast to her tan, which was already dark for this time of year.

"Hi, I really need some help. This early heat has really got me. There's no wind this morning, my air-conditioner went out, and then my lights went out too. I can't wait till eight in the morning to have somebody from maintenance show up. Could a big, strong man like you, help little old me out?" She smiled a sly smile and nodded towards her door.

Chapter Six

The downstairs apartment was illuminated by a vast array of candles. They flickered to the opening door, the shadows retreating along the walls. Kevin's head was overcome by the smell of her perfume, now mixed with the musky tinge of the apartment. It was the first time he had been inside her home, but he knew the view. Working his olfactory senses to the max, they slowly picked-up a soft, homey smell. It was faint, but there was a lingering aroma of fresh baking. Had this little tart been holding out on him? Was she actually a nice woman who came home and baked bread and goodies?

Kevin allowed himself a discreet peek into the kitchen. His disappointment would have been evident in better lighting, as the smell turned out to be an old TV dinner tin that once held a peach cobbler desert, still sitting next to its wrapper on the cluttered stove.

"Do you know where your box is?"

"Yes, but you never seemed interested in it before," she giggled, and led Kevin to the bedroom where the musky scent became even heavier. He struggled through the cloud toward the closet where the panel was. It needed no more than to be opened and a switch flipped back to the "on" position.

"Well, that took care of your lights. Let's try the thermostat," Kevin said, but no sound emanated from the air conditioner when he tried to set the temperature controls. "Sorry, but it would be my guess you are out of luck on any cool air for today. Might be a little hot sleeping without it."

"Oh, it's always hot," she sparkled. "Thanks for turning me on."

She laughed, but was heading towards the door as she did so. She wouldn't be removing that little outfit for Kevin's benefit.

He trailed back upstairs and forced his door open, letting it thud against the wall. Swinging an arm back, he closed the door and went to the TV, switched it on, and adjusted it to channel 54. He switched the out-line with a knob attached to the converter box. All this, just to make sure the power-outage had not affected his camera, of course.

Melanie's well shaped rear-end walked out of the picture. She hadn't wasted any time stripping off her clothes after he left. There was no sound to be heard, and she was more attractive that way. Kevin waited a moment, then turned the TV set off, not sure what he had hoped to see.

Chapter Seven

Work went smoothly over the next few days for Kevin. Golf would have helped to stretch his muscles from the twelve and fifteen hour shifts, but there was no time for that. It was Friday before he realized it, and the thought of a little company came to him with pleasure. He knocked-off early from the rewiring, and got ready for the barbecue.

"What was her name? Oh yeah, Karen." The image of a rather large and burly woman with a little mustache played across the screen in his mind. "If her arms are bigger than mine, I'm leaving early for sure," Kevin thought as he pulled into Paul and Becky's long driveway. Settled back along the Truckee River on Mayberry Lane, the old home was out of view from the street, and Kevin felt himself being transported back to an easier time as he slowly drove under the canopy of mature trees. The MG fishtailed along the rain-rock, and when he skidded up to the other cars he brought along a cloud of dust. He waited twenty seconds, then exited his car once the dust had made its way onto the windshield.

The front porch offered an open door behind the screen, and a yellow "bug light" did its job by attracting a large number of moths. The steps were illuminated by both the porch light, and a floodlight over the garage that Kevin swore cast a light that was gray.

Inside, a "big-band" sound played on the stereo. "Great, she's going to be twenty- years older than me," Kevin mumbled while loping up the stairs. A somewhat older woman walked into the room from the kitchen as he let himself into the house. She was pleasant looking, but her dress gave her a rounded, frumpy look.

"Hi, I'm Kevin, you must be Karen."

"Hello, Kevin, delightful to make your acquaintance. However, my name is Caroline Setter. My daughter, Karen, is giving Becky some help in the kitchen.

A rush of relief ran through Kevin, and he felt a twinge of guilt at the realization that his smile was bigger than it should have been. There were noises coming from the kitchen, then the noises became people and Paul walked into the room with his arm around a tall, plain woman. Her hair was pulled back in a severe twist, allowing full view of her square glasses.

When Paul introduced Kevin to Karen, a minor smile escaped her lips, and she self-consciously reached for a single strand of hair that had worked its way loose from the small blue ribbon on the back of her head. Her thick fingers were sprinkled with rings, and while Kevin and Karen chatted, she dipped a single manicured nail into her gin-and-tonic. It repeatedly tapped an ice cube, producing a resounding chime of ice against crystal. The movements capsized a small wedge of lime and it was forced to the bottom of the glass. Kevin repeatedly glanced at the glass as the lime spent the next ten-minutes trying to work its way back to the surface with the help of a tiny shield of bubbles. Conversation was sparse, but pleasant.

Later, Paul dragged Kevin to the back porch and pointed out how clear the pool was. He had spent the last two weekends working on the filter, alone.

"I would have helped if you had called," said Kevin.

"I'm saving you for the roofing I want to do in June, it'll be real hot by then."

"Thanks for thinking of me, but I'll only be available if there is another dinner included. And Karen has to be here too."

Paul smiled and gave Kevin a poke in the ribs. "Right! Get your ass in the house and ask her out for tomorrow!"

"I was doing fine until you wanted to show me some water."

Waldo the dog joined them and helped guard the steaks Paul was marinating, and Kevin went in search of a date. He had promised his daughter, Sally, they could go to the "Sierra Safari" zoo in the morning, and Karen agreed to come along. He sported a mile-wide grin the rest of the evening. It was great to find a woman who could join-in on such short notice. He wrote down her address and phone number, and placed the scrap of paper in his wallet for safety until he needed it the next day.

In the morning he picked up his daughter from his old wife, and patted his old dog. Her new husband gave him his usual look of disdain. That aside, it was a delight to see his daughter, even if only for a few hours. The star in his life, she could do no wrong. His heart leapt and ached at the same time. Words of pride, admiration and love for her boiled at the surface of his emotions, but all he could manage to say, was "Howdy".

"Hi, Daddy. What are we doing today?"

"Well, I thought we decided on the zoo."

"Oh, yeah. I forgot. You know what? I'm thirsty."

"Wow, what a shock. Every time you get in the car, you get thirsty! How do you feel about some company today? I met a really nice lady last night who would like to go to the zoo with us."

"Who is she? Is she really nice?" Sally queried while jumping over the door and into the passenger seat.

"Well, I had dinner over at Paul and Becky's last night, and they said to say hello. Becky wants to know when you are going to start coming over to go swimming again. Paul finished the new rock-work, and the filter works now, so there aren't any strange things floating around in the pool."

"That was really gross last year, Dad."

"I know, and it's all fixed. We had a barbecue on the patio, and while we were eating I met their friend, Karen Cannon."

"Does that mean I have to ride in the back? I'll get squished!"

"Well, yes, I think it would be nice of you to let her ride in the front seat. You'll be all right for a trip to the zoo. How about if we pick her up, and then stop and get a Slurpee?"

"Cool."

During the ride to Karen's house, father and daughter got caught-up on the happenings of the past week.

"Honey, I won't be able to see you next week, I'm doing a lot of extra work at the club. We'll have to make it the following week-end."

"Well Daddy, that means you have to take me to the arcade at the Hilton."

"That seems fair."

The dealing was done, and they pulled-up to a nice, two-story home in an older area of town.

"Wow, she has *real* trees, they go all the way to the roof! Can I try one out?"

"Sure, you go ahead, and I'll see if Karen is ready."

Chapter Eight

Kevin ran to the front door and attacked the doorbell. In the fun of talking with his daughter, he had forgotten what a nice thing it was to be taking a date, too. There was a chime, and he tried to compose himself, but his heart was still pounding when Karen opened the door.

"Hi, Kevin. I thought I heard a car pull into the driveway."

"Howdy," he cleverly stammered.

Her jeans were washed and worn, but fit well, and the glasses had been 86'ed. She squinted in the sun, but he could see those warm blue-green eyes, and her brown hair had grown overnight to shoulder length. As they strolled out of the courtyard they saw Sally already perched on a high branch.

"Hey, who's that terrific climber in my tree?"

"Hello, way down there," said Sally, as she waved at the lowly adults, and joked that they would both have to wait for her to get down from the tree before they could go to the zoo.

"You know, this is quite a famous tree. Bob Miller used to climb it back when everything around us was just open range.

"Who's Bob Miller?" Sally asked.

"Bob Miller was the last Governor of the state of Nevada, sweetheart. Now, could you climb down from there, please?"

"I am! How do you know he climbed this tree?"

"He carved his name in the trunk. You can look at it when you get down to planet earth," said Karen. "Actually," she whispered, "it is my cousin, who happens to have the same name. However, a little celebrity helps the story."

"Why Karen, you sneaky lady! I was going to say "jeweler", but you hardly look the part today. You're not wearing much gold today."

"Nope, a simple ring and a necklace are fine with me." She smiled again, while reaching up to help Sally down from a low branch. "Sally, this is where Bobby Miller wrote his name. He was way too tough a guy to put a heart and arrow on the tree, so he made a skull."

"It looks more like a pumpkin, with beady little eyes!"

"Well, it was a long time ago, and the tree has grown some since way back in the Stone Age when we were young."

"Yeah, I guess if he was a kid back then, it must *really* be a long time ago."

They piled into the roadster, and were on the way to the zoo before Sally reminded them about stopping for Slurpees, which are mandatory for road travel, just like gas and oil, so they loaded-up.

Sierra Safari was always filled with some new exotic animals and run like a huge petting zoo. More fun than the larger zoos went to as a child, and Karen seemed to have a good time also. Not only did she know all the animals' names, she could even pronounce them. And best of all, she was willing to pet most of them. She would miss that shoelace the ostrich ate, but concessions have to be made for the fun of walking among the animals. They spent so much time having fun, they didn't even have time for lunch before Sally had to be home.

The MG rushed her back, and after making plans for a few weeks in the future, Kevin promised to call a few times in-between. Walking back to the car, he noticed how terrific Karen looked. He hoped his ex-wife had seen her from the porch.

"Want me to put the top up?"

"Nope, this is great with the wind in my hair." Kevin looked over as they drove off, enjoying the look of satisfaction on her face. Her auburn hair was flowing in laces across the headrest, and she was smiling.

"I'm starving, how about dinner?"

"Sound's great, Kevin. What shall we have?"

"Well, I've kind of been looking forward to Chinese food. How about the Crystal Palace?"

"Mmm, I love their 'General's Chicken'. There isn't any better in town."

"OK, but I need to change my shoes first. The smell from that goat misbehaving on my Reebok's might not be compatible with the chicken."

"At least you still have both your shoe laces!"

"True, true enough. Do we need to stop at your place?"

"No, I'm fine for now."

They arrived at Kevin's apartment in about 15 minutes, the ride over filled with small talk. Nothing of great importance, just a chance to relax with each other.

"You know, I think I even made my bed today."

"I'm impressed, I know I didn't make mine. You mind if I turn on the TV and catch a few minutes of the news?"

"No, go ahead, I'll just wash up and change my shoes." Kevin stated. He had his head buried in the sink when Karen shrieked, and he grabbed a towel while exiting the bathroom in hyper-mode.

"What kind of stuff do you watch? This looks like some cheap, voyeuristic dream channel."

Kevin bounded down the hall and lunged at the TV.

"Oh, well, uh, that's something that just happens to be on my converter box. Let me fix this so you can watch the news. See, you have to change it to the regular channels. How about channel 8, or maybe 2, or here's the channel 4 news." He looked back at Karen, and she gave him a quizzical look.

"Hey, I'm really starving, and my shoes don't smell like the zoo anymore, I promise. Let's go eat."

They spent a great amount of time deciding what to order, finally deciding on three different main dishes along with won tons and pot-stickers. Karen ate with gusto, and they laughed as the food nourished their bellies, and the company nourished their souls.

Kevin convinced her to give him a quick synopsis of her life, and how she became the owner of Grayson's Jewelers. She spoke on, as long as he gave her some gentle prodding, and he found himself swimming in her moist blue eyes.

"You are not listening, I said at first Dale ran the business alone," she laughed while loosing the grip on one of her chopsticks. It clanked against her plate, rice vaulting into the air and spilling across the table.

"Wow, dinner and a show," Kevin said, while smiling broadly and convincing her to continue. She did just that, explaining that after a few years, she wanted to be more involved. She had starting with the bookkeeping, then went to classes and became a gemologist. It had been a fortunate decision, as her husband had passed away a year afterwards.

Karen immersed herself in the business, hardly noticing the passage of time. Over the next two years, the store did quite well. This past Valentine's Day, however, things got a little ugly. While Karen was in the back of the store, two gunmen came in, late in the evening before the close of business. They turned the store's sign to closed, reached down and locked the glass doors, and walked into the back. They had Karen's assistant in tow.

The two ladies were tied-up with duct tape, and almost everything of value in back was removed and placed into a couple large duffel bags. The ladies were threatened physically, but neither was injured. They were left in the back of the stores while the thieves made their escape through the rear delivery door. At least they weren't left tied-up with the front door open.

Or maybe it would have been better if they had been. It was a long stretch 'til morning when the day crew found them; cold, tired, and scared. Fear turned to anger, and the assistant quit the next day. Karen stayed away from the store for weeks. The police were of little help, but Becky was able to do a lot in the way of restoring Karen's confidence. She was continuing with counseling, and this was the first date she had been on. In fact, she had not been dating anybody before the robbery, and the past few months had really been tough.

"Actually, I am very lucky that the store was robbed, if you follow the logic. I was so scared, but I will *never* be a victim again. I am too strong for that now. My mom has been driving over to visit every weekend, just to keep my spirits up and to remind me to enjoy life. She and dad live in Bridgeport, California now. It's funny, I think they like visiting me on a one-to-one basis. They never seem to come-up here together." Karen drew a hand up and placed it gently against her face, her eyes looking at something far away. "I knew life could be short after Dale passed away, but I forgot to enjoy what I had."

"That's such a good point," Kevin added, but couldn't think of the next line.

"You know, Becky and Paul gave you some high praise. She gets irritated when you and Paul are out together too much, but she did say some nice things about you."

"Well, they're my only friends. I don't stay in touch with anybody else," Kevin stated sadly while giving his head a little shake. "It's kind of strange, even though I have been divorced for a few years now, I just don't get around to seeing any other friends from when I was married. Most were friends of *ours*, and it's awkward. By the way, did Becky tell you what I do for a living?"

"Did you say wives, or wife's?"

"Wives, plural."

"How plural?"

"Two. I've been married twice."

"I see. Ah, no, they didn't say what you did for a living. Well, not really, I mean, yes, Becky told me. But she said I should act dumb if it came up in conversation, because you don't tell many people."

"You're the most intellectual person I've had a conversation with in months," Kevin said while cracking open his fortune cookie. "You shouldn't ever act dumb. I work with a bunch of Neanderthals. And they think that word means you come from a country near Sweden. I don't tell many people, because, well, it's supposed to be kind of a secret. The people I watch are not supposed to know who I am, but that doesn't mean I can't tell anybody."

"But you don't tell any others, apparently. I know what you mean about not having a lot of friends. It is so tough to find time to see other people. I'm just a single lady, trying to get by in this world like everybody else. It's hard these days. You do seem to be calming me down though."

"That's great. Some men excite women, I just calm 'em down."

"Don't go feeling sorry for yourself. I hate that. You know that is not what I meant. I feel very comfortable around you. You are not as serious as the buyers I work with everyday. Must be your easy smile and laugh."

Her eyes had turned a deeper blue and were studying him closely. He blushed.

"OK, I'm glad you're relaxed around me. You know what, I need some advice about somebody I work with," Kevin said, while discarding the current fortune and casting his lot to a second cookie.

"Anyway, this guy I work with is a bit frantic sometimes. He called me the other day so he could, um, so he could go home early. I didn't have to go in that day, but I thought I did. I mean, I had a meeting scheduled, but it got changed, and Billy knew about the change, but didn't tell me. So, I go down there and let him leave, then find out the meeting has changed. I got about four hours sleep that day. I don't function that well with less than six or seven hours."

"Everybody is different. My husband used to work till two in the morning and then get up at 6:30. On the weekend, he still got up early. I like to lounge around a little in the morning."

"Well, help me out here. I need a good joke to play on this guy. Got any ideas?"

Her face became rounded as she gave him a mischievous smile. "I am really not much of a jokester, but...do you want to make him mad, or just embarrass him?"

"Wow, I hadn't thought of it that way. Embarrassing him would be fun, but I just want to get even for having to come in for no reason."

"Why don't you get *him* to come in early, or on a day off? Can you change his schedule without anybody knowing you did it?"

"Actually, we just started some extra projects, and I'll bet I could put him down for an extra day. When he shows up, he'll know I did it, though."

"So what? He knows what he did to you, right?"

"I guess so, yeah, you're right. I'm just a wimp about that stuff, confrontation. But, I'm learning. Are you ready to go?"

"Yes, that was a great meal. It was really nice meeting your daughter. Dale and I always wanted to have kids, but things didn't go so well for us. I had two miscarriages, and then we stopped talking about it. Looking back, I think he started thinking that it was too much to ask of me. He was a little older than me and we just settled into our daily routine and got comfortable with where we were."

Karen had a sad, far-away look in her eyes, then snapped back to the present.

"I really liked your daughter," she said, and her face brightened. "She has your personality you know."

"I hope that's a good thing, I'm rather fond of her."

"Well, I'm becoming very fond of you, Kevin."

The smile she gave him was warm and happy. He returned the look as they walked into the still night air. The clouds had parted above the hills towards Fernley on the highway to Las Vegas. The other side of the valley was lit-up, as if it were a fairy tail land somewhere off in the distance. Vegas was always good for a few fairy tails, Reno was a real town.

Chapter Nine

Kevin pulled the rag top up on the car, and they could no longer see the stars. Their conversation was light, but genuine. Karen promised that he would be able to see her in a few days, and Kevin stared at her lips so long he missed her turn-off from the highway. He promised he would call, and they both slept soundly in their own beds that evening.

When the new day dawned, Kevin nearly danced from bed. His eyes were clear and so was his mind. There was still a spring to his step as he made his way to the coffee pot in the kitchen. By the time he was out of the hot shower, the heavy aroma had forced its way to the bathroom. Dark and steamy, his morning cup was often the only thing that got him out the door. Today was different. The smell filled his lungs, and his thoughts ran to the woman from the night before. The sweet picture of her seemed to be in contrast to the thick coffee, but it was enough to drive his day.

Taking the stairs two at a time, he thought of all the guests he had seen take a header down the stairs at work, but he refused to hold the hand rail. In the morning air was the smell of someone making those thick waffles, swimming in syrup. Breakfast was only necessary if you were really hungry, but even if you had to take it intravenously, coffee was a physiological need. Like pizza.

Before Kevin reached the hallway to the surveillance room, he could hear Dave Baker the casino manager shouting about camera coverage. Fran was taking the brunt of the verbal blows as Kevin slipped past them and moved quietly towards the surveillance room. Baker's shirt collar was way too tight, the veins in his neck pinched and purple. His temples beat a fast rhythm.

From inside the sanctuary of the surveillance room, they could still be heard. Dorothy looked slowly at Kevin, her right eyebrow making a waving motion as it climbed to her dirty blond bangs, then back again.

"Howdy. How long has this been going on?"

"About ten minutes. We had a really bad night. First, a bellman punched-out a drunk. Then a valet driver ran over some guy's foot, and to top it off, a guy in pit three won sixty-five thousand on a six-deck shoe, and we have no film. None.

"Decks worked up?"

"Of course. Every ten-value card has light scratches in the middle. Perfect for viewing from third base on the table. Great scam. Sitting at the last spot, the player always knew when to double down if there was a ten coming, or to let the dealer hit his own hand with it," Dorothy explained with resignation. "The scratches are real light, but they got dirty as the dealer handled the cards and they started to show. The decks were on the table for twelve hours."

"No shit! They didn't get changed at the end of the shift?" Kevin asked.

"The floorman said he didn't want the player to split with the twenty-thousand he had, so he left the old cards on the game, hoping he would stay."

"Great, cost us another forty-five grand. So, what's Baker screaming about?"

"He figures graveyard should have been panning around with the cameras more, and we should have seen the action, even if we never got a call from the pit. He's right, you know. Billy was just too lazy."

"What about the pit manager? Didn't he ever call up here to check on the guy's play?"

"Come on, Kevin, you expect John Grant to even be in the pit? He's just walking around to save funeral expenses. Probably in his office having a drink during the start of the shift. When he did come out, he just asked the pit boss if he called up here, and went back to his office."

"Who was the pit boss?"

"Shelton, that cocky, little shit."

"Not anymore, that'll be it for him."

"No doubt."

The noise outside had died down. Looking at the monitor, Kevin could see Baker stomping away. Fran was trying to compose herself before entering the room. It didn't work.

"Asshole!" Fran screamed as the door closed behind her.

"Baker, or Billy?"

"Both." Fran's face was contorted into an upside down triangle. "Baker is being such a jerk, I can't believe it. He thinks the floorman did the right thing by trying to keep the player on the game. Those cards needed to be changed, whether the player liked it or not, after eight hours. If the player hadn't been scamming us, and he walked when they got changed, then so be it. Leaving them on the table all that time was stupid. But to top it off, he thinks the whole thing is my fault because with all the extra time the guy played, we should have noticed."

"He's just trying to take the heat off himself. Did anybody call him to let him know the play was going on in the pit?"

"I don't know, probably not. He's going to have to go see Weston about this one. Then, I'll have to go kiss Weston's ass. And I'm going to have to hide Billy for a while. Either that, or fire him, which is what Weston will want me to do. Kevin, why don't you take Billy with you for a few days."

"What? Why are you punishing me?"

"I'm serious. I know you need help with the wiring. Just take Billy along for a few days, and I'll tell Weston that we are using him for something other than surveillance for a while."

"Great, I needed to get back at him anyway. I'll have him do the elevator shafts, it's nice and dirty in there."

Dorothy had been taking-in the conversation, her head swiveling back and forth like at a tennis match. She smiled a contented smile.

"No smiling!" said Kevin. "No smiling."

The smile stayed, and so did Fran as Kevin left the room. He waved at the camera as he walked down the hall. His guess was that they were both laughing now.

Later that afternoon, Billy met Kevin in the back of the poker room.

"Hey, I get my ass chewed. You gon'na keep me out'ta trouble for a few days?"

"I don't know, Billy, is that possible?" Kevin asked.

"I just do what they say. They say work with you, I work with you."

"Well, I'm almost done in here, but I need another spool of cable. I've got the cart over there, but no more red lines. Go down to the receiving dock and get me one, please."

"Yup, I can do that."

Twenty minutes later, from the top of his twelve-foot ladder, Kevin could see Billy walking back into the poker room. He wasn't smiling.

"Hey, receiving is closed for the day."

"Oh, sorry. You'll have to get the key for the dock from the vault. Just sign it out, then take it back after you get the cable."

"On my way."

Kevin went back to finishing the camera mount. He called the surveillance room and checked on the picture it was sending. Mitch let him know over the radio that it was clear. The mount was able to swivel, and the zoom was fine. Mitch watched as Kevin walked over to the front of the room for a cup of coffee and a donut. He was on his second donut by the time Billy showed up again.

"There's no cable down there! I had to go to the vault, then to receiving, then upstairs, then back to the vault to take the key back."

"Oh, sorry. I was going to call Mitch to let you know. I don't need anymore cable tonight. I'm done in here.

"Mahn, you being a prick."

"Yeah, I think I'll call it a night. Why don't you come in early for me tomorrow?"

"OK, I'm sorry. I jus forget the meeting was changed."

"Bullshit, there's no way you could forget that. If you did, you would have come back at 8:00 a.m. too."

"Yeah, yeah, I'm sorry, but what about tonight? I'm already here."

"Sorry, but I'm tired. We'll start at 8:00 a.m. tomorrow. See you then."

Billy's mouth was twisted towards his left ear by an invisible fishhook.

"Hey, Billy, don't forget to punch-out," Kevin said over his shoulder.

Chapter Ten

Becky pressed the speed-dial on the phone in her kitchen and waited. She knew the sound of the ringing phone, and she knew the PBX operator at the other end of the line. When the call got switched to the detectives' room, she knew the voice on the other end of the line. What she didn't know was when her husband would be home.

"Hi, Trish, it's Becky. Don't take this wrong, but I'm really unhappy to hear your voice."

"No, no, I understand. You guessed right, we're all still working. I think Paul is down in ballistics, but I'm not sure. Let me page him."

The phone went dead in Becky's hands. By the time she called back, Paul was on another line. Trish spent a few minutes with her, trying to calm her down.

"You know, it's not every night, but it just seems like when I make a special dinner or something, Paul is always late. It's so aggravating. Sometimes I wish he was an insurance salesman, so he got home at a normal hour."

"My husband says the same thing about me, Becky. He goes crazy at work all day, then finds himself alone with our kids until all hours when I'm on a case. Oh, here's Paul. Hang in there, honey."

Trish looked-up at Paul with a knowing glance.

"Hi, sweetheart, I've been thinking of you all day. I wish I could be there right now, but we're buried. I should be out of here in about forty-five minutes. Can dinner wait that long? I'd really love to look across the candles at your beautiful face."

"Smooth, Paul. You're getting much better at that. You promise to be here in an hour? If not, your dinner goes to Waldo."

"Poor dog, I mean, he's probably been smelling that great meal cooking all day and is jealous of us. I promise to be home soon."

"You're on the edge, baby! See you soon." Becky hung-up the phone gently and looked out the window at the trees as they swayed slowly in the light breeze. Her eyes were cold.

The conversation was much the same as a hundred others between them, and between every officer in the department over the past six months. Cases seemed to be backing up, and overtime was going off the charts.

Paul looked at Trish, and she in turn looked across the room. "You guys start wrapping it up for the night, let's get home to the loved ones," she said.

Kevin was heading out into the night at the same time. He tried to concentrate on his driving, but there was someone on his mind. He knew Billy was still bemoaning his loss of income for the evening, but it was Karen who had been in his thoughts all day. Now that work was over, he gave in. Her beguiling smile played across his mind over and over. After gassing up the MG, he went in to pay his $14 bill. Inside the Quick Mart, next to the obligatory three video poker machines, was a small refrigerator. There was a single, deep red rose in a clear vase on the first shelf and he took it to the counter.

After cleaning up at his apartment, he headed back into the night air. It was warm, no need for a coat. Now if he could just remember where her store was….

Kevin tried to walk normally with the rose behind his back. Taking on an air of casual indifference, he pushed on the glass door. That unfortunately did not produce the results he had counted on. There was a sign in front of his nose that read "Pull", and apparently you needed to read it before making your move into the store. He pulled.

Inside, the air was clean and cool. Display cases were filled with diamond earrings, bracelets, necklaces, the usual. In a large case were the wedding ring sets, and a quick glance in its direction was enough. Any longer a look sent most men into a panic, and Kevin was no different. He looked across to his left and saw Karen with a customer. She winked, then turned her attention back to the woman in front of her, a rather heavy necklace draped across her hands. It glimmered as it moved, the track lighting doing its job. She was moving her hand up and down, and her head rocked back and forth like a church bell, but there was no chime.

"Oooh, it's so beautiful, but my husband will kill me."

Karen had her now. "Just smile at him all night, and keep telling him how smart he was to have found a woman like you."

"You're right! He's the one getting the bargain here, he barely deserves me."

"That a girl! That is the attitude you should have. Now, would you like to wear it home, or should I put it in a nice gift box for him to give you?"

"Wrap it up, and I'll work on my attitude until I let him give this one to me."

"Terrific. Now, do you need a pen, or will you be using your credit card?"

"Oh, honey, you know I've always got a pen for my checks."

Karen glanced over at Kevin and he showed her the rose from behind his back. The other sales person gave Karen a surprised look, but she just smiled back.

Once the customer's check was safely in the cash register, Karen came out from behind a counter filled with watches. She gave Kevin a kiss on the cheek, and he felt his skin warm to her lips as his face turned a bright crimson.

"That's so sweet, Kevin. I just love these dark-red roses. Mmm, it has a beautiful aroma. Must be grown someplace close. The hot-house ones have no fragrance at all."

Kevin managed to nod his head in agreement while Karen carried the bulk of the conversation for the next five minutes. She agreed to have dinner with him the following evening, but it would have to be a late one. The store stayed open till nine, and she wasn't going to leave her saleswoman there alone.

"Why don't you pick me up here, that will get us out a little earlier."

"All right, see you at nine."

He waved through the window after he maneuvered the one-way door and whistled on the way home. When his alarm went off in the morning, he jumped up and ran into the new day. Things would go well, of this he was certain.

Inside the confines of the Royal, Kevin walked through the employee break-rooms, then past the computer office. For two years, he had done just that, and every time he walked-by, he would search-out the little blond near the door doing data entry, or talking on the phone. Today, he forgot to look. Making his way towards the surveillance room, a voice marched up behind him.

"So, what's the story? You just ignore me now?"

"Oh, sorry Antonia, I was just, well, I just have a lot of plans going through my head for all of the wiring that needs to get done."

She ignored the cheapness in his voice and continued on.

"I don't see you for a few days, and you just forget about me? Boy, you guys are tough. I came by the cave yesterday, but you were busy somewhere downstairs."

"Yes, I was. We're adding a number of cameras, and the poker room was first on the list. To be honest with you, I'm enjoying doing something besides sitting inside and looking at the monitors."

"I see. Well, you better stop by and say hello to me when you go by."

"I will, see you later."

"Bye-bye."

She turned and walked away, her hips swayed like he had never noticed before. Boy, they were really moving. Maybe she was interested in him after all. He stared down the hall until she turned down the stairs. Then he thought of Lester sitting next to her in the car.

"Geez, she's as bad as Melanie!"

"What?" asked Dorothy, as she walked out of the surveillance room.

"Nothing, I was just talking to myself."

"Right, I didn't see anything. You can roll your tongue back-in now."

"No, I just...."

There was no sense trying to convince her of anything. She just snorted and slipped past him. As she did, she gave her hips a little swing back at him and they both laughed.

Kevin started right in with his next camera mount. It was the last one that needed to go in section four, by the poker room. Billy caught-up with him about 8:15, and as much as Kevin hated to admit it, he was a lot of help. Running back and forth, and making radio calls was tough while you were doing the installation work alone.

"Well, Billy, do you want to start on the elevators tomorrow?"

"Not tomorrow, man, I got a weekend coming up."

"What? What day is it?"

"It's Tuesday coming up."

"Right, I knew that. So, you're going to take your days off? You don't want to make some extra money by doing a little overtime?"

"Not a chance, mahn. I be done *today*."

"All right, Billy, see you in a few days. I'll probably work straight through, myself. I can use the extra cash."

    Billy took off, and Kevin glanced down at his watch for the tenth time in the last hour. He had worked almost twelve hours, but it was still too early to go get Karen. Instead of taking off, he just sat atop his ladder a few minutes and tried to think over tomorrow's job. It was no use. He cleaned up his tools and went home.

    Kevin changed clothes and got ready for his evening. Turning the front-door knob, a voice from behind gave him a start. His blood thinned quickly, but he realized one of the "ears" on his console was just doing its job. As his heart sank back into his chest from his throat, he listened to the conversation.

    "It ain't no big deal, we just don't have enough "squares" to lay-em all off to. I'll have more in place tomorrow."

    "Bullshit! Listen good, you *"fuck"*. You screw this up, I'll drop you into Pyramid Lake myself with a slot machine around your neck."

    "Yes sir, I'll get it done."

    "Get it done right. Rich, help him out."

    A door slammed and there was silence. Kevin waited, and when he heard nothing else, he headed outside. Had he waited a moment longer, his interest would have been peaked enough to delay his date for at least a few more minutes.

Chapter Eleven

Inside the casino's penthouse, Vincent Vellardi was finishing his dinner. He stabbed viscously at the pink meat, but ignored the baked potato that had absorbed much of the juice from the thick cut of prime rib. In between bites of meat, he gnawed at an unbuttered roll and pointed a fist repeatedly at his two minions. They were invited to listen, not to dine.

Vincent worked his smooth, manicured fingers into his neckline and undid the top button from behind a blue silk tie. His mood improved enough to stop pointing, and he continued with his orders for the day, the voice giving away his tough, east coast upbringing.

"This fellow, he's not working as I had hoped," Vincent growled. "Rich, I want you to explain the situation to him. Put him at ease and relieve him of his duties. He can take the heat from his guys, and we can get cleaned-up here. I don't want nobody but the two of you with connections here, understand?"

"You don't want him connected at all?"

"That's right, Rich."

Rich nodded, never allowing his eyes to stray from Vincent's hard gaze. It was now his job alone, Toni was around for the subtle work.

"Toni, why don't you take-off, that's all for tonight."

Without a word, Toni walked across the plush carpet and out the side door, then Vincent spoke again.

"Watch yourself with that one. I wanted Toni to know how serious this is, but inexperience can be deadly."

"Yes, sir."

Standing, both men straightened their suits and Vincent left the room. Rich happily called room service to order *his* dinner and have the remaining dishes removed.

In the large bedroom, Vincent slowly unbuttoned his vest. The evening's work was done, and it was time to call his wife. His voice took-on a tone as smooth as the jacket and vest he carefully removed, while telling her how much he missed getting together with her for dinner, and promised to be home in a week.

Chapter Twelve

Kevin smugly pulled on the glass door this time, but it wouldn't budge. He looked anxiously through the windows, scanning the empty store. To his relief, Karen came out from the back room and opened the door.

"Hi, handsome! Come on in, it will just take me a couple minutes and we can go."

"Howdy. You look nice tonight. For a second there I thought maybe you forgot."

"No, I did not forget what we talked about less than 24-hours ago!"

"I didn't mean it like that. I just got a little paranoid, I guess."

"Happens to men too, does it?" Karen asked, her voice trailing off as she walked towards the back of the store.

"Well, no, not very often, but once in a while."

"Right."

There were a few little chores to be done, and Karen waved back at him to follower her. Behind the counters and into the back they walked while Karen pointed at a video monitor.

"You are not the only one that does surveillance work, you know."

"Yeah, I was wondering how you knew I was at the door so quickly."

"I heard you when you tried the door. And,............I checked the monitor ten or twenty times since we closed."

The micros system in the cash registers were "z-ed" out, and the day's receipts put into a safe. Then, with the alarm set, they had thirty seconds to get out of the store. It was plenty of time.

"You like Italian?"

When Kevin answered in the affirmative, Karen directed him to "Italian World" on old Forth Street. Highway 40 used to be the only link for gamblers from California to reach Reno, and on weekends in the 1950's traffic was so tight you could have walked on the chain of cars along the road. Now it was a forgotten part of Reno, with dilapidated single story motels, dusty parking lots, and wheezened owners who insisted on still trying to eke-out a living.

The restaurant too, was old, but sported a great view. House lights stirred among the trees below, giving the Truckee river movement. It was as romantic as when the restaurant opened fifty years ago.

"How long have you lived in Reno?"

"I told you Karen, about 15 years."

"And you have never been to this restaurant?"

"No, I'm not a big *diner*, I guess."

"Well, you have missed out, mister. The cannelloni is out of this world, and anything on the menu is better than any other restaurant in town."

"Relative own the place?"

"No, I am serious, the food is terrific."

One entire side of the dining room was six-foot windows, and their table provided the proverbial "front row seats" to the beauty below. Karen ordered what turned out to be an explosive Merlot. They toasted "to new friends", and worked on the French bread and olive oil.

While getting into a discussion on the merits of living in a small town they were interrupted by a thin, bespectacled man in an ugly brown sports jacket.

"Howdy, Kevin. I'm surprised to see you here. Excuse us for a moment," he said in Karen's direction while pulling Kevin towards the other end of the room. It was an agreed upon act, as his 140-pound frame could not have willed Kevin away from the table alone. "Don't say anything, just come see me tomorrow. I'll be there at nine, you will be there before ten." His stare sliced into Kevin's eyes for a long time before he walked away.

"Sorry for the interruption. He's an old friend and I owe him a little money. He's shy."

"Really. I rather thought the opposite," she murmured.

The air was thick for a few minutes while they drank their wine. By the time their meals arrived the storm had passed.

The flavor of the Merlot danced over Kevin's palate and mixed with his savory chicken picatta. Each bite had capers, soft and pungent, melting away with the buttery sauce before he could roll them on his tongue.

Karen attacked her cannelloni and insisted that her dinner had to be better than Kevin's.

"No way, that was a terrific meal! Yours' could not have been better."

They smiled and headed towards Karen's house. Once they arrived, she turned the key and freed the large front door from half of its shackles. The outside air rushed into the warm home, pulling Karen and Kevin shamelessly into the parlor. Her heels clicked across the hardwood floor towards the living room where a colorful Persian rug graced the middle of the floor and was held down by an ottoman and two easy chairs. The tassels at the end of the rug swished as Kevin closed the heavy door behind him and a handful of rose petals danced below the vase they had departed. Along the back wall, a long green couch provided a perfect setting for two soft, muted photos. They were works in black and white of a cabin in the trees, and a single, lonely boat floating aimlessly on a lake.

"I only wish I could blame somebody else for the mess in here. Actually, it's a good thing you didn't see it earlier today. How about a drink? I have a nice dry Chardonnay, or maybe you would like a little more Merlot."

"Whatever you want is fine with me. I'm not much of a wine drinker, but those two are my favorites. If the Chardonnay is chilled, that would be great."

He followed her into the kitchen, realizing the "chilled" part had been unnecessary. Along the right wall was a large, glass-fronted cooler housing an endless selection of wines, each held at the perfect temperature. From the ceiling, every imaginable cooking utensil was hanging with-in reach, and across the spacious counters were a dozen cooking and baking devices. It reminded Kevin of the restaurants at the Royal, only cleaner.

"My husband really wanted me to stay home and cook," she said, while nodding to a photo on the counter in a beautifully polished, rosewood frame. Inside the warm housing was a picture of a younger Karen and a man. He must have been six-four, and it did not appear that he had been over-eating. The look on his face was one of ease and contentment, a bit like a young Robert Redford. Kevin disliked him immediately.

"Great, I have to compete with a ghost that was rich, and good looking," Kevin thought.

"Gee, he looks like a real nice guy," said Kevin

"Really? I am happy to hear you say that! I think some men were insecure about Dale because of his looks. I swear some of them hated him, based just on that."

"Karen, that's so silly. Why would anybody hate him based on his looks?"

"Maybe they didn't like him because he was rich," Kevin mumbled to himself.

"What?"

"Nothing."

"Well, I'm happy you are secure in your self-worth. Besides, you're pretty handsome yourself."

Kevin's wilted self-confidence took a turn for the better, along with everything else that had wilted.

"Here is a really good Chardonnay. The glasses are in the last cabinet on the right. You know those old movies where the woman says 'I'll just slip into something more comfortable'? Well, I'll be back as soon as I find something uncomfortable that doesn't make me look fat."

She slipped out of the kitchen, and Kevin got a better grip on the wine bottle. He was certain everything was going to work out great, but that little voice that whispers in all men's heads was giving him something to worry about, the little jerk. He had just about finished killing the cork when Karen returned in a white robe.

"Sorry, but this is all I could find. I guess I haven't bought any alluring evening-wear for a long time."

Kevin thought for a moment. "That's fine, you don't need some flimsy nightgown to interest me. Talking with you at diner was more than enticing enough. I'd like to propose a toast to the start of a good friendship. The sound from the glasses was a single, high pitched chime and the wine had tiny ripples running from the edge to the center of the glass, then back again.

"Did you want to catch the news?" Kevin asked.

She didn't answer, just walked toward the bedroom. Glancing back over her shoulder, Karen caught his eye. He followed.

The bedroom was awash with moon light swimming-in unabashed through the wooden shutters. There was a faint smell of lilacs, and two candles burned on the bed stand, their flames moving in opposite directions. Feet gliding towards the bed, they sat hesitantly, but their eyes entered into an eternal pact. Kevin tasted a drop of wine on Karen's lips. It was sweet, then tangy. Her lips were sweet, then sweeter; their supple softness amazing. He lingered slightly, then leaned back and took another sip of wine. Her eyes were still closed, and he noticed a light eye shadow that was highlighting her tender blue eyes. It was unnecessary.

She loosened her robe slightly, turned, and brushed her soft hair away from her long neck, exposing it like a pearl in the moon light. He could not resist leaning forward and engulfing it with his lips. First, a brushing of the lips on the side, below her right earlobe, then a stronger kiss in the middle of her neck, just below the hairline. He could feel a shiver run down her back, and it worked its way down his own back, too. She was lovely, and he was mesmerized.

"Interesting house you have here, a two-story, with the master bedroom downstairs."

"Dale's idea. The house was my parents, but I really like the area so we built a second story on it. Came out better than we could have expected. There were two bedrooms and a den along this wall, so we just used half the space to expand the kitchen, and half for this room."

When their eyes met again it was as though they had known each other for years, and soon the moonlight and Karen's perfume were too much for him. She wrapped her arms around his chest and helped him off with his sweater. The moon walked across the sky as the candles burned down to their wicks, and their hunger was sated.

In the morning, as he opened his sleepy eyes, Karen set a tray down on the bed. A tiny white rose accompanied the bacon and eggs.

"When we stay at your place, you get to do the cooking," she whispered, giving him a kiss on the forehead.

"Good morning. I can't believe you got up and made us breakfast. Guess I was so tired, I didn't even hear you. You made last night just terrific, I wasn't expecting anything more."

"Well, I want you to feel comfortable."

"I'm very comfortable. I don't want you to get the wrong idea, but I need to work today."

"So do I, but I'm going to put it off as long as possible."

She helped him finish the last piece of bacon, then gave him a slow kiss that tugged at his soul. When that was done, she took him by the hand and helped him out of bed to the bathroom. There was a clean towel, washcloth and bar of soap awaiting him.

The water splashed and a heavy mist swirled around his eyes, and his heart.

"Boy, do I owe Becky a 'Thank-you' for this."

He smiled in the shower, then remembered he had to see Tolan before work.

Chapter Thirteen

Kevin drove past the town of Sparks to the Mustang exit. Not quite what you would call a town, there was a 24-hour bar on the right side of the highway, and a wrecking-yard on the left. The ranch was past the wrecker, down a poorly kept road. It wound along past low sagebrush and rock like so many roads in the Nevada desert, but this one didn't promise a miner gold, it promised the carnal goods that only a single state in the nation sanctioned.

As the street led him to the buildings a million men before him had been drawn to, the road became a single lane across a small creek. The tiny bridge looked sturdy enough, but it ran on a blind corner and Kevin wondered how many before him had been forced from the bridge and into the slow moving stream by a drunk in a Cadillac. Ah, what to tell the auto club.

The buildings, shrouded behind a massive wrought iron fence were home to fifty wayward souls burning unbridled coals. They worked twenty-one days straight, then took the worst part of their month off. The main building was a bright pink, but behind it the trailers the ladies called home, were plain. Above the gate and attached to the neon sign was a camera, the only visitor Kevin would get until he was safely inside. He pressed the buzzer, waited, and soon the gate's lock dislodged itself from the fence. Once inside, he was met by a stern, orderly woman dressed in a gold pants-suit.

She said hello and ushered over six girls. Each was in a colorful nightgown, and he could have his choice of one or more. Two stood as if they were annoyed to have been called away from their conversation across the room. The others tried to be interested, one of them even smiling brightly. Kevin let-on that he wanted to go to the bar, and the madam said, "Sure, have a drink, we never close."

She turned, unimpressed, towards her desk, as did most of the young ladies who sauntered back towards the two red, crushed-velvet couches. There was a skylight in the center of the two-story ceiling, and the room moved with changing light as clouds passed the sun above. A short blond in an even shorter, blue teddy helped Kevin over to the bar. She batted her eyelashes and told Kevin how cute he was. "I'll bet you're a lot of fun, and you know that I am." She sat him down gently, crushing her breasts into his arm.

"I saw you looking at me when you walked in. Wouldn't you like to get a closer look after you have a drink?"

"Honey, I just came in for a drink, honest."

Her look gave nothing away, and her voice let on that she would be waiting for him on the couch. When she left, Kevin turned towards the bar.

"Here's a beer. Gim'me eight-bucks," Tolan insisted, wiping the moisture from his hand with a soft clean towel, and leaning back against the side of the bar. To an outsider, his glare was almost comical on this wisp of a man, but outsiders didn't know the Spiderman as well as Kevin.

There was a paper clip on the bar, and Kevin used it on a few folded bills from his front pocket. It wasn't enough to make Tolan happy, but Kevin promised a return visit in a week. Staring back at Kevin was the perfect poker face, and absolutely no emotion leaked from the heart within. Kevin took a few sips of his beer and turned on his heel. He smiled at the blond as she got back up from the couch, but a flat wave of his hand was the "no-thanks" sign and she lost interest.

The ranch was bugged, even the rooms that the girls worked in. How do you explain the job of the person that listens to those microphones? What would you put on your resume? At the bar, Kevin had known not to mention anything important, he simply put his payment into the glass jar where others put their tips and "good sense" money. That same tip-jar was generously filled by anyone who was too well known to take a chance on gossip; a local news star, a politician, a businessman from Ohio. Nobody was immune from a little squeeze, but the Mustang always kept quiet about its friends and neighbors who understood how to share.

Tolan gave out an occasional loan, and he never worried about collecting, because he could always drop-off an occasional scorpion in a client's bathroom. Living in the Nevada desert he had the advantage of collecting quickly anytime one of his clients had a rapacious arachnid stumble into their home on its own. And he never lost a client from a scorpion bite. What you wouldn't see was his real calling card.

Problem accounts were treated to a visit by a brown-recluse spider. The Nevada native, more deadly than a black widow, usually lives in a small nest by a warm desert rock, but for Tolan's problem children, the aggressive spider had been known to take-up a spot near the pillows on a bed. If you found one, it was probably too late.

Heading straight to work, Kevin tried to convince himself that Tolan wouldn't send him any visitors just because he left only $500 and not the $1,000 that was due. After all, he was almost current, and had been paying on time for months. He struggled out of the car, then struggled into the cover-all's from his trunk. They smelled worse than the ranch had, but he wanted to cover the clothes he was wearing today because they were the same ones he had worn the day before. Kevin was an hour and a half into his work when the thought of punching-in came to mind. He picked-up his radio, called the cave, then asked for Fran.

"Hi, Kevin, this is Fran, what do you need? So you started work around 9 a.m., but you didn't use the time clock, and you are not sure if you punched-out last night either. Maybe you are spending too many hours here."

"I've just been trying to get things taken care of," Kevin said. "And, if I don't come by the cave, I forget to punch in. Do you want me to finish the elevators and stairwells, or get the baccarat room next?"

"You better take care of the stairwells, then get to the roof as quickly as possible. There are guests in the penthouse, so you can't drill through any walls up there to run the lines. Make sure you keep it quiet. Then, you can go on to the elevators and the baccarat room."

"All right, Fran. Thanks."

Fran seemed very accommodating. Pleasant even. This was a new side of her Kevin had never seen and it made him nervous.

By noon, he was thinking about Karen. "I should just wait, then call her after work. No, it would be better to call her in the morning. Of course, she might be waiting around tonight for me to call, and be mad that I waited until tomorrow."

Up the back stairs towards the 29th floor Kevin climbed, his feet dragging, and his ring tapping against the metal handrails. The tennis shoes he usually wore were better suited to this climb than the leather soled loafers he had on. It was as though his shoes were lined with magnets, doing their best to stick to the metal stairs. Closing his eyes, and shaking his head he realized how tired he was. Perhaps the busy week *was* catching-up with him.

At each landing between floors he checked the camera mounts, radioing back and forth with Mitch. The cameras were directed at each floor's emergency door. When George came on the radio Kevin knew it was after 3p.m. Almost done with the preventative work, he finally reached the 26th floor.

New cameras were necessary for the top four floors even though there were already security guards stationed at the end of each hall. The suites on these floors were for the real "high-rollers" that the Royal was seeing more and more of, the kind that played $2,000 per hand at blackjack and didn't flinch while loosing a couple hundred thousand dollars.

On the 26th floor, the double Jacuzzi suites were three rooms, and the players always seemed to have a few "friends" with them. Either they were 25 year-old blond "nieces", or they were tough looking bodyguards. Those with the bodyguards seemed to like the $5,000 minimum baccarat tables.

On the 29th floor, the penthouse didn't get used too often. This year, Kevin only remembered three or four guests in it. One had managed to win almost four million dollars. He had three girls with him, and insisted on leaving the main door to the bank of rooms open at all times. From the camera above the elevator, you could pick-up the girls walking from room to room. They were never in more than a g-string. He no doubt felt safe, since you could only get to the 29th floor from a single elevator on the first floor. There was a guard in front, and you needed your room key to run the elevator.

The camera's for the penthouse had to be almost invisible, providing security without making the casino's richest guests feel intruded upon, while still showing the elevator, front door, second bedroom door (which opened to the hall), and the emergency exit and stairs.

"This won't be too tough a job," thought Kevin, as he walked up to the 29th floor. "Half the cameras are already in place. I can finish the hall next week when there isn't anybody staying here, and for now I'll just do the access area." Kevin had been on the upper floors two months earlier while testing his listening devices. He had placed one in each hallway from 26 to 28, and a couple of the Jacuzzi rooms along with one in the heating duct above the penthouse. They worked, and since they were tiny and could never be traced back to him, he left them intact. Kevin listened first to a wild party in the Jacuzzi room on the 26th floor.

Over his "ears-two" he was able to count at least ten different voices and names. They all ended-up in the water it seemed, and the cocaine that was being snorted must have cost thousands. He listened for an hour from his apartment, then began building a permanent console on his dining room table to monitor and record all six devices he had installed.

While building it, he made a call to Mitch, in the cave, to say he had heard earlier about a big party happening on the 26th floor. In the morning, Mitch let him know his call had come too late. The Jacuzzi had overflowed, with a veritable cascade of water running down the crooks and crevices to the casino floor. Plastic sheeting had to be placed over a bank of slot machines. Weston was less than happy.

"Tahoe-one, this is Kevin in surveillance, I'm going on the new-tower roof. I'll be accessing the security panels over "29" while I'm up there."

"Tahoe-one to Kevin, I copy. Do you have a work order, or is this preventative?"

"Uh, preventative today, you'll have to see Fran for any additional information."

Kevin slid his identification card into the reader and walked outside. The skyline showed just a few clouds holding steady over the mountains in the distance. The crisp, fresh air rushed into his lungs and he marveled at the panorama surrounding him.

White outlines along Mount Rose showing that not all of its snow had melted yet. He walked across the roof and tapped against the pole holding the southwest camera. The camera was too high to do much good. Whenever there was a vehicle stolen, surveillance could see which way the car was driven, but not much more.

To the left of the camera pole was an access panel. Not the usual opening for heating ducts, this one was large enough to crawl into and do repairs to the penthouse ceiling. Kevin snapped open the padlock and pulled one of the heavy doors upwards while checking for spiders, his skin rippling momentarily. Down three short stairs, Kevin peered across the four-foot high room, and then duck-walked across the room for 50 steps before reaching his targeted coaxial-axial wiring, and grimaced at how little extra cord there was. He frowned, realizing he would have to string new cord all the way from behind the elevator shaft. He searched his blue coveralls and pulled out a splicing kit, then spoke out-loud.

"I'll just add a little cable here and put in a bypass with an adapter. That will save me some work. What the hell, I can haul the cable up here later for the final job. Right now, it's 'Miller Time'!"

Kevin stood-up, but the short ceiling stopped his momentum. "Stupid, fucking, son of a…" stars danced around him. He stretched his face and pushed his eyes back into their sockets while the lights flashed off and on repeatedly. When the dizziness subsided, it was replaced by a dull throb. Slowly this time, Kevin got up in a crouch. "Now I really need a drink!"

After locking the "floor-door", he headed to the stairs. Knot on the head and all, he decided to use the elevator for the trip down and even remembered to clock-out.

"Hey, I'm taking off. How's it going today?"

"Just great, Kev'. I understand it's your fault I'm working 12-hours."

"Nope, I'm doing the same thing, buddy. You're just doing it in this little room. See, I can come in, I can go out. In, out, in, out."

"Jerk! Hey, take a look at this guy on eleven," Dan said, while slashing his arm across the room towards one of the monitors on the wall. "We've got him in eighteen-five, fifteen thousand of that in markers. He goes to the ATM, gets thirty-five hundred, and now look."

"That's a hell of a lot of pink chips!"

"No shit, Sherlock. They're getting another fill for the game. He's got all eighty $500 chips the game had when he got there. Amazing! The guy gets down to his last thousand and now look, forty-grand."

"Yup, down to the felt, and they couldn't snap him off. Sometimes the gaming gods just want you down to your "case-bet" before they throw you a bone," Kevin said.

"Forty-grand is a hell of a bone."

"Yeah. Did that wheel get worked-on last month?"

"It's wheel two, I know the bearing's needed to be cleaned and greased, but that's just going to slow it down a bit. The dealers have been getting a good spin."

"It's not the bearings that should worry you, it's the frets."

"Kevin, it's a roulette wheel, not a guitar."

"Right, but each pocket has its own sensitivity. Each metal spacer is called a fret, and if some are loose, while others are still tight…well, the ball just dies when it hits those loose ones instead of bouncing around. If the player knows there are a few loose ones in a certain area, then they get a hell of a return on their money. Look, he's playing a single section. His chips are loaded on 11, 7, 20 and 32. I'll bet you anything that 26, 30, 11, 7, and maybe even 9 are loose. When the ball hits one of those, it'll only bounce two or three spaces back, and then he's got a winner."

"All right, so what are the odds here, professor?"

"Well, the ball's going to hit one of those about once in 7 spins, and if he bets on four spots, and they keep dropping in, then he gets one every 28 spins, and we pay him 35 to one. That's an overlay of about 17%. He's got a huge edge, it just took some time for him to start winning. You better call Fran. Then run back the tape for the last half-hour and see what the ball looks like when it lands in that area."

"Thanks for the help, but do you really have to leave?" Dan asked.

"You're welcome. Hey, who's that guy right there?" Kevin asked.

"Who knows, just another guy in an expensive Italian suit with lots of bucks going to the penthouse."

"He looks like somebody that was in the paper a couple months ago."

"Could be, rich people get publicity."

"Right."

Chapter Fourteen

Walking back to his car Kevin thought about how to allocate time for work, and for Karen. He longed to see her, but also wanted to finish his camera work. If he could get done with the new set-ups, he would have a nice steady schedule at work again. That seemed better than just seeing Karen for an hour here, and an hour there.

He drove by Grayson's for a fix, then went home to bed. Upon waking, Kevin lay motionless in bed, thinking of the man he had seen in the expensive suit the night before. He stumbled from his cocoon and sat at the kitchen table. The listening console was still on, and Kevin knew the voices he had heard a few days ago were from his third device, located above the penthouse.

The more he thought about it, the more the guy in the suit looked like Vincent Vellardi, but Kevin was going on a black-and-white photo he had glanced at in the newspaper.

Kevin sat at the table, rubbing his face up and down with his left hand, then up into his hairline. He sat there until he had convinced himself how important it was to know what was going on in the penthouse. So important, that he should put together a special camera just for that purpose. With the bits and pieces in front of him, he could make an electronically controlled lens. To run the camera, he would have to solder a supply line to a small video recorder he had, then attach it to the "ears-two" he had in the heating duct above the penthouse. He would get video feed from the VCR whenever the audio device kicked-on.

When he was done building, Kevin looked up from his work and rolled his head around. It creaked, and he moaned. Across the table sat that damn typewriter, mocking him and stubbornly waiting. "Low priority, low priority," Kevin said. The typewriter did not respond.

Stretching again, he grabbed his coat and rustled in the pocket for his ledger sheet. The paper came out reluctantly, and he crossed out another $500. That still left $19,500 to Tolan if he could keep ahead of vig. It was an impossible amount with his pay, and his eyes glazed over.

Captain Crunch joined him at the table and he munched on the hard cereal, periodically cutting the roof of his mouth on the sharp edges. He decided to go ahead with his plan, and was at work in less than a half-hour. The new camera and VCR made his trip to the 29th floor a long one. Not only did he have to lug his new items and toolbox from the car to the elevators, but the journey included getting off on the 25th floor to avoid security. Most of the hallways and the elevators were being monitored by the security department, so it was easier to call them on a hall phone and tell the dispatcher what he was doing rather than have a nosy guard inspecting his box if he tried to get on the penthouse elevator. There was a twinge of guilt mixed with excitement as he circumvented the very security he had set-up.

    When he was back inside the crawl space he felt safe again. He duck-walked over to the heating ducts leading to the penthouse and removed a few tiles, and then opened the side of the aluminum ducting and looked down through the vent. He added six-feet of cable to the listening device, and tore a piece of duct tape off the roll with his teeth to stick the device to the aluminum pipes. It tested fine. Then Kevin slipped the VCR into the space below the tiles.

    "What the hell you doin', mahn? Fran's goin' crazy look' in for you."

    "Hey, Billy! Geez, you scared the shit out of me. I'm not doing anything, just working, you know. I'm not sure where to put the last camera-line down here. There's no room here to work in, and I, ah, I guess I'll have to run everything back along the original lines."

    "Listen, I don't know what-cha doin', I just come up to find ya. Like I say, Fran's looking for ya. No radio?"

    "Uh, no. I guess I forgot it today."

    "I let her know I found you, but get to a phone and call the bitch, she been on my ass all day."

    "Yeah, I'm on my way right now."

    Kevin caught his breath and rolled his eyes. Billy was easy to fool, but if it had been Fran, well he might as well just head on home. He checked again to make sure the activator started the camera, then replaced the tiles. Back out on the roof was some fresh air, and Kevin worked his way down to the house-phone in the hallway.

    "Sorry, Fran. I just got caught-up on this camera above the 29th floor. I was hoping to finish it yesterday, but it will have to be strung back across the original lines, and that will take another day or so."

    "Kevin, you don't have that long. We can't have you up there all week when there are guests in the room below you. You need to finish today, or wait until some other time."

    "Sure, no problem. I know a way of speeding-up the process. Oh, and could you have Billy come back up here with another spool of blue cable? Thanks."

Chapter Fifteen

Kevin made a quick trip downstairs to give Karen a call from a pay phone and they made a date for late the following evening.

"What-cha doin' now, mahn? I haul the damn cable back up there, and you're taking a break down here! You could have gotten it yourself. I ain't your fetch-an-carry slave. You still mad about the meeting thing, well we be even now, you cahn go screw yourself!"

"Geez, settle down. I had to run down her to call Ka...ah, Fran, cause the phones in the hall don't call out. I mean, the one in the hall wouldn't dial, it was out. So, I came down here, that's all."

"Yeah, well you're *not right* lately," Billy whined.

Kevin's stomach rumbled. He couldn't run up to the employee cafeteria like most of the workers, but a quick sandwich was in order. Maybe he *was* acting a bit strange, but he really needed to eat.

The "Sandwich Post" was four miles away, and Kevin decided to take his meal home so he could grab a few more items from the kitchen table.

Inside the apartment, his answering machine was flashing-out a tune. The message was from Paul, upset at being stood-up for their golf game today.

"Whoops, better give him a call. Hi, Paul? Yeah, it's Kevin. Look, I'm really sorry about golf today, I just forgot. Work is totally nuts, and really, it just got past me."

"Work, huh? Becky said you might have something else on your mind. She mentioned you were out with Karen a couple times this week. How's that going?"

"Great, just great, terrific lady. But it's work that has me a bit discombobulated."

"Wow, good word! If you say it's work, then it's work," Paul laughed, then continued. "Listen, I can't get out to the course anymore for a while. Today was my last chance. Shot a 79, and you missed it. Since you missed today, and next week is out, how about just sending me the forty bucks I would have won?"

"Hey, last week I was just building-up your confidence. I'd have kicked your butt today, and the next time we play, I'll prove it." Kevin's chest was pumped out and ready to take on the world.

"Fair enough, but it may be a while. I've got a couple new items on my desk. Call me next week or so."

"Got the Vellardi case too, now?"

"How the hell did you know about that?" Paul asked while looking furtively across the room of detectives.

"Packard. He's got a big mouth, or well, he doesn't know how to whisper. I heard him at the course the other day."

"Well, forget about it. It's federal, so just forget about it."

"All right, my secretive buddy. Sorry again about missing you today. Say 'hi', to Becky, for me. I owe her one."

"Yup, she already knows. She's been on the phone with Karen everyday, it's amazing how much they talk these days. Don't blow-it, that's one terrific lady you're seeing."

"How right you are. Talk at ya later."

Kevin turned towards the table and noticed that familiar smell. "Damn, left the Weller on again. Maybe I *am* under a spell."

He shut off the soldering gun the correct way this time, then grabbed a few parts and his radio.

"Back to the salt mines," he said to the empty room. The typewriter sighed, and went back to sleep.

He didn't want to announce his arrival to the security office, but he needed to call-in.

"Tahoe-one, this is Kevin in surveillance, do you copy?"

"Copy, this is Tahoe-one."

"Hey, Leonard, I wasn't sure if you were still here or not. Pulling a 12-hour?"

"Affirmative. Our fearless leader, Mr. King, insisted on it. He will be in later tonight. And what can I do for you?"

The response caught Kevin by surprise. Leonard sounded almost human, coming close to telling a joke.

"Well, to be honest with you, I needed to ask about the camera in the stairwell on 29. When I worked on it earlier, the picture was way off. Can I........"

"Negative, please do not work on the cameras above floors 25 tonight. You know we do our own work on those."

"Take it easy. We're on the same team here, I'm just trying to save you guys some work since I'm up here already."

"Thanks, for the thought, but we will finish the work ourselves. Tahoe-one, out."

"Gee, and have a pleasant afternoon too, you jerk."

That was it, from now on, Leonard would be called Lizzardo. He was a cold-blooded reptile after all.

After reaching the roof, Kevin bent down to open the access panel, but it was locked. His blood ran cold, and he got that tugging feeling in his scrotum. If Fran had been up there looking for him he was dead unless he had replaced all the tiles over the penthouse.

He reached for the keys in his pocket, and turned over the lock. It was the same one. There was a spool of cable that Billy brought up, and a red seal on the ground.

"Maybe nobody came in here after all. I probably locked the doors myself," Kevin said with a hopeful voice.

The words echoed inside the long, tomb-like room as he pulled the door up.

Inside, the walls were finished in a flesh colored stucco that was so rough, it hurt your hand if you leaned against it. The floor was mostly concrete, except where you could crawl even further down to the ceiling fixtures. Kevin decided to go ahead and run another line across the crawl space towards the elevator. Unsure at first, he believed this area could be accessed via the elevator shaft.

Later, his box of parts and tools all packed-up, he headed out to the roof. Putting the panel doors down and snapping the padlock, the seal caught his eye again. It was an unused slot machine seal, clean and unweathered. The number on it was 00227722.

Computer driven slot machines have a central control, and a plastic seal is placed around the opening to the motherboard. To get at the chips inside, the seal needs to be broken. It is an easy way to make sure no one has tampered with the motherboard. If the seal number does not checkout against the latest "logged" entry, there is a problem. The game chip is only checked on large jackpots, and when it doesn't checkout, the State Gaming Control Board is called.

"I'll think about this later," Kevin thought, as he headed down the stairs. He wanted to get on with his real job. He had almost finished when the cable ran-out, and another call to the cave became necessary.

"Sorry Kevin, everybody else is gone. It's just George and me in here tonight. You don't expect Fran to be here after 5 p.m., do you?"

"No, I guess not. I'll come get the cable myself. Thanks anyway." The phone clicked loudly. "Unbelievable, another trip downstairs! Whew, these coveralls are really getting bad."

He climbed back out of the elevator access door in the side of the shaft and back to the roof, then on to the third floor. When he got to the main hallway, Auggie Taylor was passing by.

"You know," Auggie said, "nothing good ever happens while walking down the hall to a break, and then you have to walk all the way back, and it's even worse because your break is over, and you have to go back to work, and that's really not good, you know?"

Auggie was not a well person. Kevin liked him.

"Now Auggie, I do remember a few good things happening on the way to a break."

"Yeah, like the time you were going to the lunch room at Harrah's, and I was coming through the arcade at the end of the hall."

"Huh?"

"Remember? You had your hand out to push the door open, but you were looking at me, and then Jennifer the cocktail waitress opened the door and walked out, and you mauled her right in the hall."

"I didn't *maul* her, I just brushed her a little," Kevin pleaded.

"Right, you buried your hand up to the wrist in her tits as I recall."

"All right, but that didn't turn out so bad."

"She never went out with you."

"That's not the point. She was so terrific about my groping her. She just kept right on walking, looked back and said, 'How about dinner first, next time'. You know that was really nice. She could have been really bent, but she was great."

"Yup, she was really *fine!*"

Auggie turned left into the employee cafeteria, and Kevin continued on, back towards the small set of stairs at the end of the hall. It was nice to run into someone that he used to work with. They had last worked together on "day-shift" at the Sundowner. What a job that was. Some days you went an hour or two without a single customer on the craps game. Brutal. If you got along with your fellow dealers, it really helped. Of course Auggie was always trying to "get along" with them.

The day-shift dealers Kevin had worked with were more family oriented than the swing-shifters. The swing-shift work-day ended at 2 a.m., and the dealers always wound-up at the bar waiting for the toke-committee to finish counting their tips. Once their money arrived, it was easy to go back to playing video poker and washing the evening away with cocktails.

Dealers always take great care of the bartenders. Of course, they take great care of each other, too. The problem is that you wind-up spending more time with your fellow workers than with your family, if you still have one. Then you have to use that great casino line: "I had a few drinks, you better drive", thereby absolving yourself of any guilt over the rest of the morning......... "I wasn't driving".

Kevin thought about the old days, when drinks were free at the bar because the pit bosses could "comp" them. All those free drinks, all those times you worked with a dealer the next day, that you were *free* with the morning before. He was glad he had been married while dealing, and worked day shift.

The rest of the evening was uneventful. More work was done by Kevin on his *real* job in two hours than he had done in the past day.

Chapter Sixteen

A strong wind rustled around Kevin as he strolled out to his car. It was warm, his hair swirled. The soft feeling made him relax. Running into Auggie had been a nice happenstance. When they worked together, there was a lot of fun and jokes, but he realized that his career was standing still, like so many other casino workers.

The gaming industry had gone through a huge transformation in the past twenty years. Where once there was a definite hierarchy, there was now parity. In the past, you had to work your way *up* to being a craps dealer, and then you were considered a cut-above the other dealers, and you had an easier time becoming a pit boss, back when being a pit boss was a position that people admired. Before Atlantic City, working in a casino was glamorous, and a pit boss was revered. Now casinos were as common as McDonald's.

The wind whistled into the driver's side of the car from a small opening where some molding was missing in the rag-top. It hissed like a punctured balloon until Kevin turned a corner and caught the wind napping, blowing in only one direction, but he was practically home by then.

He turned another sharp corner and heard grinding below him. In his side mirror he could see sparks. The MG slowed and Kevin stepped out of the car. His battery was on its side, under the car.

"Un-fucking believable!" Kevin sighed. The battery had worked its way through a rusty floorboard and must have been dancing along the past two miles. "I can't believe it. How could that happen?"

Kevin put his shoes into motion and walked home. A laugh accidentally slipped from his mouth at the thought of the battery hanging-on for dear life, dangling by the battery cables. What the hell was a battery doing behind the passenger seat anyway?

Hunger, as always, came quickly to Kevin, and he searched his refrigerator for something interesting when the phone interrupted his quest. On the other end of the line was Tolan.

"Listen, Kevin, you know I don't like using the phone. And, I don't like being stood-up."

"I didn't stand-you-up..." Kevin started to complain.

"You didn't respect my time here. You dropped by, but you were supposed to be here for ten minutes, but you only gave me *five*. When I don't get the whole thing, I get a little cranky."

The voice came cold as a tombstone, more agitated than usual.

"I'll come by for a few minutes next week."

"No, Kevin, you owe me five and ten more next week. If that is too tough, you better start selling your casino chips on *Ebay*!"

"Hey, I don't even have a computer," Kevin pleaded, the thought of having to sell his prized chips giving him more of a sinking feeling than the thought that Tolan might send a friend over to visit.

"You can always use one at the library. You only got such a big piece of my time because I knew you would take care of me. Sort things out, and make sure I see you next week. Remember, 15 minutes."

Tolan hung up, and left Kevin dizzy. He was bailing, but the boat was floundering and beginning to sink. After pacing around for five minutes he gave Karen a call and asked if she was available.

"Sure, just let me get a few things cleaned-up. I didn't think I would see you until tomorrow, but tonight is great. See you in about an hour or so?"

"Terrific, I'll be there. He tried to sound enthusiastic, but his energy level was too low. The room spun just a little to the left as he hung the phone on the wall. Shaking his head from side to side, he headed for the shower. Getting together tonight would be the best thing indeed. Besides, he *needed* to see her.

"So, I'll be tired tomorrow morning. Big deal."

The shower was warm, and his head cleared, but the listless feeling remained. Kevin turned the temperature of the water to a cooler setting and let the water wake him up. A quick shave also helped, and he forgot about his debts for the night.

Kevin decided against his coat and opened the door. No car.

He walked back inside and broke his date, then made the slow walk back to his car for repairs. It was a long night.

Chapter Seventeen

Morning arrived, and Kevin pulled himself from bed and worked his way through the bathroom, kitchen, and out to his car. As the MG rumbled into the Royal's parking lot, he swerved sharply to avoid a line of pedestrians. The lot had been sectioned-off, and there, gleaming in the sun, was a large Reno Police Department "Crime Scene" evidence truck. The sides were emblazoned with sparkling red and yellow letters, belying the grim job it held each day.

An average day at the Royal included several calls for the local EMT's, as well as a call or two to RPD. At an altitude of over 4,000 feet above sea level, it was not uncommon for Reno's visitors to experience dizziness and even pass-out from the combination of alcohol and excitement. Some were just rusty at having fun, while others simply became too aggressive once the alcohol took effect. It was amazing how often a few drinks could incite a nice, stable person to try and take-on the entire security department.

Waving and buzzing in the wind was enough yellow and black tape to line a parade. Perplexed guests walked past the crime-scene just as Kevin did.

"Howdy, Leonard, what's going on?"

"Good afternoon Mr. Webb, there was an accident last night. I am sure Fran can fill you in. Please proceed to your normal place of employment."

"Sure, thanks for the scoop, buddy."

He proceeded on towards the surveillance room, passing quiet employees along the way.

"Fran, hey Fran, wait up!" Chasing her down, his steps thundered in the corridor.

"Hey, Kevin. I suppose you heard about Terry King, poor guy."

"No, I just got here. What the hell is the big secret?"

"It's not a secret, just sad. Terry was working on a camera mount on the roof and fell off. The police have been here all morning, and the Gaming Control Board too. Weston has been all over, I guess because the State Disability System will be looking us over again. I'm sure they can find a reason to raise our rates over this accident."

"Are you talking about the 29th floor roof? Wow, that's a hell of a fall. When did all this happen?"

"We have the accident listed at 0235 this morning, but the time is not exact, because all of the cameras from 25 to 29 are out. RFD didn't get called until about 0300."

"Nobody knew he fell?" Kevin asked as his head leaned forward on the axis of his neck.

"No. He came in to work on the cameras when they went down, so the security department knew their boss was on the roof, but since they were down, nobody knew he fell. The camera relay to us from the hallways is also down. Were you working on those?"

"Sure, but I was done testing them. Mitch and I were checking each relay a couple days ago. When did you say the cameras went down?"

"It must have been after 2200 hours, because Billy would have noticed during the tape-change if all the tape-ends were blank. He was working a long shift also because George called-in sick. The police have already looked at a few tapes, and I'm going to be working with them for the next few hours."

Kevin had never gotten used to military time, and it took him a moment to realize she meant 10 p.m., and Fran was halfway down the hall by the time Kevin called to her.

"Hey, with the police here, can I still get in the elevator shaft to finish, or should I start on the baccarat room?" There was no response from Fran, even though she was close enough to have heard his question. Perhaps she was thinking of Terry.

Turning back towards the employee lounge, he saw Steven Lester and Antonia talking in the computer room. Kevin realized that she was almost completely out of his mind this week.

Rounding the top of the stairs, Kevin blundered directly into Ron Packard. "Hey, Ron, how are you doing?"

As though they had never been introduced, Packard gave him a curt "hello" and walked down the short flight of stairs Kevin had just come up.

"Nice talking to you," Kevin thought.

The process for punching-in was a bit different than when he had started in the gaming industry. Big clubs were switching to employee cards. It was easier to just program each card with a job description, then let the employee "swipe" themselves in and out. The cards were also good for entrance keys to different doors, with the exception of the surveillance department, which had an older keypad entry on its door. Fran liked to be different.

The door swung open and Dan greeted him.

"Hey, buddy, I watched you on the monitor for thirty seconds. Forget your code?"

"No, I was just thinking. What was Packard doing up here?"

"Who?" Dan asked, uninterested.

"The RPD Captain, Ron Packard."

"I don't know who you mean."

"I just passed him, wasn't he in here for tapes or something?" Kevin's arm moved forward and back, as if the motion would help Dan remember Packard coming in and then going out.

"No, Fran set up a room on the mezzanine to look at tapes with the police. I didn't see him in the hall."

"You saw me, but not him?"

"Sorry, I guess I missed him. This isn't a real secure area you know, there are always people walking around up here, and besides, I was busy watching those ladies down there in section nine. They were here before, and just as lucky."

"Who, those gum-poppers on monitor 20?"

"Yeah, they must be up six or seven thousand playing those dollar video pokers, can't miss. Seems like it was the same thing last time. No tracking cards, and no taxables. They got a bunch of "hand-pay" jackpots last time they were here, too, but no taxables." Dan changed a tape, and went to the shelf for labels. "Damn lucky, no IRS to pay."

"We should all be so lucky, Dan. Hey, I know that guy on monitor eight. The one with the stupid look on his face. Bobby Ferguson. He still owes me money from poker."

Their conversation was broken-up by a call from the casino floor.

"Sky, this is slot supervisor Ned Peters. Please verify film and give me clearance for a pay-off on slot 2023. Progressive video poker winner."

"Copy, Ned," Dan said, then continued, "well Kevin, your wishes have just come true. Your buddy just hit for twenty-three thousand and change. Maybe he can pay you back now."

"That would be a nice change! You know, that's two guys I know that got lucky here in the last few weeks. Teddy Ryan was in here, and he hit two jackpots in two days, almost fifty-grand!"

"I guess his luck ran out, 'cause he got run-over while crossing Virginia Street. He didn't owe you anything did he?"

"He what? I didn't know that."

"Yeah, it was on the front page of the Gazette. Happened down by the Pioneer."

"Wow... ah, no, he didn't owe me anything, in fact, I think I owed him a few bucks. I talked to him after he hit that second jackpot. He waved to me as I was going out the door. Remember I told you I was talking to a guy on the casino floor when Weston saw me? Man, I thought Weston was gon'na shit! Came right over and told me to go home. What a tight-ass!"

"Is that Dave Baker working on slot 2023? Checking the seal himself?"

"Hey, if I was the casino manager, I would probably wonder why those machines keep hitting so often too. I mean, we don't even do the EPROM tests anymore because they keep hitting at below $25,000."

Dan's look was blank, so Kevin headed to work. Checking the supply room got him his toolbox back.

"I must really need more sleep or something, I don't even remember leaving this here."

As he headed on towards the rewiring job ahead, he gazed into the computer room again. Antonia was sitting alone at her desk. He waved and beckoned her to come out. As usual, she didn't seem to actually be doing anything.

She stood up, and the red cotton dress stuck to the back of her chair for a split second. The long legs it had been hiding were revealed as lean and tan. As she walked over, Kevin couldn't help seeing how small the waist was on this dress. She did look good, but he couldn't get over how small she seemed.

"Hey, have you shrunk, or what?"

"Hi, stranger," she purred, sliding across the room towards him. "No, I have not shrunk. You have just been ignoring me. Where ya been?"

"Working on the roof and elevators all week. Lots of rewiring to do."

"Oh gosh, be careful. You know what happened to Mr. King. It's all over the casino today!"

"Yeah, too bad. Actually, I'm done up there. Could you do me a favor?"

"What have you got in mind?" she asked with a tilt of her head.

"I need you to look-up a few people for me on the player tracking system. I'm wondering how they are doing on our slots, long-term. What do you say?"

"Can't do it," she hissed. "I'm not authorized to access that information, or give it out." She gave him a pout, then a sincere smile. "Sorry".

Antonia winked, and strolled back to her desk, slowly.

Kevin shook his head slightly and rolled his eyes upwards as he headed on. Maybe he was getting smarter. She seemed very obvious today.

The security officer on the twenty-fifth floor did not seem impressed by Kevin's request to continue working. He called to "Tahoe-one" for clearance, but Leonard's voice could only be heard by the officer, who wore an earpiece.

"What is going on? I'm on the clock!"

"I know, but "Tahoe-one" says you have to wait till he gets here."

"Great. Is he coming from the office?"

"Yes, he's on his way from the S.O."

Kevin paced the floor, then walked over and looked out the window. The day was becoming stranger every minute. He was unable to see the corner of the parking lot from this window, but he hoped the police were wrapping things up. His reflection in the window looked strained, confused.

"Mr. Webb," said Leonard.

Kevin could see Leonard in the window. He was wringing his hands as he often did when approaching an irate guest.

"I need to talk to you about last night, before you continue working."

"Sure, what's up?" Leonard.

"Well, that's an odd question. Certainly you know I am going to ask you about Mr. King."

"No, I don't know that you are going to ask me about Terry. Is there a problem?"

"You need not be on the defensive, I simply want to know what you are working on, and when you were done on the roof last night."

"Leonard, lets not insult each other's intelligence. I know you're an ex-cop, and certainly you've spoken to Fran about the jobs I've been doing the last couple weeks. I'm not sure exactly when I finished on the roof because I went from there to the roof of the elevator, then worked there for a while before going home."

"Not the roof of the elevator, the 29th floor entrance."

"Yes, you're right, but it was the *top* of the elevator that I started on, and then I worked on another three floors."

"I'll let the police know that you are ready to speak to them."

The pompous ass had just asked questions that the police were going to ask him. Kevin seethed inside as Leonard talked through the small speaker on his lapel.

"Mr. Webb, would you please accompany me down to the S.O.? There is a Mr. Kozar waiting to speak to you."

"Sure, I'll be happy to talk to Paul."

Leonard cocked his head to the side like a dog hearing a whistle.

"Hey, I know some police officers too!"

Chapter Eighteen

    Outside the security office, Detective Kozar was pacing around with a cigarette in his hand. He didn't smoke, not anymore, but the cigarette was a forced habit, something for his hand to do. He would just light it, and stare at it. The smoke curled around his arm, forcing its way into his jacket, and later this evening, Becky would know what a rough day he had endured from just the smell.

    "Hello, Kevin. Thank you for joining us. This is Detective Rollins." Hand shakes all around sealed the meeting. "You know of course, that everything in this office is taped, both audio and visual. Please be advised that you are not being questioned per se, we are only acting here currently to help-out Mr. Baker, your boss, who will be joining us in a minute or two."

    "However, as this *is* a police matter, you may request that any information you provide be done so at RPD headquarters, and in the accompaniment of legal counsel. Should you desire this, please advise us now, before we proceed."

    A fall from the roof would not usually merit such a speech, but under taping, everybody was more careful. "Paul, I'm more than happy to answer any questions you might have about my *job*. Please feel free to ask me anything about it."

    Paul started his questioning, intent on looking at his notes, not Kevin.

    "You were on the roof and working at approximately what time yesterday?"

    "Well, I was back and forth from downstairs to the roof several times. The first was probably ten minutes after I punched-in. I left the roof for the last time before going home at about 7 p.m."

    "So you were home by ten after seven, or so?"

    "No, I, well, I finished on the roof at about seven, but then I went to the elevators to do some more work. I was probably there until about nine, or nine-thirty."

    "So, you didn't go home at seven?"

    "No."

    "But you were home earlier in the day?"

    "Well, yes, I did go home to get some tools earlier."

"Will the time-clock reflect each time you were off the premises?"

"Ah, I'm not sure."

There was an awkwardly long pause as Paul looked around the room sheepishly before asking Kevin if he had seen anything unusual while he was working, and whether the outside door to the roof had been locked when he left.

"I'm pretty sure the door was locked, it's on a spring hinge, and I don't think anybody could get through it unless they had a card-key."

"Kevin, that is really all we need right now. We will be continuing our investigation and will get back to you if anything else comes-up."

"Oh, ah, well, thank-you."

Kevin was amazed at how serious Paul had become, and at how badly their talk had just gone.

It was a bit strange, Paul never really asked him about the job on the roof. Fran had probably already told Paul what he was doing in the crawl space, and Paul was probably trying to help Kevin by pointing out the times he was off the clock, it just didn't work out that way.

Kevin gave it all some thought while walking back to the elevators. He had gone home well before Terry fell, so he couldn't know anything about that. The guard at his apartment could verify when he arrived home. It then occurred to him that the police must have already done that. Paul had mentioned they knew he was home in the middle of the day. Then again, Bob probably mentioned he went out later that evening.

The real question was could he get back to the 29th floor and retrieve his camera.

Chapter Nineteen

Confusion was getting the best of Kevin. His walk to the elevators was laborious and slow. Heel to toe, heel to toe. The ride to the 25th floor was uninterrupted and quiet. The officer there looked bored, but still annoyed at being interrupted again.
"Hey, I'm back. Let my people go."
"What?"
"Can I go to work now, or what?"
"Yeah, you're clear man, go ahead."
Kevin was a bit surprised, but refused to show it. He reached down for his radio to call engineering, but it wasn't on his tool belt. In fact, his tool belt was missing too.
"Great, no tools. Now where in the hell did I leave everything?"
He walked in a small circle, starring at the space 20 degrees above eye-level where this type of information is always found. His small circle widened until it reached the phone at the end of the hall.
"Hey Dan, it's Kevin. Is my tool belt down there?"
"No, you probably left it where you were supposed to be working, or in the detention room, with the police."
"I was only in the S.O., not the detention room, and I know you were listening, you jerk. Now come-on, is my belt down there?"
"No, and I'm busy, bye."
"Shit. I'll have to use something from the supply room."
Kevin made a trip down to the surveillance room again. As he passed the computer room, he saw Mr. Lester alone at his desk.
He pushed open the heavy door and stepped into the air-conditioned comfort of the accounting offices. This computer room was just one of many around the building, slightly different because it usually housed a young beauty named Antonia.
On a property like the "Royal", the main source of revenue was gambling. Twenty years ago, most properties in the state of Nevada were more than happy to let all the other departments lose money. The games department would more than make-up for

any shortfall in the restaurants, or the hotel. Not anymore.
Now every department was expected to pull its own weight. Some might only be able to break-even, but nobody was to show a loss. Table games, which for so long had been the champions of the industry, were now only responsible for perhaps a quarter of the gaming revenues. Keno and poker might make a few percent, like the sports book, but the bulk of the income was from slot machines, and slot clubs were started for this very reason.
The slot club functioned by getting the player's names, and making sure they got a little something back for their money. Player's used to get comped because they knew a host, or by how many discarded paper coin rolls were lying around their machines. Ah, the good old days. Now each player got a card like a credit card, and inserted it into the machine they were playing. Every pull added more information to their account, and every pull, more "comp" or complimentary dollars to return to them in the way of free meals and rooms.
"Hi, Steven, I was hoping you could give me some information on a couple of slot players. The first is Teddy Ryan, oh never mind about him, ah; just give me the address of Bobby Ferguson. He lives here in town I think. Can you pull that up on the screen?"
"Well, sure, let me switch screens, and here we go. All right, Robert Ferguson...there are two listed here with addresses in Reno. Age?"
"Oh, maybe 45 or so."
"Well, there's one who's 42, and one that's 60, so, Mr. 42-years old is living on...Sorry, no address."
"Well, what do we have on him?"
"No address, phone or occupation. I guess his occupation is playing out slots. He's had a lot of play here the last few months. He's in almost $200,000 and winning, let's see, $168,000. Lucky son of a bitch. There's a social on him, if you want it."
"That's not lucky, he's losing $32,000!"
"No, his cash-in is $201,302 with a play-through in the millions, but actual coin-out with the hand-pays, is $369,000. He's winning a hundred and sixty-eight thousand."
"Wow, how can anybody be that lucky?"
Kevin looked up from the computer screen. It was so clean, almost sterile compared to crawling around in the casino's ceilings. Maybe that was why Antonia liked this guy. He was neat and clean.
"Where's Antonia?"
"I don't know, had to run off for something. She's always doing that. Here's your other guy."
"Don't worry about him, he's dead."
"Really, that's too bad. Look, thirty-nine years old, and another lucky son-of-a-gun. Hit us for almost 150K. How did this guy die, carrying the winnings home on his back?"
"No, he got run-over on Virginia Street. Probably drunk from partying with all his winnings."
"Must be what he was doing with them. Look, he lived in the "Lucky-Seven" motel, on old Highway 40 in Sparks. He wasn't spending any of those winnings on that flea-bag place."
"What does that date here mean?"

"That's the last action on this account, twenty days ago."

"Ah, Steven, could you keep quiet about this info? It's important that nothing leaves this office, all right?"

"Sure, no problem. I envy you, it's like you're a spy or something."

"Yeah, double-o nothing," Kevin said while laughing, then thanked Steven and walked back to the door. As he walked out, Antonia walked in. Her perfume was there just before she was.

The tool belt made its way to Kevin's waist as he picked it up from the floor of the storage room. The black flashlight dug into his ribs, but everything stayed in place. That was important when you were twenty-feet up a ladder.

When the elevator job was half done, Kevin looked at his watch. Where had seven hours gone?

"Might as well give it up for the night. I need sustenance."

It was nice to get so involved in your work that the day shot past you. When he concentrated, his work was excellent. But now, with the current job done, his mind returned to what had occurred that morning.

He was dying to take a walk to the roof and retrieve his equipment. It would be nice to keep his job. Walking back to the cave, he saw the casino was packed. Weekend crowd. If it looked like this everyday, he could probably get a raise. The clubs in Las Vegas had this all week, but Northern Nevada was a summer and holiday spot.

Kevin dropped his tool belt in the same storage room, knowing that tomorrow he would remember where it was. Accessing the cave, he caught George with a magazine in his hands.

"Hey, with all this to watch, you have to read a magazine? And you didn't even hear me at the door?"

"Shut-up! Who the hell are you, my mother? I hate this job, so once in a while I do a little reading. Big deal. The only action is on BJ-2. Guy's in thirty-grand and all he's got left is what's in the betting circle."

"That wasn't my point, and besides, sometimes the gods just wait until it's your last chance to give you a break"

"Go string some cable."

"Yup, nice talking to you, too."

Kevin slammed the door, then turned and gave the camera on the wall a single finger salute, but it didn't make him feel any better. As he walked down the hall, the slot tag on the roof came rushing back into his mind. Kevin called down to the slot supervisor on duty and had her do a check in the logbook. It took a few minutes as the casino manager had to bring his keys for the double-keyed cabinet.

Cindy called back on the hall phone he was using and told him the number he was interested in was on the motherboard of slot 1781.

"Cindy, I really appreciate your checking for me, but I also need you to open 1781 and make sure that exact seal is on the board."

"Give me five more minutes," she grumbled.

When she called back, she gave it to Kevin straight: "I checked it myself, the numbers match and the paperwork is correct, Okay?"

"Great, thanks very much."

Kevin rolled his neck backwards until he got a resounding "pop", then headed out of the building.

He drove across the street to the Crystal Bar and got change for a dollar. Calling Becky, he thanked her for the barbecue and introducing him to Karen. She was abrupt, saying she was busy; thanked him for the call and let him know that Paul was still at work.

Two more quarters rolled into the phone and made the bells ring again as Kevin called the police station. He got patched through to detectives, but had to wait for Paul to get off another line. When Detective Kozar tried to switch lines, Kevin got cut-off. That was enough beer money spent. He headed back to the bar.

Chapter Twenty

Detective Paul Kozar never worried about a lost call. If it were from anybody important, they would call back. He ran his right hand through his thinning blond hair repeatedly. The file in front of him was a lawman's nightmare. The suspect in question had a long list of questionable activities including two arrests for handling stolen merchandise, racketeering, and everything pointed to the suspect being guilty, but there were no convictions. And, there was too much income from his legitimate sources.

He made constant trips from his home in upstate New York to Colorado, and to Mississippi. Often his next stop was Reno, then Las Vegas. He stayed in luxury hotels and casinos, but didn't gamble.

Paul watched the smoke rising from his cigarette on the desk. It went up about a foot before starting to curl and turn in a circle. Before the cigarette went out, he lit another, and put it in the ashtray with the first. He couldn't quite get a grasp on Vellardi's need to travel to Reno.

Although he had spent his share of time on stakeouts, this type of suspect wasn't likely to produce any good results for them. It wasn't like the movies, where the bad guys showed their true colors in a couple hours and you could just go in and arrest them. Usually, you sat in a small room freezing your butt off, and nothing happened. He was not looking forward to sitting in the parking lot of the Comstock or the Royal, and waiting for Vellardi to go somewhere. However, with Vellardi arriving in a day or two, Paul was going to have to do something during his visit.

The financial papers below the smoke were something to be proud of. Every operation Vellardi owned was making a great deal of money. Old mob guys have learned to be more careful with the IRS. It's easier to pay tax on at least a part of the money you are earning in illegal activities than it is to get caught for tax fraud. Vellardi was pumping money into his legit businesses so he could justify his pricey lifestyle. The question was, how much more was he earning, and where was the money coming from?

The smoke spread across the desk towards Paul as the door to the detectives' area was opened. Fred Meyer slipped easily into the room, making the doorframe appear

huge. His freckles closed in on each other as he squinted through the haze.
"I thought you quit," he stammered, swishing his arm across the desk.
"I did."
"OK," he squeaked back at Paul. "You getting anything from the Royal yet?"
"What, any ideas?"
"Intuition."
"My gut says that Mr. King did not fall from the roof as he was working on the camera," Paul stated while checking his hairline once again. "The camera was down and in need of repair, but there was no tool box on the roof with him. He was not the usual guy to repair the cameras, but he specifically wanted to be there late that night to do it himself. And, although it was a two-minute fix, the camera was down all day long."

The head of detectives looked down at Paul, giving his statements some thought, and Paul looked up, taking-in the red hair exploding from the sides of Fred Meyer's head.

"It's only been a day, but judging from your cigarettes, you have a real problem with this case."

"I might even start smoking 'em!"

"Listen, Packard is chewing my ass about overtime, but I don't care. Get some more help in here. Call Smith or Cambric and start going over King's history. I'd like something on my desk in the morning."

"You got it, boss."

"What have you got on Vellardi there?"

"Just waiting for him to arrive. Do we spend the extra man-hours on what is probably a dead-end stakeout with him this time?"

"Let's worry about that later. We've got too many irons in the campfire right now."

Paul made a humming sound as he viewed the file, half agreeing with his boss.

Meyer walked off, and Paul looked up to see he was gone. The guy needed a bell.

Paul stared back at the dwindling smoke and tried to decide which call to make first, Cambric for overtime, or Becky, to say he would be home late. Rock and a hard place.

Chapter Twenty-one

Kevin took the walk to his car very slowly tonight. He had that strange nagging feeling in the back of his head. It wasn't just the job, and it wasn't the camera upstairs that he had placed above the penthouse. Deciding that it was the lack of time he was spending with his daughter, he felt bad, but at the same time he was happy to have solved this minor puzzle.

Inside his apartment, there was a new message on his answering machine. The voice was not anyone he recognized. Then the answering machine started. He looked down the hall, then at the table. One of the "ears" was in action.

"Hi, it's Karen. Are you all right? I got a funny call at the store. Give me a call when you can."

He started to answer her out-loud. Voices were coming from the phone, and from his listening pad. He was dizzy. When the phone recorder stopped, he decided what he needed was some food, but he settled for a can of mandarin oranges and a Seven-Up.

"Man, I think that lobotomy is beginning to have an affect on me."

Kevin flopped down on the sofa, which released an audible whoosh, and he pondered how to get his gear off the roof.

Ringggg... "Oops, the phone. Hi, this is Kevin."

"Gee, what a strange way to answer your phone!"

"Sorry, it's a habit from being on a two-way radio all day."

"Actually, Kevin, I'm happy to hear you are so relaxed. I was worried because the police called. What have you got going on, didn't you get my message?"

"Yes, about thirty seconds ago. I just walked in."

"Sounds like you have a party going on."

"No, no, it's just the TV, hold on a second..."

He ran to turn off the audio console, then thought better of it, twisting the knob to record-only.

"I just walked in and turned on the TV to catch the news. So you heard there was trouble at the club last night."

"I hope that means you were not personally *making* the news. That's terrible about your manager falling off the roof. The news said it was a possible homicide."

"No, well, maybe it is. I don't really know. I think he just fell off the roof. He was working on a camera mount and fell."

"Cameras? I thought that was your job," Karen stated hesitantly.

"Thanks, you're starting to sound like the police did today. Security has cameras of their own, and I only work on them if they ask my boss first. However, security is very stubborn, and they think they know everything, so…"

"Fine, I was just worried, that's all. I will call you later, bye."

The line went dead before Kevin could reply. He squinted his eyes and thought for a moment before calling Karen back.

"Hey, it's Kevin. Did we get disconnected, or did you just dump on me?"

"You obviously are very busy. Maybe some time in the future we can see each other again. Give me a call."

Again, Kevin was left holding a silent phone. He wandered around the apartment for twenty minutes before getting the courage to call a second time.

"Listen, it's Kevin again. I know you don't know me that well, but I'm starving, and there is no one I would rather spend my evening with than you. Could we go out, now?"

The jury went out, but eventually Karen agreed to dinner.

Kevin took a quick shower, and wondered why Paul's boss had called Karen. At least it hadn't been Packard, that would be even stranger. Actually, the fact that Paul was handling the case at the club was strange enough for the time being. He wasn't losing his sanity, but his back seat was filling-up quickly. He slipped across the wet tile and grabbed a towel, then went to try Paul on the phone again.

Chapter Twenty-two

Paul spent an exorbitant amount of time keeping his desk clean. It pained Becky to drop by the precinct and see everything so neat and tidy. He certainly wasn't like that at home.

Paul reached across that very desk and answered a call from Meyer. When the boss calls, most people get that little nagging feeling in their mind about being in trouble. Not Paul, never entered his mind. He pushed himself back from the desk to the squelch of the metal chair legs. Paul missed Kevin's call again as he headed to Fred Meyer's office, striding along as though he was doing his boss a favor. Not arrogant, or even cocky, just calm and ready.

"Want to know why you have to come to my office," Meyer asked, his red eyebrows dancing like tiny fires above his eyes. "Because I'm the boss. You know why I don't have a full head of hair? Because I didn't learn to delegate blame early enough, but now I know that if you guys screw-up, it's your fault, and, if I screw-up, it's still your fault. It's a great system."

"Fred, what's up?"

"I'm talking about Teddy Ryan. He can't give us anything else on Vellardi from the morgue. You said he was vulnerable, and it was your job to convince me. Detective Sanders here tells me that he was living in a roach-motel in Sparks, but he had plenty of cash on him when he was run over. One of his buddies says he suddenly had more money than he knew what to do with this past month. I really think that Mr. Webb is hiding something. Find out what it is."

"Ryan got hit in front of the Pioneer casino," Sander's added, while pounding his left fist into his right palm for emphasis. "No witnesses, and no suspects after two weeks. The only thing we know for sure it that he was seen with a young lady earlier in the evening while playing blackjack."

"And...." Meyer asked of detective Sanders.

"He was playing up to $100 a hand, but there were nickels all over the street where he was hit. Maybe the young lady he was with saw the accident and dropped her

-74-

nickels."

"Like I said, Paul, lean on your buddy Mr. Webb."

"Kevin works at the Royal like two-thousand other people."

"Right, and he's a friend of yours, so push him till you find out."

Paul walked the white and gray speckled tile floor back to his office. Eighty-two steps. He counted them off while part of his brain ticked away on the angles of this case. The air was fine for all but the last two steps, then it got thick with smoke, and the tiles in the ceiling were yellow, not white like down the hall.

Teddy Ryan was a rounder. He worked all the angles in life and tried to stay clear of the law, but that wasn't always possible. When he was picked-up for a minor offense, he was always enough help to the police on some local burglaries or fencing to get himself released. The RPD had plenty of contact with people like Teddy Ryan. He called himself a professional poker player, but he was hanging onto the bottom rung.

Sure, some people have a tremendous talent for sizing up their opponents, and putting it to use across the green felt. Not everybody was a "real" player, like Red or Tuna. Most just hung-on by making a few shady deals now and then. Anything was better than working.

In the world of business, Vincent Vellardi had an uncanny knack for sizing up his opponents. He was a hands-on boss, unlike most people with an organizational tie. His reign was one of intimidation. You worried about him showing up, because that meant there was a serious problem, and the problem might be you. However, you had to worry about him *not* showing up, because a hit always happens when you are the most comfortable. Every time a connected boss gives you a new assignment or promotion, you look over your shoulder first. But once you've looked, it's too late. You're either paranoid, or dead.

Chapter Twenty-three

Kevin's wallet was almost bare, and he searched the little cubbyhole in his desk for a loose Franklin. Nothing doing. Well, that left only his suit pocket. "Bingo, two bills," he nearly sang while pulling them from the dark of the closet. "Damn," it was a five and a one. "Six bucks isn't going to do for tonight".

"Let's see, what can I get from Wells Fargo Visa? Oh-oh, maybe B of A Master Card....He turned the card over and dialed the number on the back. "I could have some room on this one..."

"Welcome to Bank of America. Please enter your account number, beep."

"Good evening, could I have your sixteen digit account number please."

"Sure," Kevin read off the sixteen-digit number followed by an expiration date that would soon be past.

"Mr. Webb, the reason your call was transferred to an operator is because your account is past due. Have you made a payment in the last few days?"

"Ah, yes, I have. I made a $200 payment two days ago, but my car broke down, and I could really use a slight increase on my line."

"I see. Mr. Silver, I show your account as having been extended from $5,000 to $7,000 last year. I'm afraid I can't authorize any additional increase, however I will give you credit for the $200 you say is in the mail, and allow you to charge up to $135."

"That would be great. Thank you very much!"

"Is there anything else I can do for you tonight?"

"Nope, thanks again," Kevin said, almost dancing while hanging-up the phone.

"Wow," he exclaimed. "That was easier than I thought."

While he had the phone in his hand, Kevin decided to call his friend Josh at the Gaming Control Board. The office in Carson City handled most everything in Northern Nevada, but there was an office just a couple miles away on Apple Street, there in Reno. His friend had joined the board as an "ex-lawman" from Wyoming. The board insisted that all active agents pass POST tests and attend the police academy in Las Vegas. Every agent carried a weapon. Somebody like Josh with a gun always scared Kevin a little.

"Gaming control, Winslow."
"Hi, Josh, it's Kevin Webb"
"Hey, Kev', what's happening. Somebody else fall off your roof?"
"No, but I've got a few questions about our cameras. You guy's busy today?"
Josh shook his head vigorously for those in his office to see, then added some verbal confirmation. "Naw, it's pretty slow. Picked up two guys yesterday that you had film on last month. Remember the guys with the $5 slot slugs, and one of the guys had a ratty black shirt with monkeys printed on it?"
"Oh, yeah. The guy with the pony tail, right?"
"Yup, same one, and his buddy. They were at the Legacy for the third time. They busted 'em and called us. I'm glad you called, actually. What can you pass on about Mr. King? Any new cars, or houses? Any funny stuff going on?"
"Nope, not that I'm aware of."
"Well, call me back if you pick anything up on him. What about his pay?"
"I could check with Ferguson at Human Resources in the morning, but you could probably get that easier than I could."
"Tomorrow? Aren't you at work?"
"No, I'm at home, and going out tonight, if you must know."
"Listen Kev', I've got to go. I'll talk to you later."
"But, I..."
It was too late. The line was dead.
"What the hell was that?" Kevin wondered aloud. "It has got to be a full moon!"

Chapter Twenty-four

When Kevin hung-up the phone, he reached over to the phone book and explored a listing for the Cattle Company restaurant on Wells Avenue. Their food was better than the usual fare found in the casinos, and they had *real* atmosphere. If you wanted privacy, the booths were perfect with their floor to ceiling walls, and the waiters were attentive enough to make you feel like you were the only people in the whole restaurant. Just thinking of the place made Kevin hungry.

It was too warm for a suit, besides, Kevin didn't like the one he owned. Just a nice pressed shirt and some slacks would do fine. Completing the outfit was a pair of $9.99 shoes he had picked up at the grocery store.

On the way out the door, Kevin took a final look at his audio devices. This time they were all lit. The recording started and stopped after a certain decibel was reached or lost, and didn't take-up much tape that way. Unfortunately, being started upon noise, you often lost the very beginning of a conversation, or listened to a blank tape for a while because someone slammed a door. Maybe he would come home early tonight and give a listen.

Yeah, right. If Karen just tilted her head a certain way, he would wind up in bed with her. But he wouldn't beg! He might whimper a little, but he wouldn't beg.

Karen's house looked bright as a star when he turned the last corner. He knocked upon the heavy door, trying to see-in through the small slats of glass that graced its center. Kevin heard a loud thump, and with all the strange events this week his heart began racing. She looked so terrific after she opened the door, that his heart continued running laps in his chest.

"Before we leave, I want you to put that ottoman in your car and get rid of it," Karen demanded. "I just did a "Dick Van Dyke" over it. It just leapt-out and tripped me, it's always had it in for me. What is so funny... I just told you I almost broke my neck, and you're falling into my rose bushes. I hope you get stuck by the thorns."

"I'm sorry, but I got this great image in my head, you know, you dressed in a suit, and falling. I swear, I was worried before you opened the door."

"Oh, and I suppose you're no longer worried about me? And I wasn't going to go out with you tonight. I'm not sure I can trust you. However, that laughing just cost you at least a lobster tail. Where are we going, or was I supposed to cook?"

"No-no, you said to 'pick you up', and I already made reservations. But they aren't for about a half-hour."

"And?"

"And what?"

"And *where* are you taking me? Please try to keep-up with the conversation. I'm the one that just had a terrible fall."

"OK, Humpty Dumpty. I made reservations at the Cattle Company. Sound good?"

"Sounds terrible. Do I look fat to you, like Humpty Dumpty?"

"No, you look great."

"Correct answer. We can go now."

"Uh, I don't have room for the ottoman in my car."

"Well, it can stay for now. But if you show up some time and I am lying dead on the floor, it will be your fault. At least that's what the police will think."

"I'll take that chance."

"Well, how cavalier you are with my health," she replied, swinging her hair sideways with a flip of her head while leading the way to the car.

"I'll protect you. I'm even going to get the car door, so you don't get hurt opening it."

"My hero. Will you cut my steak for me, too?"

"If the knife's sharp, I'll probably have to."

They drove wordlessly into the night, but before reaching the restaurant Karen demanded to know where Kevin had been the night before. He told her about the dangling battery, but she looked leery about his explanation.

"Reservation for Webb, party of two."

"Yes sir, that will be just about ten minutes. Care to have a spot at the bar?"

"That will be fine," Karen purred.

"Sorry, did you feel left out of the conversation?"

"No, but you might not want a drink, and I do," Karen stated. "I had a terrible day at work. The phone kept ringing, and then two of my salespeople didn't show up for work. Sometimes, owning a store is a like getting popcorn in your teeth."

Kevin's mouth moved, but words could not be heard over the squeal from the dry ball bearings in the barstool. He started over. "Karen, I haven't always been a peeker you know. I used to own a sporting-goods store. Remember the "Weekender", at the corner of Virginia and Del Monte?"

"Yes," she acknowledged with a nod, "as a matter of fact I do. The prices were very good there. In fact, I bought Rich some golf clubs for Christmas there three years ago."

"Oh, so you were the one."

"Sales were that bad?"

He shook his hand and denied there was a problem with sales. "I just wasn't ruthless enough. If we got a good deal on something, I kept passing the savings on to the customers. Never really got ahead money wise, and when sales went flat I didn't have the capital to hold-on."

"Under capitalization is a major downfall. Over half of all new businesses fail due to a lack of funding. Sometime you just have to make certain choices and live with them."

"How many crash due to bad partners and greedy wives?"

"That's the other half. Same story there, you make a choice and stick with it while it is still working. Picking a good partner in business, as well as life is tough."

"Damn near impossible, in my case."

"Been married twice you said?"

"Yup, I was double-dipped."

"I won't ask what you were dipped-in. But maybe, the third time is the charm."

"Perhaps. If I get the courage to try again. I don't want to get called-out on a third-strike."

"Interesting metaphor. Move on. Life is short, and only as fun and exciting as you make it. You have to decide what you want, then unleash yourself and go after it."

"Wow, you sure have loosened up after just one drink."

"Mr. and Mrs. Webb, your table is available now."

"Hello, ah, Jeannie, I am not sure I want to live with a sporting goods salesman so we are not married."

"Oh, well, ah.... here we are. Can I get you another cocktail before your waitress arrives?"

The hostess never even looked at Kevin. Karen had taken over, and instead of being insulted, he just sat back and smiled. She had gone from librarian to corporate raider in just a few weeks.

"So dear, what am I having?"

"Do you like steak and lobster?"

"Yes, Karen, I do."

"Teriyaki?"

His head bobbed an approval.

"Medium?"

"Got ya Medium rare!"

"Kevin, if I give the waitress the order, do I have to pay for the meal too?"

"Oops, I was going to stop at an ATM. You may have to pay tonight. I've got exactly eleven dollars on me."

"You're lucky I'm so fond of you. Not every woman would let you get away with that."

"It's the truth. I guess I can use my credit card here, just as well as at an ATM."

"Nope, it will be my treat, but I may need to take the cost of the meal back-out in trade."

"If you twist my arm, I'm sure I can comply with your wishes."

The waitress arrived and introduced herself. "Did you folks decide what you want?"

Kevin nodded back towards Karen. "She's doing just fine, let her order."

Karen had no problem fulfilling the request.

"I'm glad you took care of that. I can't pronounce most of the wines on this list, and I sure don't know which ones are best," Kevin said when the waitress had left.

"Neither do I, but if you act like you do, most people believe."

"Ah, finally I learn your secret. And I was beginning to think you were a ruthless business woman who would stop at nothing to get ahead in the world."

"Honey," Karen started, her voice taking on the tone of a schoolteacher. "I am a good business woman, but you don't have to be ruthless to make it. You simply need to know your products, and your customers, and then do what it takes to survive."

"You're right, I suppose. But maybe there's something inherent about it all. I don't come from a family of entrepreneurs. They always worked for someone else. I wanted to break the mold, but it turned out that I just *went* broke."

"Rich always told me that some people are sellers, and some are buyers. You have to "sell" yourself to your employees first, then they can take care of the buyers."

"Mmm, right now, I'm just happy to be working for a steady paycheck. My job a few weeks ago was pretty mundane, but lately, I haven't minded going to work so much. I suppose some of that has to do with you."

As they worked their way through a warm spinach salad with croutons that Karen pushed to the side of her plate and ignored, they continued with their philosophical discussion on bosses and employees. The food, as always, was good, but the company made it fantastic.

"You know, maybe I just didn't get the whole idea, the big-picture. I can't always see what's coming up. And I wanted to do everything myself."

"Well, you need to be *wide-eyed* about everything," Karen stated while starting to use her fork to point, then catching herself . "So much can get past you while you're doing things that should have been delegated to somebody else."

"You're right. I wasn't forceful enough. You should have heard this guy a few days ago. Man, he was shouting at somebody to 'just get it done', and he sounded like he would kill the guy if he didn't."

"Well, I don't think you have to go to that extent."

"You know the guy that fell off our roof, he's our director of security. There was no reason for him to be doing the work up there on the roof, that job should have been given to somebody else."

The wheels and gears had been turning in Kevin's mind all day. Finally, they meshed together

"Honey. Kevin, hello. Mr. Zombie!"

"Huh?"

"Sweetheart, don't worry. You'll get another chance to be a boss and run a business. Finish your steak, I'm ready for dessert," she stated with a wide smile and the anticipation of something terribly bad for her.

He looked out the opening of their booth. The crowd had been barely present for the past hour, but now they were starring into the tiny booth, listening, waiting.

"I'm too full to finish. Are you sure you want dessert?"

"Yes. They have a great chocolate pie here, sure you don't want any?"

"Nope, not my style. If they don't have 'Baked Alaska', then nothing for me."

Kevin tried hard not to drum his fingers or play with his spoon during the fifteen minutes it took to get the check. The pie looked good, but his throat was dry.

"Honey, you are doing it again. Going into a trance is not good."

For the first time since they met, he was thinking seriously about something other than her eyes, her lips, her very presence.

"I'm a little befuddled."

"So I see. I am happy to have such an affect on you. Or is it something else?"

He staggered a bit towards the door, with her on his arm. At the car, he fumbled with the keys and finally reached over the half-open window and pulled up the lock.

"Did I leave a tip?"

"Yes, you left a whole eleven dollars. I slipped in another twenty. Are you all right?"

"No, I'm really confused about something. You're smarter than I am. Maybe I should let you in on this, I just don't know."

"Try me."

"I already tried you. I like you. In fact, I think I love you, and I'm worried about screwing up our relationship by letting you in on what I'm trying to figure out."

"That is really insulting. Nothing you confess could make me love you less."

"Isn't that from a song?"

"Sure. I steal one line, and you catch me. Let me help," she pleaded, while stamping her foot.

The night air helped clear his mind, but it seemed too cold to leave the top down. After he had secured the "rag-top", he thought of how to explain his predicament.

Chapter Twenty-five

Kevin wasn't in the best shape to make any decisions, and he had to ask Karen which way to turn out of the parking lot.
"Did you want to do something else?"
"Sweetheart, do you want me to drive?"
"No, I'm not drunk. I just don't know which way to go. Did you want to catch a late movie, or just head home? And who's home?"
"You couldn't sit through a two-hour movie in the dark if you were nailed to your seat. You might be able to stay-up for another two hours in the dark if I keep you company though."
"Sure, why not."
"That doesn't sound too convincing. Talk to me," she implored. Her thin eyebrows dipped low and she tried to catch his eyes. "What's racing around in your head?"
"Nothing. Well, I'm just not sure what's going on at work. I've been so busy the past couple weeks I'm not sure what's happening."
"What *do* you know about what's happening?"
"It's nothing outrageous. Just that, well, I'm paid to be a snoop. I'm suspicious of everybody and everything. Not you, but at work, everybody. Did I tell you that I get my check in the mail? Nobody is supposed to know that I work in surveillance."
"But you told me, and Becky and Paul know. Are there many others that know about your work?"
"Sure, Gaming Control, and RPD I guess, and my ex-wife."
"So you have a guilty conscience about spying on people at work. It's understandable. Don't let it get you down. That's what they pay you for."
"Sure, but they don't pay me to, well, it's only supposed to be at work."
"What does that mean? So you worry about your job, even when you are not at work. Lots of people do that. You just need to relax. Take me home, and we'll sit in the

hot tub. I'll rub your shoulders and kiss your ears, and I promise, you'll forget about work." The corners of her lips and her eyebrows moved upwards at the same time, as though they were connected by string.

She was right. He forgot about work as soon as they hit the steamy water. She wasn't always right, though. He almost confessed about his listening devices. She didn't need to know about those. So long as they went to her house, and not to his "recording studio", he was fine.

At three in the morning Karen woke Kevin from a dream. He didn't really remember it, but he was arguing and mumbling.

Kevin apologized, and against her wishes, headed home. He needed to listen to his recordings, and see if there was anything new. He slipped off his shoes and grabbed a Seven-Up, knowing he was going to have some explaining to do in the morning.

"Let's see, nothing on secondary receivers. Activation on one through six only."

Kevin picked-up the phone and called work.

"Hi, Billy, it's Kevin, how are you?"

"Great dude. You gon'na come down for some early work, maybe give me a break?"

Kevin closed his eyes and shook his head in silence. "No, I'm still working on cameras. I have to finish the Baccarat room too, so I'll...

"I don't think so mahn, you be coming in at three like the rest of us bats up here for a while." Billy's smile was bright in the surveillance room.

"What?"

"Dont'cha look at the schedule mahn? You done playing outside for a while,"

"When did this happen?"

"Yesterday. I think Fran, she gon'na call ya in the morning. Sorry friend."

"Well, shit!" Kevin said while pounding the table. "So what else is going down?"

Not much. I'm sittin' here alone, so nobody gon'na steal my pizza. Oh, and it's because Mitch got the boot."

"What the hell for? He works hard."

"Something about not watching the pit enough. There were some players crimping cards, and we got taken-off for a little, so Mitch goes, and I sit alone watching the pit on graveyard."

"What about the cage, and the slots."

"Yeah, they're up on monitors, but low priority, mahn. You better concentrate on the games department when you here."

"Whatever you say buddy. Hey, we get any play from that guy in the penthouse?"

"I don't know, who's up there?"

"Could you call the desk and find out for me please."

"You got it. Back at ya in five." Click.

Seemed like everybody was hanging up on Kevin this week. Hadn't Billy ever heard of a "hold" button?

Kevin pulled the input lines off the primary console and attached a back-up, just in case there was anything happening while he listened to the tapes.

He was bored in two minutes. Doors closing, phones ringing, but no conversation. There might be some problems with the output device getting past the

Reno/Tahoe Airport. He was certain that he had earlier turned the system to record-only. The phone rang, causing Kevin's arm to jerk forward with a life of its own. Seven-Up flew across the table, and tiny bubbles danced around wires, diodes and tapes.

"Hello? Yeah, Billy. You won't believe what I just did. Spilled my damn drink across my tapes, er...across the table."

"What?"

"Nothing. What did you find out about the penthouse?"

"Some guy named Wallace, Frank Wallace. Ring bells for ya?"

"No, must not be a player."

"You're wrong, Shelly down at the desk say he's been up there for a week, and it's on a marketing comp. Must give us some pretty good play."

"I guess you're right, thanks."

This time it was Kevin who hung-up without a goodbye. He ran to the kitchen and grabbed some paper towels. They weren't the "quicker-picker-upper", and he had to go back for more. The tapes looked hopeless. After drying-off the console, he tried to save his tiny spools of tape. Listening to each one in turn, there were some sections that would no longer reveal any audio output. The sounds he *was* able to hear were no more exciting than earlier. From the non-damaged areas, he was able to hear a few names, and an order for dinner. The television was playing in the background, and if he was correct, Rich and Frank both wanted their pasta cooked firm to the tooth.

"Great, I'm looking for a plot, and some high roller wants his dinner cooked a certain way. I must have a hell of an imagination."

Sleep came singing from the bedroom and Kevin succumbed. The bed was unmade, but still inviting. He scrunched down into the mass of covers and slept soundly. When the phone rang at seven-thirty, he didn't even jump, just rolled over and answered.

"Hi Kevin, this is Fran. Listen, I need you to come in late today, not until three. We will be a little shorthanded, and I need you in the box all night."

"No problem, I'll be there. What about the cameras for this weekend?"

"We'll have to put those off until later in the month."

"What about..."

The line was dead again.

"What is this, hang up on Kevin week?"

At eight, Kevin forced himself out of bed. Those nagging questions had all gone away, with the exception of Paul. He called the RPD detectives office.

"Good morning, detectives, Reed speaking." His voice was a stilted staccato.

"Hi, is Paul around?"

"Who's calling..."

"Ted, it's Kevin Webb, is Paul around?"

"Detective Kozar is on assignment, can I take a message?"

"Geez, you guys sure got formal all of a sudden. Tell *Detective Kozar* that I'll be at work after 3 p.m., and I'd like him to give me a call."

"He has your work number?"

"Yeah, Ted, it's Kevin. Tell him to call me, all right?"

"I'll do that Mr. Webb."

"Wow, you spill one Seven-Up, and look what happens!" Kevin chuckled to himself, but the little man in the back of his head didn't see the humor.

In the dining room, there were lights on five of the seven consoles. Two had no tape spool, as he had run out. He turned-up the volume so the words weren't just leaking out, and gave a listen.

Guests in Jacuzzi suite 2712 were talking about a gallstone operation, while some guests in suite 2612 were discussing the lack of hand-towels, and complaining about a horrid plane ride. His job down at the club suddenly seemed exciting.

Kevin started the tape from the penthouse, room 2900, and let it run while he got some toast and cereal. It was mostly the TV and an occasional yes-sir, just like last night.

"Boring, boring," Kevin was saying as he washed out his bowl, still listening.

"We're out of here on Tuesday, no sense hanging out any longer. Not with people pitching off the roof. You finish up with the Palace, and when Frank finishes with the numbers from the Crystal, have him meet us in Denver. It's time to dump everything for a while. It's not worth the fuckin' aggravation. And get Toni back up here."

"Yes sir, I'll take care of it."

The room was silent again, and the tape stopped. Nothing too strange there, except the casinos that were mentioned were part of the City Casinos group. Kevin realized why he hated big companies. These guys were just some managers, and they were using a *very* expensive suite to do business, all expenses paid no doubt.

The alarm rang from across the table. It would have been time to go to work, but with the 3 p.m. start, he still had several hours. His line of sight took in the typewriter. He tried to ignore it, but there was a stain from last night's spillage under it.

This necessitated actually picking the typewriter up, and moving it. When all was spic-and-span, he placed the heavy Remington back where it had been. He leaned forward towards the paper against the platen, and felt as though he was being sucked into the life of the typewriter. His eyes watered, and he felt a bit woozy. Finally he gave in, took a seat, and started typing.

The words flowed as if water were running from his head and his heart, straight down his arms and into the keys. He played them carefully, then violently. The story took on a new life of its own, and Kevin was surprised by his sudden burst of emotion. When the page filled, he pulled it out and reached for a new sheet. The dozen or so pages had soaked-up some liquid, and they crinkled in his hands. His head swiveled back and forth but there was no other paper.

Inserting a moisture thickened page, he went on with a few words. The letters came out smudged, and as the keys struck, they made an annoying scratching sound. He stopped.

His head went into his hands and he rubbed at his temples while the Royal returned to his thoughts. He wasn't going to be a paid writer at any time soon, and those lines to the penthouse needed to be moved before he lost his only revenue.

Kevin wondered why Paul wasn't returning his phone calls.

Chapter Twenty-six

From the stale confines of the RPD detectives' office, Paul Kozar was thinking almost the same thing Kevin was. He needed to get back on the roof of the Royal, and let his imagination go to work. There didn't seem to be what looked like a scuffle on the roof, and no reason to believe the deceased had left the roof at the hands of another person. He may have decided to stand on the wall to work on the camera pole and slipped off his perch.

There could be some moisture outside at two in the morning, but there were no footprints on the ledge. A screwdriver and a wrench were found in the parking lot, but there was no way to know if it they were Terry King's without a fingerprint check. The wrench was scratched and bent as though it fell from the roof also, but he didn't need it to lower the pole.

No, those were the least of Paul's problems and questions. The real question was about the occupants of the penthouse. They had not heard or seen anything, and with five feet of open space and a concrete ceiling between them and the world outside, their lack of knowledge about what had transpired above their heads was understandable. However, *who* they were, was not understandable.

When officers canvassed the area, they came back with a name. In the penthouse, which was registered under the name Frank Wallace, was a familiar face, Vincent Vellardi. Vellardi was too smart to throw anybody off a roof, and his underlings should know better, but still...

At least Detective Kozar had plenty of time. He knew Vellardi would not help increase the suspicion about him by leaving town quickly. He would act like nothing had happened. And even if he were guilty, he'd never act it. The guy was stone cold.

Paul reached across his desk and answered the ringing phone. Actually, it was more of a dull "buzz" than a ring, but there was definitely somebody on the other end of the line.

"Yes, Fred, I know it's a high priority. I was just thinking of driving back and checking the roof again, maybe something got past us."

"Give me something to give to Packard, you know how he is. He gave us Vellardi's file and I'll bet he's got all kinds of stars dancing in his head. He would love to nail him with a murder rap, but Vellardi's no idiot. He didn't come out here to set himself up for a murder rap. Reed is working on King's background and you should go on back to the Royal, then call me. We might want to talk to Vellardi. I don't want to spook him, but this is a nice chance to get at him."

"How come our information on his arrival was a week off? It would have been great to be on top of him since the day before yesterday."

"I'm not sure. I've got two plain-clothes officers in the parking lot right now. Do you want to use Reed as a back-up?"

"No, I don't think Vellardi's going anywhere. He's always here for at least a week, and he's not going to take-off now."

"It's your call. Don't forget to call me before you leave the casino"

"You got it, boss," Kozar promised.

Chapter Twenty-seven

"Kevin, come in here for a minute!"

It was Steven Lester, his voice strained and angry. He rushed out of the office, arms thrusting the door away.

"What the hell have you been telling everybody? I helped you out with a little information, and I got a write-up. Antonia was right, you're a jerk!"

"What? I haven't been talking to anybody. With the exception of the police yesterday, I've just been working on cameras ten-hours a day.........no conversations."

"Yeah? Well I just screwed-up my chance for a raise. My review is in two weeks, and all my boss is going to remember is that I gave out privileged information."

"Are you talking about those two slot players? I could have gotten their account information from the club desk downstairs..."

"Well next time, you'll have to."

"Wait a second Steven, I wasn't working on anything specific. No reports filed, so who the hell got uptight about this?"

"I don't know, but next time you need something, forget it!"

He slammed the door hard enough to cause his co-workers to prairie dog over their consoles. His arms were still waving as Kevin walked up the stairs. Well, he never did like Lester, anyway.

Kevin couldn't get the keypad to accept his code and finally knocked on the door. He felt like poor-old George.

"Hey, Kevin, come on in."

"George, I was just thinking about you."

"Take the left-side of the room tonight. We've changed a few monitors, and I need you to work mostly on pits one and two. Table seven has a pretty good card counter working. I confirmed him at 90-percent accurate to the count. There are a few others today, also."

"What's up with day-shift? Nobody wants to "back the guy off"?"

"No, bunch of wimps down there. The lady on nine is worth looking at."

"Yes, she is. That's a very low-cut blouse. Can she play?"

"Who cares? No, really, she can't, but I think the guy on third base can, or he's using a computer. He's up about ten thousand. When he got to the table he came-in two-hands of $500 in cash and hasn't looked back."

"That's a six-deck shoe. Did he start on a fresh shuffle?"

"I don't know, it could have been."

"Well, I was just wondering if this guy was part of a team. You know, a few counters sitting at different tables, and when the count is high enough in the players favor on a shoe, the guy with all the money gets called in and makes his big bets."

"I just told you he was up ten-thousand on that table."

"Yeah, and there he goes. How long was he there, just the one shoe?"

"Yup, I figured maybe a computer because he stood the whole time and seemed to be watching first base when he first got there."

"Well, I'd probably be watching the lady with the blouse too. Was she moving her hands around, like she was signaling the count to him?"

"I don't know, you'll have to run the tape back. He's going to pit two now. You stay on that, I'm running to the bathroom."

George walked-out and left Kevin alone in the room. He was keeping a trained eye on the "money player", when he remembered what Lester told him Antonia had said. It hurt. How could she tell Lester he was a jerk?

The player on table seven got-up and walked to the cashier's cage to cash in his chips. Kevin followed him over and recorded on his sheet that he cashed out thirty-eight hundred. The player never smiled. He didn't have that little "skip" in his step like most of the big winners did, he was all business.

Kevin called the pit and asked about the other player. Keeping an eye on him as he again walked around the pit, it seemed more and more like he was looking for a signal from a counter about a good shoe.

Team play was something that had to be taken seriously, especially on the six-deck shoes. If the counting player on the game keeps track of the cards that have been played, he knows when the edge is in the player's favor. The counter bets the minimum at all times, and uses a numerical value for each group of cards to track where the odds are. The big-player is called-in when the count is good, signaled the correct count, and then proceeds to make bets in the $500 to $1,000 range. That means the team of players have their big bets out only when they have the edge, and there were some decent teams still playing at casinos around the country. "Jerry's" team and the "Ken Uston" group had been very effective in the 1970's and early 1980's. Now the best team was a bunch of guys that had originally met in college at MIT.

Kevin hung up with the pit and called security. He requested a "radio" sweep of the pit, to be sure there weren't any computers in use. George always thought somebody had a computer because he refused to believe anybody could memorize all of the play variations that had to be implemented for different counts. It didn't take "Rain Man" to run-down a six-deck shoe, but you had to be good.

Before security could do their sweep, the "big-player" headed to the cage. Kevin again followed him, and noted his cash-out at $9900. He must have kept some chips in his pocket, because he had taken more than that from the tables. At $10,001, the cage would demand a photo ID due to the Nevada Gaming Control Board's Reg-6 laws and ask for a social security number. Gaming control and the IRS are everywhere these days!

When George returned, he viewed the drop-off in activity as his signal to go home. Fran had staggered the shifts to make-up for the loss of Mitch, and Kevin would be alone for a while.

Once George left the room, Kevin pulled his brief case up to the desk and popped it open. Inside, the contents were a mess. After sorting the tapes, he re-threaded some questionable ones and gave them a listen. They were ruined. The next batch wasn't much better. He had given-up the idea of checking the rest when the phone rang.

"Hi, is this Kevin? Can you talk."

"What? Who is this?"

"It's Steven Lester."

Kevin stammered a surprised "hello".

"Listen, I'm sorry about earlier, I was really hoping to get a raise so I could move into a new house. Are you there?"

"Yes."

"Well, I've got a problem. I just ran a program on our last one hundred slot winners with jackpots over $5,000. The guys you asked about earlier were on the list for eleven jackpots. That's way above probability for the past two weeks. Then I notice there are three other people with eighteen jackpots between them. That's twenty-nine percent of all the big jackpots, to just five people."

"That does seem a bit out of line."

"Well, yeah, its high, but that's not the strange part. Since all five are club members, and use their tracking cards, I can look at their over-all play. Combined, in the past two weeks, they only have about twelve hours of play, each jackpot came after only ten or fifteen minutes, now that's too weird," Lester stated, while pounding his pencil into the desk for emphasis. The lead snapped off and rolled in a perfect little circle, back to where it started.

"Anything else?"

"Every jackpot is from $10,000 to $24,000. No little ones, and nothing high enough to result in an EPROM check. This time, Lester underlined this $24,000 amount several times with a new pencil.

"All seal-checks?"

"That's right. The supervisors just check the seal attached to the mother board."

"Don't tell anybody about this, all right."

"No, I won't, and I've got more for you," he continued, the excitement in his voice obvious to Kevin.

"You want to get together later tonight? I'm off at eleven."

"Sure, it's my Friday and Antonia is busy. How about the "Cue Ball?"

"I'll see you there at about twenty-after."

Strange indeed.

Chapter Twenty-eight

Dan walked into the room as Kevin tried for a third time to reach Karen.
"Grayson's Jewelry, this is Karen, can I help you."
"Yes, I'm crazy about somebody, but I can't see her tonight."
"Hi, honey. I was just thinking about you."
"I'm stuck in the small box I call home over here at the Royal. I get done real late tonight, so I thought you might want to have breakfast in the morning. Any interest."
"Yes, compound! I like to have breakfast, will you be there too?"
"Is this Karen?"
"Oh, stop. You can come by the house tonight if you want. Becky Kozar was asking about you. Tell me the truth now, what's going on?"
"Nothing, well, something, but I don't know what. It's really funny, I called to talk to Paul earlier, and he never got back to me. The detective on duty acted like he didn't know me."
"Honey, I trust you, but I guess you need to try calling Paul again. Come by after work and I'll have coffee ready."
"I've got an errand to run so it'll be midnight or so. I love you."
"I am happy to hear that. See you later."
Kevin heard a strange muffled sound again. He had heard it earlier, but it was so faint, he had forgotten about it. He picked-up the phone to see if there was a voice coming from it.
"Shit."
"What?" asked Dan.
"Nothing, I left a radio on in my briefcase."
He opened the case, and caught part of a conversation. He would swear he had turned the console off, but there it was, with the lights on.
The conversation was heated, with one gruff voice giving a lecture and somebody getting chewed-out.
"That's it. You've fucked-up this whole place. Now we'll have to shut it down for months. Get them together at the shop and take care of them. Rich, get us set for Denver. And you, get out of my sight!"
"Yes sir," came the soft, faint response.
There was a TV playing in the background, but the conversation was apparently over.
"What the hell is that?"

"Nothing, Dan, my radio."
"Yeah, right."
"Really, it's nothing. Hey, where's our schedule for the week?"
"I just walked in the door, how should I know?
"Oh, here it is, sorry," said Kevin.
"Are we sure it wasn't you who fell off the roof on his head?"
Kevin brought the 29th floor up on monitor eleven. All he had was a single mounted camera above the elevator. He was in time to see a woman leave the second bedroom and head down the hall, and he watched as she scooted quickly towards the stairway. Kevin followed her path by punching in camera numbers on his keyboard, starting with the stairwell. The views flipped by every two seconds, giving him a chance to catch her when she had walked to the floor below.

He peered into the fuzzy split of four video feeds call a "quad-shot" and waited. Finally, on the 25th floor, the woman, clothed in a light-blue dress, exited the stairwell and walked to the elevator. Her head was down. On the mezzanine a pretty woman got out of the elevator. She wore a light-blue print dress, with a large matching hat that obscured her face.

"Hey Kev', you in a trance?"
"No, just looking at a pretty woman."
"Yup, happens to me too."

The hours dragged by. Finally, eleven o'clock rolled around and Kevin was able to grab his briefcase and head for the door. When he got outside the building there was an RPD plain clothes unit in the parking lot., the same model they had used for years. The running lights were off, but there were two officers in the front seat.

He wondered if Packard had anything to do with this, or even his friend Paul. The "Cue Ball" was a few miles away at the corner of Keystone and Second Streets in an older, somewhat depressed neighborhood. It was a good place to shoot pool though, especially with the food they served. Great cheese burgers!

When Kevin arrived, Lester was nowhere to be seen in the crowd of mostly college kids, and for probably the first time ever, he was too keyed-up to eat, hanging close to the door. When Steven did arrive, they squeezed into the video-game area.

"Listen, Kevin. I'm in deep trouble," Steven whined, his eyes peeking carefully from behind his glasses. "Somebody pulled my work up on the computer system, so they know I'm still looking into the names you gave me. There is definitely some kind of a scam going on right now, and we've got to figure it out before we both lose our jobs."

Steven's words had come-out in small bursts, between breaths, and Kevin took-in what he had said, the confirmation exciting, but chilling.

"Yeah, listen, did you have anybody looking over your shoulder after we talked the first time? Anybody see what you were doing, or hear you on the phone?"

"It *is* a possibility, but I don't remember that happening. Who were you talking with yesterday?"

"Well, you may not believe me, but I swear I didn't talk about this with anybody. Only Dan was in the office when I talked to you on the phone, but I don't think he could figure anything out."

"It's too crowded and noisy in here. Let's walk up the street to the Gold Coin Casino."

As they walked out the door, Kevin caught a strong smell of "Escape". His eyes darted around, but there were no ladies near-by. Halfway up the block, a police car drove slowly past the two men on the street. The officers watched Steven and Kevin closely from their cruiser, and Kevin resisted the urge to turn and watch as it passed out of sight. Suddenly, Kevin caught that perfume again, and as he turned toward Steven, a gun muzzle made a new home in his face. It was enormous, and the smell gun oil, gunpowder, and perfume all mixed together in sickly-sweet way.

"Walk this way gentlemen," a familiar voice commanded. Antonia was still in her Spring dress, but the hat had been retired.

Steven tried to speak, but was cut-short by a burly man showing a knife. He forced them around the corner towards a waiting car.

"Well, *Toni*, what's going on?"

"Shut-up Kevin. You guys got lucky and stumbled on something you shouldn't have, and you fucked it up. Rich, get them in the car."

Kevin was surprised by his own question, the gun having grown to about three feet by now. From the corner of his eye, Kevin caught Steven in a whirl of motion, grabbing for the knife in his back.

Bad move.

The knife moved quickly, just high enough for Kevin to catch a glint of moonlight coming from the blade. Taking Steven's cue, Kevin lunged towards Toni, but she was too quick. Twisting sideways, she slammed the butt of the gun into his cranium. The next blow was from the concrete sidewalk as it rushed up to meet him.

First stars, then black.

Kevin tried to shake the cobwebs, his face scraping against the cold, rough concrete. Beside him was Steven, twisted into in a fetal position. His was on his left side, his right arm was behind his back as if his brain had stopped on the final thought of getting at the knife Rich had been holding.

Kevin's arms were pinned under him. He willed himself to roll over, and through blurry eyes looked at his hands. The left was the aggressor, holding a knife, and his right hand the victim. The blade had been thrust straight through, making it appear to be a magic trick, but there was nothing magical about the pain he felt. Rumbling from deep within, a howl Kevin could never have imagined raged from his mouth as he pulled the long knife from his palm. Both hands shook as the serrated edge cut against bone and tendon. There was a whirling of white light, and it stopped just long enough for him to realize his right eye and chest were screaming also.

He rested.

"Steven, can you hear me?"

Kevin pushed his way to his knees and crawled towards the still body. With his left hand, Kevin gave a shake and the body rolled-over, motionless. Steven's esophagus was exposed, like a botched tracheotomy. He had died quickly. Why Kevin had been spared he couldn't fathom.

There was a fine steam rising from Steven's open wound as Kevin peered through it and down the street, learning what deathly-quiet meant. Faintly, a car engine droned, and he tried to focus on the lights coming his way. As it got closer, there was no mistaking the RPD cruiser.

Kevin staggered to his feet, then fell to one knee. This wasn't going to go over too well with the police. Two men on the sidewalk, one dead, and one bleeding from knife wounds. One knife, one set of bloody fingerprints. He stood up and looked around for the knife, then back at the car. It was less than a block away. No knife.

"Fuck! There's no way to explain this."

The words came quickly from his mouth, but his ears took them in slowly, as if he was speaking underwater. As the neurons crashed around his jumbled mind, he realized maybe it was better to get the hell out of there. He got back down on his knees and searched the grass next to the sidewalk for the knife, and finally it was in his grasp. Staggering away, he moved towards a small yellow house with a picket fence. He was just able to thrust himself over the spiky protuberance, thundering to the grass beyond. His eyes worked hard, but the rest of his body refused to join-in. He lay there momentarily, the cool moist grass wetting his arms. The distance between Kevin and the police car shrunk with each passing second. Grasping the fence, Kevin pulled himself up like a fighter trying to beat a ten-count. His abdomen cramped and breath was elusive.

Worked his way upright, a crouch was the best he could do. He used the fence like a blind man, and each unbalanced step left him feeling as though he was heading down again. Light flooded-in from an open gate at the back of the home, offering salvation. Twenty steps, then ten, then five and through the gate. Across the alley he could see his car on the street. If somebody in his current shape could be considered lucky, he was, for he had avoided parking in the lot across the street, and his pummeled body could never have made the longer trip.

Behind him, the police were out of their car. By the time the lights started flashing, he was driving away.

Chapter Twenty-nine

The rear view mirror revealed a tired, older face. Blood was splattered across Kevin's forehead, and it cascaded like a waterfall into his nearly closed right eye. The MG's tires squealed as the car turned onto Keystone Street, and then again as Kevin shifted into third-gear and headed up the I-80 on-ramp to the highway. Veering sharply to the right, the wheel slipped in his bloody hands. Pain shot from his right hand to his head. For a short moment, he had forgotten about the gaping hole in his palm. From the other hand, he threw the knife across the top of the car and onto the dirt shoulder of the highway.

Lightheaded but determined, his mind raced as fast as the MG. His apartment was out of the question. Karen's home would be safer, if she truly believed in him. He wondered about her safety, and what she had wanted to talk to him about earlier. She obviously had questions about him, but there didn't seem to be many options at this point.

The cold night air crashed into the car, coming to the aid of Kevin's senses, but doing little for his eye, and he wondered if it was blood, or tears that he could feel running down his neck and pooling-up on the collar of his shirt. The thought came to him that perhaps Rich and Toni had been watching him from somewhere out of sight, and he glanced repeatedly into the rear view mirror. Even as the time approached midnight, there was too much traffic for him to know if he was being followed. His brain clicked back to the car he was nearly forced into. It was starburst blue, probably a Lexus. But then again, he just didn't know. Anything after 1990 looked the same to him.

Off the freeway and through a stoplight, he headed towards possible sanctuary. He eased off the gas and let the MG slow to a crawl, then pulled up to the curb a block away. There was a glow from the porch light, nothing seemed amiss. Continuing up past the house at a snail's pace he checked the cars parked along the street. They were all empty.

Kevin leaned on the car horn, then made a U-turn. He kept honking the horn as he slowly worked back toward the house. Karen opened the door and took a tentative step outside. As she did, the little MG sped-up and swerved in front of the porch. There was a slight screeching, and she jumped back to the safety of her home. A second set of headlights suddenly appeared from up the street.

Kevin screamed for Karen to get in the car. She hesitated.

"Karen, please, you've got to get in, they're coming! Hurry!"

She took a single step and stopped, as her good senses came into play, but the oncoming car forced her to make a quick, bold decision. She got in the car. With more screeching, the door slammed itself shut. In front of the car was a small running fence protecting a canvas of flowers that were peeking-up for the first time this season, but they quickly became a memory.

"Oh, my God! What's happening? Kevin, look-out!"

He swerved left onto the street, in front of the oncoming car. A tap on the brakes and then a sharp turn had the vehicles heading safely in opposite directions.

"That was close, thank goodness you got in."

"You're damn right that was close. You're crazy! What am I going to say to the Phillips?"

"What?"

"Stop the car."

"Are you serious?"

"Serious? You're out of control. My neighbors, you almost ran into them, and my poor little daisies." Her voice was high-pitched and quick. "Kevin, what am I sitting in?"

There was an audible gasp as she brought her hand up from the seat. Karen's sight traveled from her bloodstained hand to Kevin's face, and her eyes were wide as she gulped gallons of air.

"Oh Kevin, I'm sitting in blood. My God, what has happened to you? Stop the car."

"No, I can't. I'm in trouble. We need to go somewhere, maybe out of town. I thought that car was somebody else following me. I don't think you're safe at your house. They tried to kill me, and they killed Steven Lester."

"Who's Steven Lester? Kevin, slow down, there's blood all over you, all over the gear shift and wheel. We've got to get you to a doctor."

"I can't go to a hospital. I don't know who to trust. You are the only one I can trust in this whole town. Not the police, not the gaming control board, not my bosses."

The words were jumbled and confused. Then Karen's calm voice convinced him to pull the car over so she could drive. He couldn't refuse anymore. The adrenaline was still pumping through his veins, but too much blood was working its way out. Before he could get his door open she had come over to his side to help, and she was stronger than he expected.

"How bad is this? What *do* you know about what is going on?"

Kevin tried to answer, but she continued before he could form a coherent sentence.

"You must be light-headed. I'm going to stop at my store for some cash. I've got first aid supplies. I'll take care of you."

The words were more than music, they were a symphony. She hadn't asked if he was in the right, or in the wrong. Only if he was all right. He closed his eyes and they were at Grayson's.

"Oh, I don't have my purse, my keys."

Kevin leaned against the door, trying to get out and help. The sights around him were diminishing. His feet were in mud, his right arm unable to find the door handle.

"How do you open the trunk?"

"That's the hood, it's ah, what?"

"A crowbar, I need to break the glass on the door to get in. Don't worry, sweetheart, I'll get us out of here before the police arrive."

The glass front door was no match for a woman protecting her man and the shattering of glass was followed immediately by the howl of the alarm. Kevin was waving at the cobwebs overtaking his mind, and the siren's scream was deafening. His right eye had closed completely, and he had trouble focusing on Karen as she walked around inside the dimly lit store.

When he looked up again, the road was rushing past him and the jarring motion of the changing gears was turning Kevin's head into a heavy-metal concert, the amps right up against his ears. He tried to talk, but his lips were puffy, and his tongue had grown thick. He wasn't able to get the window rolled down, before throwing-up.

"Hang-on, we are almost there. Just a couple more minutes."

His mind was in reverse. He had no clue where they were, or how long they had been driving, but the car was motionless. Unsnapping his seat belt, he pulled on the door handle. The door swung open and the cold floor kicked his head.

"Honey, I'm sorry, I thought you could sit up. Look at me Kevin, stay awake!"

Karen was floating around him. No legs, just shoulders and a head.

"I cleaned you up a bit, but you need a doctor, you need lots of stitches. Do you understand what I'm saying?"

He dutifully shook his head. It hurt.

"I drove us to the Mt. Rose storage yard. We're inside the building. Do you feel safe enough to go to the hospital now? We can change vehicles, leave your car here. We just need to get you into the van. Can you stand-up?"

"Cerbanly, I'm fimb."

"Kevin, I need to take you to the hospital. We'll keep driving. Maybe Carson Memorial, or Tahoe Central."

"Central? No hospital."

"OK, take my arm."

On the way up the Mt. Rose highway, Kevin was able to roll down his window. The cool air felt good this time. For the next hour, Kevin told himself that he was coherent; he was fine, he was in control of his faculties.

"Karbin, I fink I really am all right. Please, jusp leb me go to beb."

"You probably have a concussion. You have a huge knot on your head, and you've lost so much blood. This is the toughest decision I ever made, trying to decide between the common sense of getting you taken care of, and believing that it is as dangerous as you say, and passing on the hospital."

"No, I'll be fimb. Jusp let me svep a libble."

"I've got a cabin at Tahoe and we are almost there, but if your speech doesn't improve, you're going to Tahoe Central."

"My spebch is fimb."

Kevin laughed, shocking them both. He even smiled. He loved her.

Inside the cabin, Karen helped him to the bathroom. The light above the sink blinded his left eye. When he could see again, he took stock of his reflection.

"Wow, I look like Rocky Balboa."

"Honey, you look like shit. Excuse me."

She busied herself removing his clothes. As his shirt came off, there was a gasp as she saw the wound in his abdomen. It wasn't deep, but it traveled a good ten inches. Kevin looked down and noticed for the first time that his right hand was bandaged.

"You do good work. Do you think this lump on my forehead will leave a scar?"

"I don't know, Honey. I did my best. You have become quite a challenge. Let me start a bath for you, then some ice for your head. Here are some aspirin and a Valium."

"No Valium, I have to keep my wibs aboub me."

"Kevin, take a drink."

Her voice was like nothing he had ever heard. Commanding and soothing at the same time, it traveled around the small room and settled softly into his ears. Valium and a bath, good combination.

His eyes were shut, then the left one flickered open. It was light outside. Karen worked the rocking chair beside the bed like a metronome. Swish-click-creak, swish-click-creak. Six hours had passed.

"How do you feel, sweetheart? I've been so worried. You've been mumbling all morning. Is Vellardi the guy that did this? And what's a seal chick?"

"Huh?"

"You were talking in your sleep. Mostly mumbles, but you said something about Vellardi, and the damn seal chicks. What's going on?"

"Oh, I'm dying here. Did I get really drunk, or do I have a sock in my mouth?"

"No booze, just a Valium. Do you remember how you got like this?"

"Yeah."

"Well?"

"Well what?"

"Are you going to tell me you are all right, and what's going on, or do we go to the hospital?"

"No, I mean, yes, I'm all right, and it was a seal *check* I was interested in," Kevin intoned. "Hey what's up with my eye?"

"It's swollen shut and looks terrible."

"Thanks."

"Well?"

"Again?"

"Yes, tell me what's gong on! I left my house with the front-door wide open, you drove through my yard, and I broke into my own jewelry store. Could you let me in on why I'm putting up with this."

"Uh, yeah, shoot, where's my briefcase?"

"I don't know, sweetheart. We left your car at the storage area. Do you remember?"

"*Yes...*"

"Fine. Now, what else do you remember?

Kevin looked around the cabin, then slowly back towards Karen. She deserved to know everything. At his point, that only seemed fair. Maybe she could figure-out what was going on.

"Got anything to eat?"

"You are really pushing it, buddy!"

"No, really. I'll let you know everything, but first let me wash my face. I feel pretty funky."

"There is food here, but we could use a few things. If I run to the store, you will fill me in on *everything* when I get back, right?"

"Promise."

Her lips brushed ever so lightly across his own, warm and soft. Her love and concern charged into his heart, and it beat so hard he thought he would pass out.

"I'll be right back."

Chapter Thirty

Karen proceeded cautiously out the front door. She had run a comb through her hair and looked great. Kevin pulled his legs to the side of the bed and swung them over the edge where they dangled like two boat anchors above the hardwood floor. He stood up with the room swimming around him, then steadied himself on the night-stand. When the floor stopped moving, he reached up to see if there was a vise around his head. He took a few steps, but the bathroom got smaller, slipping farther and farther away.

At the long journey's end, Kevin saw the reason for his discomfort come flashing from the mirror. The face he had grown so accustomed to was no longer there. In its place was that of a fighter, and not a winner. He had gone at least two rounds with the floor, and there were three cuts around his eye.

"Why the hell couldn't I fall on the left side once in a while?"

A hand towel helped clean his face with the aid of his left hand. The right was nicely bandaged, and there was a bandage on the side of his head. The hairs pulled against the tape when he raised his eyebrows and it now appeared he had a quickly receding hair line.

After a moment of holding the sink, the voyage back into the other room was possible. The two-room cabin looked comfortable to Kevin, rustic and warm. There was no clock, but the morning sun had risen above the pines, and it was fighting to peek-in around the curtains. In the streams of light Kevin could see dust particles floating about, weightless. He hoped they were dust particles.

Looking at the bed, it was obvious Karen had never crawled in with him. She probably didn't get a wink of sleep. A vehicle outside drew him immediately to the window, and his heart pounded as it pulled into the driveway. There was a serious face in the driver's side window. Upon exiting, the tall woman glanced around furtively, then headed towards the front door. She was grim, her walk determined.

"I got a paper, but everything happened so late, they probably put their final stories to bed before you abducted me."

"Well, that's a hell of a way to put it!"

"That is what my neighbors are going to say, especially after the police report that my store was broken into. You have been quite a reckless cowboy. No, no, you stay inside, I only have the one bag."

The bright sun was both a pleasure and a punishment as the rays pierced into his head through a single eye and settled there, searing his brain. Blinking, Kevin was able to see again in a few moments and he felt well enough to enjoy the cool air which carried the heavy smell of the pines to his nose. The beautiful morning was forced to stay outside, and Kevin wondered when he would be able to enjoy it again.

Pouring more coffee, Karen pulled a few things from the grocery bag and sliced him a tomato. Then she served it on a small plate with a donut.

"Your time is up, spill your guts!"

"A tomato?"

"It is good for you. You lost a lot of blood, and you need some vitamins."

He looked at the table and smiled. She could be so funny.

"A while back B.K., that's 'before Karen', I was a little bored with my job. I played some golf with Paul, and saw my daughter on my weekends. That was about it. Oh, and I promised my car that it would get a new coat of paint."

"Life in the fast lane?"

"Right. I was bored. So, to keep myself occupied, I made electronic listening devices, trying to improve them with each new model."

"Does the word 'Watergate' mean anything to you?"

"No, I wasn't after any big secrets, I was just nosy, and I don't even know if that has anything to do with what is going on."

"You did something else, too?"

"No, no, let me finish, then maybe you can help me figure all this out. I put some of my devices in the penthouse suite at the Royal and gave them a listen on occasion. I heard almost nothing until the last two days, you know, I wasn't listening every minute, but I had a sound activated recorder with a tape going."

"Why? You are *not* the police," Karen said, having saved her most confused and agitated look for this very moment.

"I know, I was just listening because I was a snoop I guess. It's stupid, but I just did it, OK. Besides, I'm not too sure about the police at this point."

"Why don't you call RPD, talk to Paul, and tell him what you know."

"Because I think the police are in on it. Maybe the gaming control board, too."

"In on what?" Karen asked while brushing strands of tired hair from her eyes.

"Let me have some more coffee, OK?"

"Keep talking," she said.

"Remember you said I mentioned a seal-check in my sleep?"

"Yes. Here is your coffee."

"Every slot machine at the casino is like a computer, they're still one-armed bandits, but everything is run on programs. The randomizing quality of a machine works like a box full of separate outcomes," Kevin stated, while making a box with his hands, the right side crooked from his bandages. "The computer picks a new outcome each time the machine is played. On a draw poker machine, you have a box of approximately 165,000 different hands, and only four of them lead to a royal-flush, so the machine gives you fair odds of about one in 40,000 of hitting the jackpot."

"And the casino gets to keep a little money along the way to those 40,000 hands," Karen said, then began moving her left hand in a circular motion to help Kevin get to the point.

"Right, and every play still has the computer picking one of those hands, so every time you still have the same odds against you. But as a computer, it simply does what it is programmed to do. So, suppose you have your own chips made with a special feature that is only activated when a certain number of different coin combinations are played. Then you know when the machine is going to give-out a royal flush, or a similar high-paying jackpot. On our dollar machines that's about $5,000 and the $5 machines start at $20,000."

"Kevin, I understand what you are saying, but how could all of this be done?"

"Well, we are extremely careful about the chips that are in the machines. Most of the machines come from the factory with a motherboard ready to go. The boards are kept inside a metal compartment in the machine, and each has a plastic tag around the opening with a number embossed on it. That tag is called a seal. When there is a jackpot of over ten thousand dollars, the slot supervisor checks that seal number against a reference number in a special book, accessible in the main cage. That log-book can only be taken out of its locked box with the keys of the casino manager, and the security shift-manager."

"So you think the whole place is involved in something like that?"

"I don't know, but I really exposed myself a couple days back when I checked a lost seal. I needed to know if it was in the log book, or was unused. I saw it on the roof, just a single tag, and it had the same number as one that was already on a machine."

"So somebody made duplicates," Karen said, as she wet her lips with her tongue.

"Maybe so. A supervisor, or a slot tech could be opening a machine, cutting the seal, and replacing the original chip with their own chip. Then they just replace the seal with a duplicate."

"Would you be able to see them doing that?"

"Probably not. The supervisors and key-people are in and out of the machines so often for coin fills, coin jams and the like, that after a while you stop watching. And that's only if you aren't distracted."

"Did you ever get distracted?"

"Yes, now that you mention it, I used to have a regular visitor in the cave. Guess who?"

"Your boss?"

"No, Antonia, the woman who clunked me on the head."

"Is she cute?"

"Stop!"

"That means she is cute. So you think she visited at an appointed time?"

"Now I do. I guess the reason I mentioned the seals in my sleep was because of the questions about 'em, but this is all just theoretical. I don't know any of this to be fact."

"Go on to the part where you said they killed Steven, and this lady hit you."

"Oh, yeah, Steven Lester had come-up with a list of players that were repeatedly hitting big jackpots. He was a computer programmer and ran part of the slot tracking system. Antonia worked with him, and she and another guy... I don't remember his name, attacked Steven and I. They tried to get us in a car, but Steven fought back, got stabbed, and they left us on the sidewalk outside the Gold Coin Casino.

"You just left your friend?"

"I had too. It was too late for him. There was a police car driving by, so I took off. I guess I wasn't thinking too well."

"What made you think of all this slot stuff to begin with?"

"When I was up on the roof working, I went through some steel doors to the top of the penthouse, where I put the camera."

"What camera?" Karen asked, exasperated.

"Oh, yeah, um, anyway, that is where one of the seals was, on the ground. At the time, I thought it was strange, but I suppose I forgot about it. The night I finished working up there, Terry King fell off the roof."

"Or was pushed. And the camera?" Karen continued, her eyes widening.

"Well, it's a camcorder that is voice activated. There might be something on it."

"Showing the roof?" Karen asked.

"Uh, no, the penthouse."

Karen looked at Kevin in disgust.

Chapter Thirty-one

The cabin dwellers finished their coffee and stared questioningly at each other. Karen walked off to the comfort of a warm shower, leaving the room with just the one occupant who spent the next twenty-minutes looking through the top of the curtain lace at several tall pines beyond the cabin. The setting was warm, homey. Had they come under different circumstances, things would be perfect. There was a stone fireplace against the east wall, and enough wood for a few days. Kevin sighed, and for the first time felt the pull along his abdomen.

Raising his shirt, he saw more tape and gauze along his chest. Not knowing the extent of his own injuries, he felt confident they couldn't be any worse now than how his chest was going to feel when all that tape was pulled-off, taking a slug of hair with it. Staring at his chest, he remembered how Steven Lester had looked on the sidewalk. It was very sobering, and there was a chill along his spine that reminded him how vicious the attack had been, and how lucky he was to be alive.

Looking up, he could see Toni shoving the revolver in his face, and the sounds around him. What a shock it must have been for poor Steven to find himself being abducted by the woman he was dating. Then his thoughts turned to his briefcase. Were there any decent recordings on those remaining tapes? What about the conversation right before he arrived at the Cue Ball? Was that on tape, or was he listening to that live? He couldn't remember.

"Wow, you look great! Were you able to get any sleep last night?"

She was already dressed, but was busy towel-drying her hair. Her head was tilted and she gave him a weary, but charming smile.

"Well, I suppose I dozed off a few times, but I was a little worried about you."

"I know, you're terrific. I am so overwhelmed by your ability to take care of me last night, and now. It's, well, just terrific."

"Thanks. I was thinking, is all of this really worth doing for the casino?"

"Me, or you?"

"No, I mean, is all the risk you mention worth it to the casino to go through?"

"I don't think so. There are a lot of safeguards put into place by the Gaming Control Board, and I don't think the casino would risk its license."

"So who's getting the money."

"That's the million dollar question! There are about 2,000 slot machines down at the club, and each one gets a lot more play than you might realize. The 'hold', or win, might only be 4% on average per pull, but they get so much play! If you take the total amount of every play, it is easy for the casino to do ten million dollars in 'drop', or total action. Their four percent win is $400,000 per day."

"But you have analysts, right? How much could be stolen before they noticed?"

"That remains to be seen. The Gaming Control Board keeps track of each casino's total drop and their win. They would be all over us if there was a large fluctuation in the percentages. If all that play was on a single machine, then the numbers would be perfect by the end of the month, but if the play is spread out over 2,000 machines, then there is some room for the percentages to move. It is gambling, after all."

"So.........how much are we talking about?" Karen queried.

"I can't say exactly, but there have been months where our win was below four percent, and some where the number was well above it. Another thing, the board is looking for changes in the hold, or win, not necessarily a low win percentage. What if those chips had been in place when the casino opened, and new machines got new ones when the supervisors had time to change them? Then there wouldn't be any changes to notice."

"Do they compare numbers to other casinos?"

She had both hands up with the palms twisted toward her face and they framed her puzzled-look permanently on his brain.

"Yes, but each casino can set their machines to pay a certain amount, and every club has different machines, and we change machines all the time. It's just not possible to have any exact numbers."

"So, if there could be a ten-percent fluctuation that would go unnoticed, that would be $40,000."

"Right. Now the casino might not risk its license for that kind of money, not when they know they can make ten times that by playing fair. However, somebody that was well connected, with a large enough bankroll to pay some people on the inside to make the initial changes, well, it would be worth the risk. Plus, I heard the guys in the penthouse talking about going to two other casinos that are owned by City Casinos, which owns the Royal."

"So, you think maybe it does have to do with the casino ownership?"

"Depends on who *owns* what," Kevin said with a sigh and shake of the head. "There were clubs in Vegas that had a skim of the profits going to mobs in Kansas City, New York and Chicago for years. It could be that the Royal's management was just new and easy to fool. You know our general manager, Robert Weston? He's only 37 years old. Maybe these other guys got in on the ground floor, so to speak."

"Why fool with all these small jackpots? Why not just do a couple big ones each month?"

"Safe-guards. Every jackpot of over $25,000 has to have an EPROM test. The seal on the game is checked, then cut off, and the motherboard is exposed. The main function chip is removed and checked against another chip that is housed in the main cage. If the electronic check is not exact, then we have to call the Gaming Control Board."

"Still, somebody has to collect all those little jackpots, if we can call $20,000 little."

"Yes, but there are enough people out there that are willing to do something like that."

Karen finished drying her hair and slung the moist towel over the top of her rocker, then slumped down into the cushion on the seat. Her lips formed the next question, but she let-out a long breath before continuing.

"What about the IRS and taxes?"

"Wow, good question," Kevin mumbled. He looked around the room and came back with more answers. "Well, whoever claims a jackpot should have to pay taxes, but you can go to any casino and ask for a loss-statement. They don't put a lot of effort into getting those too accurate. In fact, Steven Lester got involved because I was looking into the account of two different players that I now think were claimers."

"But they can't just go around killing everybody that knows about this. Even for $40,000."

"That's per day. It adds up to about $15 million per year, and that's for just the one casino."

She shook her head in amazement. "You have put a lot of thought into your plot."

"Not enough to know who's to be trusted. One of the guys that Steven checked on was a friend of mine. I wanted his address, but I found out he was killed in a hit-and-run a couple weeks ago. Maybe it was an accident, or maybe he forgot to give-up what he had collected." Kevin sighed across his chapped lips. He was getting dizzy.

Three hours later the two were still discussing all the other possibilities storming across Kevin's mind. They talked at length about the police, and the gaming-control agents. It might be easy to bribe an officer of either force when you had $15 million to work with."

"You mentioned Vellardi a few times while you were sleeping. Who is that?"

"I'm not sure exactly, like I said before, I know the name from somewhere, and I think he is a well-connected crime boss. I do know that Paul was working on his case, so he may be one of the guys in the penthouse. I heard somebody up there saying 'we don't have enough squares to lay-em off to', and that might mean people claiming jackpots for them.

"That sounds like a heck of a coincidence."

"No more of a coincidence than my playing golf with the RPD Captain, and him whispering the guy's name to Paul, but loud enough for me to hear."

"You didn't tell me about that."

"Well, I don't know if he wanted me to hear, or maybe he was watching my reaction. Maybe he thought I knew Vellardi personally. I don't know. Listen, my brain is leaking out my ears and I'll bet you could use some sleep. Join me in bed?"

"What about lunch?"

"No, just sleep right now."

The increasingly more beautiful woman beside him nodded a weary yes. She slipped her pants suit off, and hung it back in the closet before crawling into bed with her weary warrior. There was an overwhelming comfort lying in Karen's arms, and sleep was oh so tender on their minds. The sun dropped below the tree line before they stirred. Karen rolled over and turned the bedside lamp on. It was a bronze cupid holding up a bow-and-arrow that became the stem for the shade. Set-off in light orange and green, the Tiffany shade glowed warm in the room.

Kevin's eye looked better in the dim light, and the swelling had gone down considerably. She wasn't sure if the green and purple color was from bruising, or the lampshade, but she gave him a loving smile as his eyes fluttered open.

"Sleep well?"

He looked around the room and thought for a moment before answering.

"I was hoping it was all a dream. Where are we, exactly? I mean, do you own this place, are we safe here?"

"We're up at the lake. I don't think the Philip's or any other neighbors know the address, but they know I have a cabin. If the police look through my house, they will eventually come across this address somewhere. There are pictures in photo albums."

"Where's my car?"

"At a storage facility near the base of Mount Rose. I have a boat and jeep there."

"I saw the closet had clothes here for you, but I don't have anything else to wear. Got any clothes stashed away?"

"No, but we will figure something out. I think you should call Paul. Let him know we are fine, and tell him about this Toni bitch."

Kevin managed to raise one eyebrow while Karen continued.

"You're mine now, so nobody gets to you without going through me."

Kevin didn't argue. He was still trying to figure out how he got so lucky, and so unlucky in the same month. What he didn't know, was that there had already been some calls made to the police.

When Kevin called the Reno Police Department, he was quickly patched-through to Detective Kozar. Inside the detectives office were a dozen officers, their phones burning from use, all working the current case. Working along with the officers was a stale cloud of smoke, and several witnesses who had been called-in to give statements.

"Detective Kozar, who is this please?"

"Paul, it's Kevin. I know there is a lot going on, but you would be amazed at how much more is going on at the Royal."

Waving his hand through the blue smoke, Kozar snapped his fingers, then waved his finger in a loop and pointed towards some electronic equipment. The closest officer started the tape and monitoring devices, while Paul mouthed out "forty-four", while flashing four fingers at them, and the trace started immediately.

"Kevin, how are you? What's going on?"

"Cut the shit, Paul. I'm in trouble, but you can help me out of it."

"We've know each other for a long time, friend. I know you have a good reason for what is going on. Where is Karen Cannon?"

The tone was assuring and true, but Kevin had known him too long to believe it.

"Nope, I took her someplace safe, you'll never find her."

Kevin cupped the receiver and told Karen he thought Paul was in on it.

Kozar felt a huge lump in his throat, and he tried to keep his eyes from watering. The movement in his stomach was quick, an undeniable desire to purge its contents. He couldn't believe his next comment, as he too, cupped the receiver.

"It was him. Says he picked her up and we won't find her." He continued speaking to Kevin after removing his hand. "Listen Kev', why don't you come down here and we'll work on this together, we need your help."

"Paul, that's insulting, I'm not an idiot," Kevin said.

"Kevin, I talked to Tolan today. He told me you had somebody come-by and pay-off your account. Where did you get twenty-thousand dollars?"

Kevin slammed the phone back into its cradle. The cabin was very dark, its walls closing in on him. The silence was not alarming, it was oppressive.

"That bad?"

"I'm screwed. They're all in on it, and I'm screwed. I should have kept the knife."

"What knife?"

"The knife Rich stabbed Lester with. The prick stuck me in the palm of the hand with it. I tossed it into a field as I got on the highway."

"Kevin, you were very bloody. Wherever you fell on the sidewalk there is going to be blood. In a few days, the police will be able to match that to you. This really is not good. Does Paul think I'm involved?"

"No, he just thinks I grabbed you to rob your store and pay off this guy I know. Is it getting really dark in here, or is my life just flickering out?"

"We need to leave here," Karen said. She jumping up and walked across the room. "I've got a friend who lives in Carson City, but he's in Europe right now. We can use his house, I've got a key."

"You've got this guy's house key?"

"Jealousy should not be your greatest concern right now! Besides, he's gay."

"I didn't have any problem about the key."

"Yeah, *whatever*. He is almost your height, so you can have a nice change of clothes."

"Yuck."

"Knock it of, I have seen *your* clothes."

"Right, let's go."

"Hand me those keys, you are not driving."

"Hey, I really need my briefcase. Can we drive by the place you left it?"

"It's the opposite direction, but if you need it....."

On the way back down the mountain, Kevin tried to sort out who else might be involved. There wasn't going to be any way for him to extricate himself from his predicament without some very strong evidence against those who were actually responsible. His thoughts were becoming as black as the night. Clouds had covered the moon, and the headlight's cast strange shadows along the side of the road.

In the distance, a deer bolted from the shoulder of the highway and stopped. Kevin knew just how it felt with its eyes filled-up by headlights and a car bearing down on it. The deer was smart enough to head into the trees as Karen slowed to make a left turn. Up the street a block, she suddenly turned the vehicle around and stopped. She was smarter than Kevin.

"See anything?"

"Where? Over there, across the highway?"

"Yes. If we are lucky, the police have not learned about my storage facility yet."

Karen eased the gas pedal down. The van sped-up and crossed the road. Pulling into the driveway, she pressed her code into the keypad and the gate jerked to a start, then groaned until it came to a shaky stop, the chain twitching.

Chapter Thirty-two

Cold to her touch, the knob twisted easily. The door complained, but allowed them to enter the cavernous building. As Kevin lumbered towards the MG, each step created a range of sounds playing off the galvanized steel walls and came back to his ears at twice the volume it had innocently left his shoes. He viewed his old friend with its broken headlight and dented fender and groaned deeply. Inside, blood coated the leather seats and the steering wheel. There were stains on the dashboard, but no briefcase.

"How many pints of blood are there in the human body?"

"Now, or yesterday? You are very lucky I didn't drive you to the morgue."

"Well, that's a cheery thought."

"You are very lucky!"

"Not so lucky. Where's my briefcase?"

Thinking back, Kevin knew he was listening to a conversation on the way to his meeting with Steven. Things were a bit hazy after that. No, it was before the meeting, right after he saw Toni coming out of the elevator after her visit to the penthouse.

He explained to Karen that one of the voices had commanded that a listener "get them together and take care of them". He wasn't sure what that meant, but it sounded ominous.

"Take care of who?"

"Rich and Toni were going to take us somewhere. Maybe to your house."

"How would they know about me?" Karen asked, perplexed.

"Maybe they knew about you from Toni, and maybe they were going to take all three of us to your store. That would be a good place to kill us all. It would have looked like a burglary."

"Kevin, you certainly have a good imagination."

"Would you have believed any of this two days ago?"

"I can hardly believe any of this now," she said, biting the inside of her left cheek.

Kevin grabbed his toolbox out of the trunk and tossed it into the back of the jeep.

He paused, then went back to the trunk and looked at the crowbar.

"Is that what you used to break the glass at your store?"

"Yes, and I did not want to leave it at the scene of the crime".

"Well done, but let's toss it out somewhere and let the insurance company pay-off on a burglary."

"You're so bad."

"Hey, justice prevails."

The ride into Carson City was only about thirty minutes, but that was enough time for Kevin to tell his chauffeur to slow down and not get pulled over. She replied that he would have to leave the front seat if he was going to be a back-seat driver.

"It's probably not safe to stop at a fast-food place, but I'm getting hungry."

"I'm sure Jeri has food, but we could use the evening paper. Check the glove compartment."

"Sorry, no newspaper."

"Wise guy, for quarters."

"Oh."

There were enough quarters sliding around in the tiny glove box to pay for a newspaper, and their questions about the police were quickly answered. On the cover of the Reno Gazette was a picture of both Karen and Kevin. The headline read: "Reno Man Sought in Abduction".

The small print was too hard to read in the car, and Karen must have been getting very anxious to get to the house and read the rest, as the final left-hand turn tossed Kevin up against his door.

"Geez, slow down!"

"Sissy!"

Karen pumped the brake and they pulled up to a very nice ranch house. There were just two other houses on the quiet cul-de-sac, each on about an acre of wooded land. The porch light was on.

"Looks like he's home."

"Some burglar you would be. He went to Europe, remember? Those lights are probably on a timer."

"I knew that. I just meant it *looked* like he was home."

"Right."

Walking around the house, Karen took a weary Kevin by the hand and led him through a small gate in the fence. A larger gate allowed access to a 24-foot boat moored on a trailer. Kevin wondered why so many people had boats here in the desert. There were lakes, but the boats spent most of their time vegetating in their owner's yards.

In back was a brick barbecue facing the stone patio. Weeping willows hung down along a path that stretched the entire yard, and there were decorative lamps hung carefully about, the whole setting surrealistic. If the killers were coming, they would no doubt work their way along the path, then through the bushes by the porch.

"Looks like a movie set."

"It really is pretty. Jeri is so talented. You should spend an evening back here having dinner. The smell from the barbecue and the plants is wonderful."

They crept around the patio and Karen used a key from the jeep's key ring to open the back door. Her breath was frosty when they opened the door and she headed straight for the thermostat. As the home warmed to their comfort level Karen showed-off the house. The furniture was modern upscale, without being garish. Homey, country living. Upscale country.

"What does this guy do?"

"Jeri is an accountant. He was able to get my books straightened out after Dale passed away. He is such a sweet guy."

"Yeah, but I suppose he could still kick my butt if he were here, right? I got beat-up by a woman yesterday, you know."

"Keep it up, and you can have it happen again today."

"Bully."

"Want me to read the paper to you?"

The paper swished in the air while Kevin reached to turn off the front porch light, then pulled the drapes and headed to the kitchen.

"So, start reading."

"*Reno Police are searching for the whereabouts of Kevin N. Webb, a local casino worker.*"

"The N. stands for Nicholas, but only my mom calls me that, when I'm in trouble. Where are the snacks? All that's in here is bottled water and Diet Pepsi. What a wuss. Where's the sugar?"

"Look in the pantry."

"Oh, yeah," Kevin said, his hands in the air. "I keep forgetting you all have pantries."

Karen continued reading the paper to herself while he resumed his quest for snacks.

"Nicholas!"

"What, I'm in trouble already?"

"It says when the police searched your home, they found electronic surveillance gear and additional devices in surrounding apartments, including a Ms. Hopper's residence, where a camera was found."

"That's bullshit! There was no stuff in any apartments except hers."

"You are *not* helping yourself."

"I was just trying some equipment. It was a direct feed from her apartment to my TV."

"Is that what I was looking at the first time we were in your apartment?"

"Uh, well, it was just a test."

"A test of my patience. You.......... are perverted. What was it, you wanted to watch her, maybe listen to her having sex?"

"No, there was no sound, just video."

"Terrific," she continued , her eyes rolling upwards. This says you are a possible suspect in the demise of fellow workers Terry King and Steven Lester. They talked to a lady who worked with Steven Lester in the computer department. She wants to remain anonymous, but says you were always hounding Lester's girlfriend to go out with you, and that perhaps you killed him in a jealous rage."

"If I get a good lawyer, I can probably get this knocked down to life in the electric chair."

"Got any ideas?"

"Yes, dinner, but there's no real food here."
"I'll find something to cook. Don't you think I'm taking this well?"
"You're the best. Did they mention my briefcase?"
"Yes, they say you may have been on your way to my house to "bug" it. However, there is nothing left but scraps, because you ran over the brief case while abducting me."
"Shit. Some of the tapes might have still had voices on them, maybe something with Vellardi, or Antonia."
"Sorry, they don't even mention tapes, just a sound recording device."
They collaborated on cooking angel hair pasta, and the spicy marinara sauce, though from a jar, was just right. The air around them became heavy, and they hardly spoke for the next hour while the dinner was eaten and cleared away. They both had their own demons. When she spoke, the voice was reassuring, but Kevin wondered, if the tables were turned, would he believe this story?
"You know, I look great in stripes."
"You will not go to prison. We can figure something out. I'm alive, and that's your best defense right now."
"Karen, do you think it's safe to call my daughter?"
"No. The lines at your daughter's house may not be wired yet, but all the calls will be easily traceable by the phone company. They would get this address."
"How about a phone booth?"
"Is it worth getting picked-up right now, just to make a phone call?"
"Yes."
She didn't approve, but she understood. There was a similar call she needed to make to her folks. Both calls were quick, but tortured. Neither seemed easier than the other, although they both used the same statement: "it was a misunderstanding, and would be straightened-out in a few days, 'I love you'".
"Hold-on, I need to call my assistant manager at the store."
Kevin waved at the phone booth.
"Yes, it is going fine. Don't panic, I will be back in a few days. Keep this between us, bye."
The van's door snapped open. "Had to let my assistant manager know I am fine. She will take care of the insurance and getting the store back open."
"You're lucky to have somebody like that you can trust."
"You are so right, Kevin. So right."

Chapter Thirty-three

As midnight rolled around, Detective Paul Kozar rubbed his steaming eyes with the knuckles on his thumbs, and his neck gave an audible crunch as he worked it back and forth. The room's occupants had dwindled in number as each hour crept by. Some had returned to other cases, some to the last accounting of Mr. Kevin Webb. A lucky few had headed home.

The thought of heading home nauseated Paul. How could he go home and talk to his wife about the current fate of their respective "best" friends? Becky was well aware as to what had happened in the past 24 hours. Paul knew more, but didn't want to be the one to break it to her. Never had he brought his work home, but there is always a first time, and that sobering fact didn't make it any easier to end his day.

Through all the back files on Vellardi, Kevin's name had never come up. On the other hand, neither had the names Terry King or Steven Lester. Surveillance and some tips could paint a picture, but it was a watercolor with no fine lines.

Vincent Vellardi had spent the past ten years painting a picture of his own. To his credit, he appeared to be a successful businessman who gave back to the community, supported the arts in New York and New Jersey, and paid his taxes. His good deeds often made their way to the local papers, and his wife entertained the right people at their country estate. Local politicians met with him on a regular basis, and he was known to support them also, but that was legal. His favorites held their offices, or continued upwards on the political scene. America in a nutshell.

The FBI felt a bit differently about the affairs of what was considered the Vellardi organization. He spoke with very few people in the business community, but those he spoke with had ties to loan sharking and the discount sale of new products. It wasn't like the old days where almost everything was said to have fallen off a truck, but the sale of new items from bankrupt companies was becoming a way of life for several well-connected businessmen. It wasn't against the law, our system has allowed distress sales to go on for years.

Vellardi was visible, but insulated. He took trips around the country, and kept his affairs in order. He called his managers "advisers", and met with them in person at least twice a year. There was nothing more intimidating than a personal encounter. The books better be straight, and the cash had better continue to flow.

The FBI was aware that some successful ventures had been taken-over by Vellardi. Lawyers could always produce documents showing a legal partnership. New partners kept quite, and were allowed to maintain a portion of their profits. You had a choice of go-along, or go-away. Vellardi had been a suspect each time a new partner "went-away", but making a case was another thing.

The Reno Police Department had as much success as the Fed's when watching Mr. Vincent Vellardi. None. He was rarely seen outside his hotel rooms, had room service doing the cooking. If he left for a night on the town, it was with a bodyguard and might include a three-minute conversation at a bar with a local businessman, and a quick dinner.

Paul read through the short list of things obtained from the roof of the Royal. It included one plastic sandwich bag, three soda cans, one Phillips-head screwdriver (fingerprinting not conclusive), half a dozen screws and bolts, one 12-inch strand of black cable, and one six-inch red plastic tie with a number on it.

"Hey, Paul. What have you got?"

Paul looked towards the voice of Fred Meyer and was amazed that he had not heard him walk into the room.

"Kibbles and bits."

"No sure ties?"

"No, but I appreciate your leaving me on this."

"I've never doubted your ability, or your obligation to the department. Look, I know you're on both sides of the fence right now, but you're still gon'na find the right gate. Knock-off for the night. I'll be here till three or four, then if you get something going in the morning, you call me at home after eight."

When Fred told you to knock-off, it wasn't a request. Paul stood at his desk, and felt his pants sticking to the back of his thighs. His shirt was wrinkled to resemble a city road map, and it was definitely time for sleep, but both men knew it would be impossible for him to get any tonight.

The doorway loomed, but his legs just couldn't get into gear.

"Buddy, I know it's a tough place you find yourself in, but go home to your wife. The words will come. Talk all night if you have to, she needs you more than I do right now."

There was no simple definition for Fred Meyer. He was one of the toughest of the old cops, and at the same time, he had that compassion. If you looked in the dictionary under the word "humanity", you'd probably find his picture.

Paul headed home, and Fred took a seat at his desk after turning the cushion over. The last two items on the roof inventory list had been highlighted. The black cable was the kind Kevin had been installing, and the red tie was a slot tag.

Meyer called the Apple Street office of the Gaming Control Board and listened to the phone ringing. It was into the graveyard shift, and the office was probably empty.

"State Highway Patrol, Reno office."

"Good evening, this is Detective Fred Meyer at RPD, I would like to speak to officer Winslow."

"I'll relay your message, and an officer will call you back at the RPD front desk."

"Thank you."

Nevada was still small enough for each local law enforcement agency to work together and share what they knew without any petty jealousies found in larger states. Meyer made some notes while sifting through the mass of papers on Paul's desk. He was ready when his phone call came through.

"This is Meyer."

"Hello Fred, it's Josh, I'm sorry I haven't gotten back to you. I can't seem to get to my office tonight. I spoke briefly with Mr. Webb two days ago. In fact, he called me, but I didn't get what you wanted. As far as the slot tag, they aren't a secure item at the hotel. They can be picked-up by a slot tech or supervisor in the slot managers office. Each should be accounted for, but there is little paperwork, and half a dozen companies make them."

There was a screech, and Josh apologized.

"Sorry, that's why I shouldn't talk on the phone while driving. Anyway, they could definitely be reproduced."

"What does that tell you, Josh," Meyer asked wearily.

"It tells me the slot techs probably walk around with the seals in their pockets from time to time, and that the Royal is too lax on their procedures. What does it tell you?"

"Josh, I've got two dead, and one missing from the club. One is the Security Manager, with full access to cameras; one is a surveillance worker who also repairs cameras; and one is in charge of the slot tracking system. On top of that, I've got a wealthy businessman with some questionable associates, and a kidnapped local jewelry storeowner. What does that sound like to you?"

"It sounds like a mess, but if you are trying to put them all together, I think you're stretching things."

"What does the Board think of the two murders and a missing surveillance person?"

"The evidence is too preliminary to support any conclusions, but I have my own doubts about the Terry King incident being part of the other murder. However, I have another problem," Josh said with a slight hesitation.

"Yes?"

"A couple weeks ago there was a Teddy Ryan who was the victim in a hit and run."

"Yes, I remember."

"The records from the club indicate that he had recently won a substantial amount of money at the Royal."

"No shit! Anything else?"

"Not yet, Fred, but we'll have auditors down at the club in the morning, hell, probably for the next month."

"Thanks for the update."

"Bye, Fred."

Meyer looked across the room and saw he was down to just two detectives. He finished his notes and headed back to his own office. He loved being a detective, but hated being drowned in paperwork. It was best to keep on top of it, and he finished a report for Chief Packard, dropping it off on his way out the door.

The night was still, and the air had turned cold. He took a few good gulps, and his breath was visible against the clear, moonlit sky. It was a good night, for he had a good grasp on this current case. It was a bad night, because problems within the casinos were never easily fixed.

Chapter Thirty-four

Kevin and Karen tossed and atop the large trundled bed. There were shadows on the walls, the moonlight slipping in from around the pulled curtains and it was cool in the room, but the sheets were damp.

"Kevin, why do you think the police are in on this thing? I don't understand that part."

"I don't know, they just seem very strange lately," Kevin said, while using his left-hand as a scale again. "I called a guy I know at the Gaming Control Board, and he hung-up on me. It was like he realized that I might be on to something."

"If we were certain that the police were not in on any shenanigans, then you could just turn yourself in."

"Shenanigans? I haven't heard that word in years," Kevin said, and he rolled-over, trying to see her eyes in the darkness.

"What if this Vellardi guy has already killed Toni and Rich, and left clues that would implicate you?"

"Great, I hadn't thought about that. Now even if the police are clean, I can't turn myself in. Any other sobering thoughts?"

"You need to find out who was in the penthouse. You need to get your listening things working, and you need your camera from the roof."

They debated their needs, and possible paranoia. The newspaper hadn't mentioned anything about the visitors in the penthouse, or any cameras above it. Kevin climbed out of bed and flopped into an easy chair, his face haggard. The problems hanging over him were the size of Nebraska, and the rope holding them all was slowly twisting, each strand straining under the enormous weight.

"I remember the guy in the penthouse saying something about them 'screwing everything up', and he wanted to shut-down the operations for a while. I don't know how long we have to get any evidence on these guys, I think we are running out of time."

Kevin slipped back into bed and closed his eyes, thoughts drifting aimlessly.

When he reopened his eyes, the room was still dark. From the corner of the room a bar of pale light shone across the floor and he could hear a trickle of water running.

"Karen, are you coming back to bed?"

The bathroom door creaked open, and Kevin's heart beat faster. The light from within pushed its way past the woman at the door. She was eerily familiar in the back lighting.

"You look different, what's up?"

"You are next, my dear."

Karen reached over and turned on the overhead light. It wasn't Karen anymore. The woman before him had worked on her eyebrows, now a light reddish color. Her hair was cut into a short "bob", and it had a red glow.

"That dress is pretty short, especially with those heels. I almost didn't get around to noticing your hair."

"That was the general idea. Get up, we have work to do."

While he tried to extricate himself from the heavy blankets, Karen slipped out of her heels and hung the dress across the rocking chair. It continued rocking on its own, while Kevin raised an eyebrow and smiled.

"No, we have work to do. We will be cutting your hair, and shaving your mustache. Maybe darken your hair a bit."

"Wait, I like my mustache."

"I know honey, and you have probably had it since you were ten, but not to worry, you can grow it back in a week. Now come over here."

Kevin dragged his stocking feet the entire 12 feet, swish-swish-swish.

"But I don't *want* a hair cut."

"Stop whining. Honestly, a little change is not going to kill you."

"OK, doctor, do what you must do."

For the next hour, the "mad-stylist" transformed Kevin into a clean-shaven, younger-looking man. With the darker hair, he looked European. Next came the clothes. The closet was packed, but each time Kevin grabbed something, Karen would put it back and choose a nicer outfit.

"Are we going overseas, or do you have another plan?"

"A trip to the Royal is on tap. Then we can figure out where we stand."

The look on Kevin's face gave him away.

"Don't worry, nobody is going to recognize you. I've been thinking all night."

No, you *were* thinking, but now you seem to have stopped. I'm not going back to Reno. There are probably a hundred cops all over town looking for me!"

"The great thing about paranoia is that you get to be the center of attention."

"I'm not paranoid, the newspaper says I'm a killer. Don't you think they're looking for me?"

"Yes, but you do not need to worry, they will not recognize you."

Karen explained that they would drive back to Reno and head for the Royal. After entering the casino, he could go to a safe place like a bathroom while she would go from spot to spot, checking things out. She could wear some of those glasses, like in *"Mission Impossible"*, and he could watch it all on a monitor from the bathroom, of course they would have to wait until morning, and then...

"Karen, this isn't a movie. I don't happen to have any magic glasses, because they cost about seventy-five hundred dollars. Besides, graveyard would be a lot better time to sneak around. Now, if I could get some equipment, we could patch into the lines that the surveillance department is getting, and we could see what they see. Wait a minute, what's the point?"

"Kevin, you need to get back on the roof and listen to those guys in the penthouse. You need to get your camcorder down and check the film."

"Right, good idea. That sounds kind of dangerous, though. I'm not Bruce Willis in *'Die Hard'*, you know. I won't be jumping off the roof with a fire hose attached to my waist. Does Jeri have any weapons around the house?"

"Sure, he showed me several perfectly good guns once."

They walked down the hall to the den. It was a working office, but true enough, there were guns on the walls.

"See, right there."

"Wonderful. Let's see, this is a 1894 Remington 'thirty-ought-six'. That should work well, and it won't attract any attention when I walk in the club with a rifle."

"So, that one is not the best of the bunch. How about that pistol?"

"I think it's a decanter."

"No, that one over there."

"That's a lighter. It'll take forty years to kill them from smoking."

"I know Jeri has a newer revolver, because he wanted me to carry it after the robbery."

"Refuse on moral grounds?"

"No, it was too heavy and ruined my purse," she said with a matter-of-fact tone.

"So, where do you hide a newer, heavy, purse ruining revolver?"

It was the first place they looked, in the desk. The fact that it had no bullets was a minor set back, but those were found in the garage, on the workbench.

"Wow, this guy has a great work shop, and it's so clean. When I had a garage, it looked like a typhoon had just blown through it."

"I will let you in on a secret, Jeri was out here cleaning just before he went to Europe."

"Well, I feel better then."

The "big game hunters" returned to the kitchen, and Kevin went over the layout of the casino, and some of the hotel floors. He tried to remember where each camera was, which were monitored by security, and which by surveillance.

"The trick is going to be keeping those guys busy while I get to the roof. If I take the elevator to the 24th floor, I can blend in. But after that, the stairs are the best route. However, there are cameras on each stairwell."

"How many officers are going to be watching?"

"Probably just one in the security office. The cameras are set-up on a revolving basis. Two seconds at each camera, then they move on to the next station, unless the officer zooms-in on a particular spot. In the surveillance room, there are dedicated cameras near each elevator, and one on the roof."

"Just tell me which hallway to go to, and I'll distract the officer," Karen said with a confident smile.

"How are you going to do that? They're not stupid, you know."

"Are they men?"

"Yes."
"Then don't worry about it, I can distract them."

Chapter Thirty-five

Kevin hated his hair. It was itchy on his neck. The hard, ceramic tile floor of the bathroom looked like a beauty salon and there were tiny hairs stuck to his socks. For a moment, he thought he was Frodo in *"The Hobbit"*. When he looked in the mirror, the face was definitely not his. Two days worth of stubble had been shaved away, and along with it, a mustache that had hung-out on his upper lip for twenty years.

The space from his nose to his lip was enormous. It had definitely grown since he last saw it. His nose had grown also, but part of that came from the bruise and three cuts across it.

"Did you know that concrete has very sharp edges?"

"What? Could you please raise your hand when you change the subject? You know, when I said that anything you told me would be all right? I lied. I can not believe you had a video camera in that girl's apartment!"

"That was hours ago."

"What difference does that make? I did not know you were going to turn out to be a twisted, voyeuristic, snack-food junkie who would rather watch a naked woman than be with one."

"Where did that come from?"

"We have been in bed twice in the past 24 hours, and you have not touched me."

"Sometimes I don't express myself as well as I'd like to, Karen. When I look in your eyes, I see into your soul, and I see my only possible future. I want to spend the rest of my life with you, and I hope it's a long life. You're more than I ever hoped for, more than I know I deserve, and I can hardly believe you are so accepting of me at the absolute worst time of my life."

"You can be almost charming when you want to." Karen said, with a flutter of her eye-lids.

"We all walk around in our little worlds, wishing things were better. No matter how good things get, we still struggle with daily life. We fight our dragons, and live to tell about it. Sometimes, there just isn't anybody to tell."

"Well, you have me to tell your dragon stories to from now on. I will do my best to think of you as eccentric, instead of neurotic, but no more "peeking". After this, you get a job where you meet people face to face, instead of through a camera."

"You're the boss."

For the next few hours they discussed how Kevin would get to the stairs, and up them without being seen on camera. The day dragged on as they waited for nine in the evening to go to bed.

At three in the morning the alarm rang. Bleary-eyed, they both staggered from the bed. They talked about being ready both physically, and mentally. Once in the garage, they decided to take Jeri's car.

"Do I get to drive for a change?"

"No, your eye is still healing."

"But I *want* to drive."

"Stop being a child," Karen demanded and turned the other way.

"I'm not."

"Are so," she shot back.

"Am not!"

"Do you suppose that it is just our nerves causing this?" asked Karen.

"Yes. Think I'm safe with this gun?"

"Probably not. Just remember the barrel points away from your body, Kevin."

"Thanks for your help, I'll try not to shoot myself."

They laughed, but the pitch of their voices was high. There was every chance the police and gaming control would be on the premises. In addition, the security department had probably "beefed-up" their numbers.

Kevin rolled down the window of the 911. The car was small, like his MG, but he wasn't used to the passengers seat. Karen, on the other hand, looked right at home. In the moonlight, she hardly looked over 21, just a spoiled, rich girl in her Porsche.

"You look beautiful tonight. This reminds me of a date I went on, once upon a time."

"That is a nice start for a story, but I think it's taken."

"No offense, but you're so much like me. Even now, you still have your guard up, like an invisible fence. You don't look through it, you look past it, past me."

"Hey, I'm scared, all right. I love you, and I do not want to lose you. I let my guard down long enough to let you inside, but tonight if I happen to be a bit defensive, it is unavoidable!"

Her voice wavered a bit, and she wiped a tear from her cheek. It was such a tender movement with the back of her hand, that he felt a tear running down his face also. He knew it was only from his bruised eye, not an emotional reaction.

"That adrenaline is a funny thing, huh Kevin."

"All right, all right. When we get there, drive around a bit, and let me take a look at the parking lot."

She circled the entire property, which seemed deserted at this time of the morning. Along the way around the block, they spotted not one, but two police cars. There were also a couple boring Chevrolets sitting side-by-side.

"Drive by those two Chevys and let me look inside."

"What are you looking for?" Karen asked.

"Well, I'm pretty sure those are from the Gaming Control Board. They aren't too imaginative." They drove slowly past and Kevin peered into the cars. "There are scanners inside with radios, and they're parked right next to each other. What do you think?"

"Chickening out?"

"No, I am ready if you are."

They parked in the center of the north-west lot, which was illuminated to almost the brightness of day by the heavy lighting from poles that sprouted like palm trees across the landscape of asphalt.

Walking up the steps to the building, Kevin tugged at his sleeves from inside his jacket, then stopped.

"Wait, I don't have a watch. We need to synchronize our watches."

"You have been waiting your whole life to say that, have you not?"

"Maybe, but it's true. The gift shop is closed. Let's see now, you got any quarters little girl?"

"Yes, I have a few. Going to call for the correct time?"

"No, this is better. There is a crane machine in the arcade that has watches in it."

"Super spy, able to work with any tools."

"I'm not being a kid, this is serious, now give me the quarters."

True to his word, there was a crane machine on the mezzanine, and to Karen's amazement, Kevin snagged a watch on his first try. It was broken.

"Probably just a bad battery. More quarters, more quarters," Kevin pleaded.

"Your poor mother must have gone broke at the amusement park."

"Naw, I used to win cigarettes for her."

"You were a strange kid."

"Nobody's perfect. There, see!"

"That was pretty cool. You won a two dollar watch, and it only cost you three bucks."

"That's right, most people would have had to spend six or seven dollars to get a cheap watch like this."

The fun was over. They set their watches to exactly 5:00 a.m., and Kevin escorted Karen to the ladies room. It was a good idea before they got started, and he had several sets of stairs to climb after the elevator ride to the 24th floor.

At 5:10, Karen walked out of the restroom, strolling calmly to the elevators, and a barely trembling finger pressed the up button. Walking into the small room, she looked into the corners to see if there was a camera. Kevin had promised there were none inside, but she was still curious.

At the fifth floor, she eased her way out and headed to the right. The new carpet felt strange under her heels, but it would be perfect. Security kept an extra eye on the health club, where on good nights, there might me a skinny dipper who snuck in after dark.

Karen walked slowly towards the door to the pool, swinging her hips. She reached out and pulled, but the door was locked, just as Kevin said it would be. She walked back and forth in front of a second set of doors and peeked in the windows. Then, back to the first door she went, slowly, and this time she dug her right heel into the carpet before pulling. The two-inch heel snapped easily under her weight. Falling back, she landed on the carpet with a thud. Her short skirt exposed her lightly tanned thighs.

Karen's heart crashed against her chest and the thumping seemed to be on both sides of her eardrums. She twisted on the carpet, exposing more of her legs to the camera in the corner. Lifting up a bit, she bent her leg and grabbed her shoe. The heal was hanging off, and it took no pressure to remove it completely. Making no attempt to cover her spread legs, she kept her right leg crossed above her knee. She scooted across the carpet just a bit more and grabbed her purse. Her dress was now up to her hips, and her thong panties were only slightly out of the light. In the security room, Howard thought he was the luckiest guy in the building.

He switched over two cameras to check the health club entrance. His cameras afforded him a rear view of a pretty woman, sitting on the floor. From the front, he was certain she would move enough to prove she was wearing nothing under her dress. The more he looked, the more certain he was. If she just sat back a little more......

Karen opened her purse and put the broken heal inside, while fiddling around for a moment.

Upstairs, Kevin had worked his way down the 24th floor hall. He had to pass several cameras to reach the emergency exit. The cameras above the 25th floor were limited to showing only the door and five feet of walkway. Kevin grabbed the cold steel tubing of the handrail and pulled himself up to stand on it. He reached above his head and pulled himself along, walking on the slanted rails above the stairs, keeping himself from the camera's prying eye. He had been certain this would be an easy task, but the strain and pain from his bandaged right hand was excruciating.

He rested at the 28th floor and looked at his new watch. It had already been fifteen minutes, and Karen might already be done. He continued his climb.

Chapter Thirty-six

Back in front of the health club, a hapless woman was struggling to her feet. The rocking motion of standing up caused her purse, which she held by just one of the two straps, to capsize. The contents slipped slowly out, as though they were the final survivors on the deck of the Titanic. Tumbling to the ground, they bobbed up and down on the frothy plush carpeting, then settled-in with a hope of being rescued. Karen bent down on one knee to retrieve her precious belongings, and as she did so, the top of her dress puckered. A single, happy security officer was now able to view her exposed cleavage, the milky white suppleness accentuated by the darker skin around her neck and shoulders.

When her chest began to flush and she felt that her show might become obvious, Karen stood and adjusted her dress, while getting the final items into her purse. The officer watching in the security office had no intention of giving up on her, she just might drop something else.

Her last move gave Kevin enough time to place his security card in the slot outside the roof above the 29th floor. He held his breath, the small red light turned green, and the door opened to the early morning breeze. The sun was still half-asleep, but its eyes were open, shooting rays of light upward from behind the mountains.

Kevin walked into the coming dawn and headed for the gate to the roof. The city of Reno loomed as far as he could see in all directions, stretching, yawning and dreamy-eyed. Far below he could hear a lonely delivery truck making its way down the empty street to his left. Soon the streets would fill with similar trucks; Bonanza Produce, Nugget Meat Company and the like. They would lumber along in short bursts, stopping at each casino and disgorging their payloads like so many slot machines across the town. There was no fear in the cool air, only resolution. Kevin needed the tape in his camcorder. It was his case bet, nothing else mattered.

His steps made a tremendous racket as the dirt and soot rubbed against the hard soles of his shoes, the echo's worked their way to the edges of the roof and spilled over the sides, taking the quick route to the ground, a long 29 floors below. He walked awkwardly in the slightly too-large shoes, the service door not as close as his previous trips here. It seemed to have moved hundreds of feet away, and each full step brought him only a tiny bit closer. The sky above him was open, but he felt as though his every breath was pulling the mountains and clouds closer as they were sucked into his lungs. He was covered with landscape and suddenly claustrophobic. He flinched noticeably as a flock of Canadian Snow Geese flew past, their perfect V-pattern against the gray clouds breaking his spell.

His feet slipped-out of their mental quicksand, and he reached towards the service door. It was unlocked. The heavy, steel door screeched skyward and Kevin peered inside as the square shadow of light grew eerily larger along the floor. At the bottom of the two steel stairs was a light switch. Kevin flipped it on while listening to the heating unit humming in the vertically challenged room. He was alone.

Crouching, and doing his best Quasimodo impression, Kevin reached the air flow-duct and panels above the penthouse ceiling. The two tiles pulled easily from the floor, but the sheet metal over the duct cried like a wounded animal. He slowed his movements. The camcorder came into view and Kevin reached warily for it as the gun he was carrying in his waistband gouged into his stomach.

While half crouching and leaning into the sheet metal, he pressed the rewind button. The tape started, but the batteries were weak. Through the ducting Kevin could hear voices. "Don't these guys ever sleep?" he wondered. Just a quick look at what might have been caught on tape was all he wanted. Just a little video with Toni, or Antonia or whatever name she was going-by today, would do the trick.

The tape was barely moving, and it left no clear picture on the tiny screen. He would have to view it later. The stop button made a loud click, and Kevin reached for the end of the PVC pipe. Sticking tightly to the metal wall, the duct tape refused to budge. Twisting the pipe slowly, Kevin pulled on the input line from the tiny camera at the end of the pipe. As his wrist twisted to uncouple the wiring, his $2 watch popped off his wrist, and rattled down the duct. Around and around it went, sounding like an empty can in a clothes dryer. The wire refused to come loose, and Kevin dropped it back into the vent. He hit the eject button on the camcorder, grabbed the tape, and thrust it into his pocket where the Velcro closure held it safely against his heart. Rushing out of the room, he ran across the roof. The gun in his belt slipped down his pants and flew out the bottom of his slacks to the floor, spinning liked a crazed carousel.

Kevin skidded to a stop and retrieved the gun, holding it as a weapon for the first time. Resuming his path to the edge of the roof, he peered over the side, but Jeri's car was nowhere to be seen. Karen was supposed to move the car to a space near the road, a signal that she was safely out of the hotel. Kevin ran a quick fifty feet to the corner of the penthouse and looked down the twenty-nine floors to the lot below. The car was still where they had originally parked.

Upon reaching the small gate that led down the stairs to the 29th floor entrance, Kevin hesitated. There were voices, and the thumping of heavy feet on the metal stairs inside, so back to the side of the building he went. Looking east, Kevin saw a window-cleaning rig hanging over the side of the building. The 27th to 29th floors on this side of the building were smaller than the lower floors and the building had a "wedding cake", tiered look. He jumped over the edge, splashing onto the fifteen-foot long platform.

"Bruce Willis, eat your heart out!" Kevin shouted. The rig was a mass of ropes and pulleys, holding it above the 27th floor landing with its small deck and pool. Walking to the right side, there were two power buttons, one red, one green. Pushing the green button, the platform immediately slopped to the left. The motor continued to run even after Kevin lost his footing and his grip on the controls. Sliding across the wood, he headed for a now almost vertical left end as the gun he was carrying slipped from his grip. Two heavily knotted strands of rope slapped against his face as he rushed by. The metal railing around the platform snapped open as his full weight was pummeled against it. Kevin grabbed at the end of the platform before blood obliterated the sight in his right eye from the cut in his eyebrow that had reopened with a vengeance.

Kevin blinked furiously while getting a not very comforting view of the cement far below him. The gun followed him down his vertical trip, and when he grabbed at the railing, the gun passed him, then continued on down towards the pool where it struck a deck chair and clattering to the ground.

His grip on the cold metal bar was not strong, and his right hand sent a new type of pain pounding across the electrodes of his brain, but still he held on. The view below was not promising. The pool was too far to the side for him to jump into, and the single dangling rope on his right became his only option.

Struggling under his own weight, he reached for the rope. With his elbow bent, he wrapped it around the thick strand attached to the metal gate, then swung over and grabbed the rope with his left hand. As he did, both legs instinctively wrapped around the rope below. He feet clamped against the hemp, his left shoe taking a suicide plunge thirty feet to the hard cement.

Above him there were voices, but he couldn't make out the faces of those taking in his predicament. With the help of gravity, he worked his way down the rope as quickly as possible. His right arm ached, and the rope burned its way into his skin. Suddenly his feet began flailing away. No more rope. He unwrapped his right arm and slid down to the end of the rope, hanging by his left hand. He was out of options and his left hand reluctantly let loose.

Trying to absorb as much of the fall on his still shoed right foot, his leg collapsed under him. His right hip took a good blow from the concrete, but he was able to get back to his feet. Grabbing his other shoe, Kevin looked up at the roof. There was nobody there. He slipped the shoe on, then grabbed the gun. The only way off this deck was through a set of sliding glass doors, and they were locked.

Kevin grabbed a chase lounge "key" and threw it against the doors. They shattered, spraying shards of glass across the room and furniture in front of him. The sleepy couple in bed sat-up, mouth's agape.

"No, no, don't get up. Sorry, housekeeping will take care of this."

The man and woman never made a sound. In the hall, he turned left, then stopped. Kevin turned and ran back to the right and looked out the window at the end of the hall. Karen still had not moved the car, where could she be?

Next to the window was a door leading to the service elevators. It was locked, but with a few hard pushes the door popped open. The elevator charged into motion as soon as he pressed the button, and arrived quickly from just a few floors down. Into the tiny, foul smelling room he went. The cleanser couldn't mask the odor of garbage carried on countless trips from the restaurants to the dumpsters below. Kevin pushed 25 and held his breath.

As the elevator surged downward, he shoved against the stop button. No alarm sounded, as it had been deactivated to accommodate the many room-service stops that were made each night. He reached above his head and pushed the panel in the ceiling. Kevin jumped as well as could be expected with his throbbing hip, and grabbed at the now exposed edge, his fingers sneaking over the rim above him. The roof was dusty and his grip poor, but there was a small, metal handrail, running around the middle of the elevator which gave his feet a semi-sturdy perch. Kevin peered into the shaft, looking for the permanent metal ladder, which hid momentarily in the dark.

Try as he might, there was no way to reach the stop button from his current footing. He climbed back down and pulled on the button. The elevator jerked into motion and stopped at the 25th floor. Down the hall there was a security officer sitting at a desk. He could see Kevin, and jumped-up at the sight of him. Running towards the door, Kevin pressed 3 and let the doors close. As the elevator headed down, Kevin headed up. Just able to pull himself through the small opening, he stood on the roof, legs spread wide against the rocking ceiling. He bent down and replaced the ceiling panel before the ride downstairs was over. As soon as the downward momentum was done, the ladder he had been searching for took him towards the 4th floor.

Halfway up the sturdy metal spire, he was able to shimmy across a tiny landing and crawl into the service ducts. He stifled a sneeze and rubbed his face, hands now covered with grease and dirt. The shaft was hot, and with the adrenaline coursing through his veins, his face and body were covered with sweat.

They should have had a back-up plan. Karen had thought of moving the car, and it was a good idea, but it hadn't occurred to either of them that Kevin might get stuck somewhere. The only thing he had said to her was if he was not back by 5:30, that she should drive to the police station in Sparks. Kevin had no watch, but it had to be 5:30 by now. Finally, his brain kicked into gear.

He struggled on his hands and knees for almost 100-feet, crawling along towards the banquet area and the sound technicians room. Once behind the ballrooms, Kevin stretched himself out over the drop ceiling. Moving a tile, he could see he was above the hallway. He had to be careful, as the tiles would never support his weight, and if he dropped one, the cameras at the end of the hall would pick-up the movement. Continuing on, he checked below two other tiles before the audio boards were below him. Locks on all the doors, but all you had to do was go through the ceiling!

There was a shelving unit against the wall, and Kevin crawled down it like a ladder. The lights were off, but he could see the room, and the phone on the desk.

"Hotel operator, this is Sherry, may I help you?"

"Yes, could you please page 'Jeri, from Carson City'."

"Last name?"

"No, 'Jeri, from Carson City', please."

"Please hold."

Kevin's breath was coming hard and heavy, his entire body screaming at him. Looking down his pants had become a quagmire of grease and blood. The wait was interminable.

"I have your party on the line, go ahead."

"Hello?"

"Karen?"

"Kevin, oh my God. You got out! I was sure the call wasn't for me, but I couldn't keep from picking up the courtesy phone. I thought it might be a trick," she said, her words spewing forth in one long breath.

"I'm stuck inside. Why didn't you move the car?"

"You wouldn't believe this place. There are officers everywhere, it is just crazy."

"I want you to meet me in the laundry area. You know where the Smuggler's Lounge is? Along the way from the smaller cashier's cage, by the Baccarat Room."

"I'll find it."

"Good. Now, with the Baccarat Room and the cage behind you, pass the lounge and go through the double doors that say 'No Exit', or something close to that. You go down the hall and turn left, then there's a door that leads to the basement. That's where the laundry is."

"I can find that."

Kevin smiled, relaxed and closed his eyes as pent-up breath escaped his lungs.

Housekeeping started at 6 a.m., and Karen would have to follow the staff downstairs to their work area, then head on down the hall to the maintenance shop.

"I'm sure you can do it. What time is it now, Karen?"

"It is exactly 5:46, did your new watch stop running?"

"No, it's still running, I just can't read it from here," Kevin exclaimed while looking forlornly at his bare wrist.

"What?"

"Nothing. Just wait by the maintenance door, and I'll see you in a few minutes."

"I love you."

"Right"

Crawling up the shelf, he wedged himself into the ceiling on his elbows, not bothering to check for spiders.

In ten minutes he had made his way to just above the tool shop in the basement. The ceiling had a wire-mesh running across the small room, and Kevin vented a little anger with his legs, causing a corner panel to give-way, and he slipped down the opening into the room. Every conceivable tool was now at his disposal. Too late. Kevin opened the door and looked directly at Sonny, one of the engineers. He had dark pouches for eyes, and deep creases in his cheeks.

"Hey, how you doing Sonny?"

"What?"

"Still got that great economy with words I see."

"Who the hell are you?" the large man asked, raising a crescent wrench above his head.

"Think of me as the guy with the gun," Kevin said.

Gravity made quick work of the wrench, and it clanked on the hard floor.

"Look, I'm not here to hurt you, or steal your tools. I just want to walk out of here and leave the building, so I'm going to put you in this little tool room and lock the door."

"Wait a minute, buddy."

"Shut-up! I'm tired and cranky, now get in the damn room and I won't have to shoot you in your big, fat head."

Sonny shuffled into the tool room and closed the door. Kevin snapped the latch shut and attached the dangling pad lock, then opened the main door to the shop an inch or so and peered into the hall. As he opened the door a bit more, a hand brushed his and Kevin fell back into the room.

"Oh, honey, are you all right?"

She looked at Kevin, and a single tear escaped her left eye. Looking into her pale blue eyes, he saw more pain in her face than she saw in his. The tear rolled over her cheek, then spread-out across a light smile line.

Across the room was a First-Aid cabinet, and Dr. Cannon worked on Kevin's puffy eye. The blood had coagulated, and it was painful to have her wiping at it. What remained on his eyelids gave his world a strange haziness. It was not a rose-colored view.

"You did great getting here, Karen. I'm a little fuzzy on just how to get us out of here though. Got any ideas?"

"I can't believe you got beat-up again. Was it Rich and that bitch again?"

"Not exactly."

"How many were there?"

Kevin said he didn't exactly know, but it wasn't important. What *was* important right now was finding a way out, and Karen felt the way he came in was their best shot.

"I'm not too sure about that, it's through a messy, disgusting crawl space."

"Honey, *you* are messy and disgusting right now. I think I can handle it."

"Succinctly put. Sonny," Kevin shouted, "I'm going to open this door again, now stand back, because if you move, I'll put a bullet in your leg."

There was some shifting of weight, then silence.

"Oh, my God, you have somebody locked-up in there?"

"Yup, and now I need to break-in, but the tools we could use are on the wrong side of the door. Kevin grabbed a metal stool and cracked it against the pad lock. Nothing happened. After a few more tries the lock snapped, and Kevin pulled the door open. "Sonny, don't move," he said, and the frightened man nodded in silence. Kevin grabbed a few nails and hammered them through the door and into the door jam, securing the door.

"Now listen my friend, you stay put for a while, and I won't have to come back here and hit you with this hammer."

Again the silent man nodded his understanding. Karen had already climbed on the workbench below the hole in the ceiling. She began her ascent without even looking back at Kevin, and he was quickly behind her. When they were up to the second floor crawl space, she turned and asked which way to go, but he stared back blankly, having yet to think of a plan.

"Did you find anything out from the camcorder?"

"Yes, batteries don't last very long...but I've got the tape right here in my pocket. Now if we go left, we can get back into the sound technicians room where I called you from. I'm not sure about going to the right."

They turned left, there feet slipping constantly as they struggled against a set of cold and dusty pipes to the next floor.

They worked their way above a hallway on their knees. The small, thin girders they were forced to crawl along made their knee's beg for mercy, but the sound tech's room came into view.

"Once we get in there, you should give me the tape. I probably have a good chance of getting out of here, and you can hide here for a while."

"Are you kidding me, Karen? I'm not turning loose of this tape until I see it myself."

"Well, we need to think of something".

"Hey, you've got tennis shoes on. What happened to the high heels you were wearing?"

"I brought a spare set with me so I could break the heal on the others and give the fellows behind the camera something to watch."

"And what exactly was that?"

"Just a woman with bad shoes, and a short dress. Actually, it was kind of exciting. Maybe there is an exhibitionist hiding inside me."

"Must be why we get along so well, opposites attract."

Chapter Thirty-seven

"How about if you call the front desk and ask for the penthouse, we can see if anybody is still checked-in," said Karen.

There was no need to call the front desk. Kevin simply dialed a six, followed by the room number and it rang in the penthouse. The phone rang twice before a female voice answered.

Kevin hesitated before speaking. "Toni...do you know who this is?"

"I'm sorry, there is nobody here by that name."

The voice was smooth and calm as she hung-up the phone. Perhaps it hadn't been her.

"I can't believe people are still hanging-up on me."

"Who was it?"

"Toni."

"And the bitch hung-up on you?"

"Twice! That's twice you used that word. You've gotten so tough."

Karen's eyes narrowed and squinted through the razor slits, while Kevin thought of the old "a woman scorned" thing.

"Listen, Karen, we came down here to see if there is any film. Well, the batteries were too low in the camcorder to check the tape, so we still don't know if there is anything worthwhile here. I can leave you here while I go up to the penthouse. I would definitely have the element of surprise on my side..."

"We already discussed going up to the penthouse, fine, but you lead, and I will follow, because I will not leave you alone again."

This was not an argument he could win, so back to the crawl spaces they went, leaving the tile on the floor.

It was quite a trip, nearly 100-yards on their hands and knees to an opening in the employee lounge. "At certain intervals, that lounge is empty," said Kevin, "and we can just drop in."

In a few minutes they were in a corner, over the heating duct. Kevin lifted an acoustic tile and let his eye pick-out the room's inhabitants. There were just three employees below them; two dealers, talking about their latest player's being a bunch of "stiffs", and a bellman. The clock on the wall showed 6:15, and in an excruciatingly long two-minutes, the dealers headed back to work. The bellman looked around the empty room and heaved a tired sigh. His tongue worked a ball of gum past his lips and to his left hand. After rolling it around his fingers a few seconds, he launched it across the room to the far wall, where it hung momentarily before slowly sliding down to the rug below. He stood, then mumbled something as he exited, just another happy Royal employee.

Kevin tried to pry-up the tile next to them, but it slipped out of the frame and he followed it to the ground. There was a cascade of dust and chalk as he starred up from the floor.

"Here, drop on this seat cushion, it's softer than the rug," Kevin said, while waving a tired arm up at Karen. She did just that, and the noise produced was heard only by the bare walls. Turning slowly towards the computer room, Kevin peeked inside. It was empty. Finally something was going their way.

The air inside was cool and refreshing. Some days, the cave was eighty-degrees, but the precious computers were pampered. Their room was sixty-eight degrees, summer and winter.

The drawer's were locked on the first desk Kevin tried, and to Karen's glance he explained that they needed scissors, strong ones.

"Like these?" she asked, hitting pay dirt on her first try.

"Terrific, let's go cause some havoc."

"What exactly do you have on your mind?"

"Just snip-snip, that's all."

She looked at her man as he tried to wink, and she felt his pain. They walked up a few stairs and down the hall. The lighting was sparse, and so was the paint, everything in gray. When they were fifteen-feet from the cave, Kevin explained what he had in mind.

"You stand right here, under this camera. When I get to the door, cut this cable, then run up the hall past me and I'll catch-up with you."

Karen nodded, as he continued towards the surveillance door. There came a loud snapping behind him, and Karen began running up the hall. Taking the pistol from his pocket, he grabbed the barrel. The butt of the gun thumped against the keypad, and red and yellow sparks shot-out from around the numbers. Popping noises followed, with a few wisps of smoke, and a black, burn mark around the entire keypad. Several of the individual numbers were welded together. Kevin savored the smell of burned electrodes and charred plastic for the first time ever.

"What did you do?"

"I locked the door to the cave, giving us time to climb this ladder and cut the rest of the camera lines. Security watches some of the cameras in the hotel, so we'll have to cut their trunk lines in the atrium elevator shaft, then we can go to the penthouse or anywhere else we want, without anybody seeing us."

"My, such a sneaky devil you have turned out to be."

"I did most of this wiring. See how the cables are rolled together so they make a tight braid, and these couplings hold them together."

"Lovely," Karen said, while following Kevin up a permanent ladder to above the cave.

"Yup. Let me cut these over here and then we can get the ones in the conduit and that's that." His hand moved with the scissors, but they wouldn't cut. "Geez, I can't cut this. How come scissors can't be used in your left-hand."

Karen took over. It took a few minutes to get them all, and by the time they finished, voices could be heard below them. The cables in the PVC pipe still remained. Kevin began trying to break the 3/4 inch plastic pipe. With Karen's help, the pipe broke about four-feet from where they were kicking it. Holding the cables up in the air, Karen was able to cut each one.

As Kevin stood up, he came face-to-face with a man in a green coat with an ugly security patch playing-out across his breast pocket. The jacket was small for his build, and there was no mercy in his eyes. His finger was on his lapel, holding down the button on the microphone attached to his jacket.

He finished his transmission to the security office, having told them the perpetrators were in sight. Kevin thought how strange it was that through all his recent tribulations he had been beaten severely, but had yet to throw a punch, and now seemed as good a time as any.

A short left-hook to the guard's cheekbone gave Kevin some satisfaction, but it would have been better if the square faced guard had fallen to the ground. Instead, he grimaced and snapped Kevin's head back with a blow just beyond the speed of light.

Blinking, Kevin realized he was now looking up from the ground. Behind him, Karen was struggling with the plastic piping. Pulling the four-foot section away from the freshly cut cables, she swung the pipe in a low arc, swishing over Kevin's head. The pipe shattered against the guards shins, and tiny, white plastic projectiles headed everywhere.

Kevin twisted around on the small of his back, his legs sweeping swiftly against the heels of the guard, who tripped awkwardly to the ground on Kevin's left side. Once prone, he made an easy target for a few quick shots to the head. Rolling on his stomach to escape the barrage of blows he grabbed his throbbing face while Karen pulled Kevin to his feet.

Two more officers were climbing the ladder to the small landing, and Kevin shouted at them. "Freeze, I have a gun". To his surprise, they stopped, giving Kevin a chance to show Karen another ladder that led to the elevator shaft.

Up the ladder Karen went, while Kevin snuck a peek back at the guards who came to the aid of their fallen comrade. None of them looked happy.

Chapter Thirty-eight

At 5:15 a.m., detective Paul Kozar's morning alarm went off. His muscled arm crashed forward from his chair, knocking the clock over, and silencing the annoying sound. His eyelids stuck together as the sore little balls inside slowly adjusted to the light in the small room, a hint of the cold dawn pushing its way into his study. Casting aside the blanket from his legs, he stretched. A nap in a chair can be no nap at all.

The room was carpeted, but the floorboards groaned under his short steps and reminded him of the creaking front door of an old cabin his uncle owned. There were a lot of good memories bundled up in that cabin at Donner Lake, and he smiled, wishing it was there he was headed. It was the only time he would smile today.

In the room next door, Becky could be heard thrashing about. Her mind had taken-in the shriek of the alarm, but her husband was not at arms reach. Paul opened the door quietly and walked to the side of the bed. To his presence she opened a single eye, and mumbled a question about how he could have gotten up and dressed so quickly.

"I'm heading back to the office in a few minutes. It's not even five-thirty, so go back to sleep."

Sleep had not been found in great quantities in the Kozar home recently, and he hungered to lie down and join her in the warm bed, but settled for a lingering kiss that he left on her dry, morning lips.

The ringing phone broke-in, and he slipped out of the room to answer it in the den. From the RPD station, he was told of the disturbance at the Royal.

He decided against going into the bedroom again, hoping Becky could get back to sleep. In the study he grabbed the socks from the floor, and experienced a weird sensation down his back as he slipped the stiff material over his feet

An orange soda from the refrigerator was as close to breakfast as he was going to get, and he picked-up his shoulder harness and went into the bathroom. When he came out, he shouldered his jacket and took his back-up pistol from a drawer. After starting his car, he put the back-up in a small holster around his ankle.

By the time Kevin was locking, then breaking his way back into the tool room, Kozar was meeting a uniformed officer at the door to the Royal. He couldn't wait to tell the story of the disturbance on the 27th floor. The words spewed forward as the edges of his mouth developed a web of saliva. He finished at record pace, and Paul tried to absorb most of the words.

Dave Baker, the casino manager, joined their discussion, and soon their group became a foursome as a third RPD officer joined and brought news of a frightened engineer who had just broken-out of his own tool room.

"So, who locked him in?" Kozar asked.

"It was the male who caused the disturbance on the 27th floor. He appears to have been alone on the upper floor, but when he was in the tool room, a woman joined him and they climbed into the ceiling."

"I'm sorry, they climbed into the ceiling?" Kozar asked.

"Yes, above the tool room."

"Mr. Baker, where can they go from there?" Kozar queried.

Baker's lips buzzed, and he ventured they could go anywhere on the first or second floors, but he really didn't think they could get anywhere else without going into a hallway that had camera coverage.

"Fine. Could you put me in touch with your surveillance department, and get me one of your security officers who has a radio."

"No problem, detective."

Baker walked over to the valet desk to use a phone. The cord was twisted, and as he pulled the receiver, the entire phone came with it. Slipping over the edge of the counter, Baker juggled it momentarily before it crashed to the floor. The heavy Mexican tile hardly noticed, but the American phone took a beating, with Baker still holding the receiver.

"Good thing we have two phones," Baker stated, his face turning red as he reeled the phone back up to the counter.

He was more careful reaching for the second phone. His call to dispatch produced the security shift supervisor, Leonard, in record time, and once surveillance was on the line, he handed the receiver to Paul.

"Good morning, this is detective Kozar. Can you give me a rundown of what has happened in the past ten minutes, please."

"Nothing unusual in the past ten minutes, except for the extra police officers running around. You have units at each entrance, plus we have our officers walking the floor and the perimeter of the building. I've got almost three hundred camera angles available, with two dozen monitors currently on one-quarter, split-screen quads."

"Nothing to show for all that? You *are* looking for a man and a woman right?" Kozar inquired.

"The report from our engineer is that the male is about six-foot three, two-hundred pounds with short black hair. The female is five-six to five-eight, with light red hair. The male has a bloody face and a bandage on his right hand. I don't think I'm going to miss them." There was just enough sarcasm in his voice to grate on Kozar's nerves.

"Thank you. I'll be with your security shift-supervisor, so please advise him immediately of anything new."

"Sure, I've got...hold on, one of my monitors just went out. I've got somebody pounding on my door, but I can't see who it is, because that's the monitor that's not transmitting."

"We're on our way."

Kozar handed the phone to Baker, then looked at Leonard, who finally said, "Follow me," and the men threaded their way through the casino towards the elevators. One of the group of five elevators had its doors open and they lumbered inside.

Kozar questioned Leonard about what his dispatch had on this incident, but there were no cameras available in that particular hallway.

"We monitor the stairs, cooking facilities, health club and the gift shop."

"This guy broke into the 27th floor from the pool, right?"

"That's affirmative."

"Well, how did he get *there*?"

"He worked his way down a window-washer's unit to the ground."

"From where?" Kozar continued.

"The roof of the 29th floor."

"And how did he get there? Kozar asked. "How could he get outside on your roof without anybody seeing him? What about the door to the roof. Isn't it secured?"

"That's affirmative."

"Well?"

Leonard stated he had no answer to the question, while squirming with both indignation and frustration.

When the elevator jerked to a stop, they hustled through the employee break rooms, past walls plastered with job descriptions and posters listing benefits. The air smelled of bacon. Not a "lazy Sunday" bacon, but a mass produced, cook it and keep it slightly warm aroma that hung in the air until lunchtime

Leonard struck a pose as they arrived. He had the pupils of his eyes pointed upward and to the left, lids parted only slightly as he listened to the small transmitter in his ear.

Once Leonard's eyes rolled back to look at the detective, he stated the employee in the surveillance room was still locked-in. There had also been a disturbance of some type above the room, and his officers were pursuing the perpetrators. Leonard headed towards his crime scene, and Kozar was left to simply follow.

There was a single officer at the scene, sitting with his legs pulled-up and his arms around the front of his knees. He sheepishly pulled his pants-leg back down and stood up.

"There's been a fight, I see," Leonard stated, immediately grasping the obvious.

"There were two of them, and I didn't want to hit the lady, so I was trying to get the guy down to the ground. She hit me with that plastic pipe."

"And that knocked you down?" Kozar asked incredulously.

"No, the guy punched me, see this welt?" He pointed to the pink and puffy marks around his left eye and cheek.

"A savage beating," Leonard stated. "You will probably be out of work for weeks. Unless of course you feel well enough to continue the pursuit."

The words were still making their way from Leonard's mouth to the tympanic membrane of the officer when he realized that detective Kozar had left his side. Making his way from the circle of shattered plastic, Paul picked-up the trail of the two officers that were following the suspects.

The description was less than accurate to the last time Paul had seen his best friend. Eyewitness accounts were often subject to each individual's own perception of the world, however. It could be anybody, and that is who Paul hoped it was. Anybody.

Chapter Thirty-nine

Kevin looked up at Karen as she climbed the metal ladder above him. The elevator shaft was hot, the air musty. It was dark, but he was still able to see Karen's short skirt and the perfect, rounded curve of her buttocks. He pondered momentarily what makes a man in such dire circumstances still take time to steal a glimpse of the female form. There was no easy answer, and he took another look.

"You are falling behind."

"Interesting choice of words, Karen."

"Do you really think there is any chance that the guys in the penthouse are still there? Why would they hang around after all of this craziness?"

"Who knows, it's just a hunch. I'm getting dizzy. I could really use a drink right about now."

"No beverages on this trip. You know, I thought that was really clever, wedging your shoe into the bar across the door so nobody else could get in here, but they will still know where we are. It won't..."

"Oh ye, of little faith. You see that line of light up there on the right? That is an access panel to the next elevator. We can change cars and take that one to the 25th floor."

"How do we get to the penthouse? There are going to be officers at the other elevator, right?"

"Well, I don't think we can get away with another one of your diversions, although I know I would be distracted."

Kevin had not made any real plans, they simply opened the door to the middle elevator shaft and waited for the elevator to make its way up to their level. It shot past them once, but on the trip down it traveled to the floor just below them. Traversing the ladder, they gingerly stepped to the roof. Kevin pulled the ceiling panel up and looked into the empty room.

He took Karen's hand and beckoned to the hole. Making her way to a seated position, she turned over onto her belly and dropped her legs through the ceiling. Her feet were still four-feet from the floor, and he could see her legs dangling on the mirrored walls.

As she inched her way over the opening, the car started on its way to a lower floor. The soft carpet came up to meet her a bit quicker than she would have liked. The control panel and stop button were now within reach, and Kevin put his head through the ceiling as the car came to an abrupt stop. He found himself in the same predicament Karen had been in a moment before, but it was his torso that was dangling in the mirrors.

"Give me a hand?" he asked.

Karen stopped a laugh and reached up to his shoulders. He slithered through the ceiling and tried to stop when his feet reached the edge of the hole, but they both wound-up on the carpet again.

"Smooth, Kevin. You do this for a living?"

"Take me for a pro, do you?"

They laughed at each other, and Karen gave him a hug. It was so natural, almost like a mother and child. Not a forgiving hug, because no apology was necessary, just complete acceptance and absolution.

They struggled to their feet, still in an embrace, both waiting for the other to speak, but words were unnecessary. Karen jammed her palm against the start button and the car jerked into motion and continued its path to the next floor. When the door opened, Kevin shoved his hand out and said, "Sorry, no passengers". The startled little man took one step forward and halted, the coffee in his cup continued on its way for a moment, then headed to the floor.

Kevin pushed the 24th floor button, and reminded Karen that the 25th floor was guarded. They would have to stop on the 24th and then use the stairs.

"Do you still have the gun?" Karen asked.

Kevin pulled it from his waistband and offered it to Karen. She took it momentarily and handed it back.

"No offense, but I feel safer now that you have that out of your pants."

The stairs were noisy, but the officer was unaware of their presence until they were within whispering distance of him. He had no options, as there was just the one gun between them. He hit the carpet, and Kevin pulled the microphone from his jacket, snatched his remaining shoe from his foot and raised it above his head. The heavy heel came down on the microphone and bounced back up. The carpet protected the electronics, and Kevin threw his shoe against the wall in disgust. Then, he gently pulled the wires from the earpiece, rendering the unit inoperable.

Kevin took the officer's handcuffs and placed one end around the door handle to the stairs, while dangling the other end at the officer.

"Please get up and take hold of this door handle." The metal clicked into place and Karen and Kevin headed towards the elevators. "Chatty fellow, I thought he'd never shut-up," Kevin said.

As they walked towards the alcove that housed the elevator to the penthouse, Kevin took Karen's hand again. He no longer cared about the pain in his right hand, he just wanted to feel her skin, be a part of her. Rounding the corner and turning right, Kevin's feet burned into the carpet. He shoved Karen backwards and she tumbled to the ground. His left hand drew the gun up from his side.

Everything around him was in perfect view. On the far wall, a picture of Frank Hawkins bursting through the line at a University of Nevada Reno football game showed detail he had never noticed; the glint of sunshine reflecting off his helmet and the grease paint under his eyes, a Budweiser beer ad along the goal line. Below the picture, an ashtray by the elevator had a tiny crack running up its base, and the top held only sand, no butts. Above all this was a chandelier with exactly 22 bulbs, and there was the smell of "Escape" in the air.

Toni was braced against the white tiled wall, her knees bent, and the short skirt pulled tight above her knees. There was a handgun fixed at the end of her slender arms, and the offensive weapon was pointed at Kevin. He noticed the perfect hair, with only a few strands making their way from her delicate ear and across her temple towards those piercing blue eyes. They seemed to be looking right through him. He could see the chamber in the thirty-eight in her hand, twisting. She was quick, so was Kevin . He squeezed the trigger and heard his gun click, while from the alcove came a thunderous roar.

He could see the smoke rise from Toni's gun. Kevin thought he was being picked-up by an unseen giant and flung backwards. His arms whipped forward towards his feet, which had suddenly come into his line of sight. There were no shoes, socks only, one with the big toe pushing through a hole. Time flooded back to its normal speed and the gun flew from his hand.

As Kevin crunched to the ground and melted beside her, Karen picked-up the gun and calmly removed the safety clip.

She moved to her knees and wasted a shot across the hall, then twisted around the corner and continued firing. There was a return volley. Bullets from Karen's gun loosened the marble around the elevator and it sprayed towards the ground. The more distinctive sound of a gun hitting the floor worked its way back to her ears, but she continued shooting until there was a louder sound, that of Toni's body embracing the floor. Dust fluttered about, powdering the face and hair of a once beautiful woman. Her eyes lay open, but her heart, if she had one, had stopped beating.

Karen turned her attention to Kevin. His eyes too, were open, but they continued to blink. The small part of his shirt that had stayed clean over the past hour was now soaked with blood. The bullet had ripped into the side of his chest, and through his left arm.

Chapter Forty

Ripping open Kevin's jacket, Karen checked his wound, and through his fog he heard her leave his side to check on Toni. Later, the sound of an elevator grinding along registered on Kevin's mind, as his breath came in short gasps. The officer handcuffed to the door behind them had squatted down, but not a sound made its way from his larynx and across his dry lips and he flopped like a rag doll when the door was thrust open. A gun was pointed towards his shackled body for a fleeting moment, then away.

Pooled-up in the thick carpet around Karen's legs was enough blood to make a vampire envious. Considering his many accidents the past few days, it was amazing there was even enough to stain her white tennis shoes.

From this scene of discomfort, she looked up into the face of a friend. He was tall, tired, and unshaven. And, he had his gun pointed at her. His eyes were quick and attentive, scanning the scene in front of him, taking in the two downed civilians. Paul cautiously picked-up the gun from the rug, then looked across the hallway. On the marble lay another gun, with a smoldering story of its own, just inches from somebody he was not aquatinted with. As he brushing the hot metal away with his foot, his gaze never left the eyes of the woman in front of him. Neither of them blinked, but her eyes were now as blank as her future.

Directly in front of him, the silvery doors of the elevator opened and Leonard burst upon the scene. Had his brave lot arrived a few minutes earlier, he could have led them to their deaths. As it was, his arrival meant a fellow officer could be released from handcuffs, but little more. It was now a police scene, and while reports would be filled out until each officer had writer's cramp, there was nothing else to do but call an ambulance, and the coroner.

"Thanks for coming Paul, I'd have called you sooner, but I was busy," Kevin managed with great difficulty, his left lung making a hissing sound.

"Great Kevin. Did Karen, here, tell you that you're a mess? You know there's an arrest warrant out for you? Of course I knew you weren't the instigator of all this. You weren't, right?"

"No, I am not, and I knew we could trust you, but we couldn't get you involved right away," Kevin replied, now completely out of breath.

"Right away! It's been three days, and it looked like you kidnapped Karen, you couldn't call back?"

Karen broke into the conversation to tell them both to "Shut-up".

"Listen, Kevin needs an ambulance. That lady over there is dead, but this guy is alive, and I intend to keep him that way," Karen stated.

"Right. Leonard, do we have an ambulance on the way?"

"Affirmative, and my medical officer will be here in a moment. Of course we will need statements from everybody, and there are questions of liability here."

Kevin looked up at Leonard and gave him the same look as so many times before.

"No, no, I need to know why this man is not being placed under arrest," said Leonard.

"Because he is not a criminal!" Karen screamed.

Her outburst set the tone for the next twenty minutes while the paramedics arrived and took over Kevin's care. He tried to make a statement, knowing his explanation would be better than Karen's, but his eyelid's fluttered shut. Sounds around him grew distant, and the last words he heard that morning were Karen's as she let everybody know she was *not* going to the hospital in a separate vehicle, and she was by his side when the door to the ambulance closed.

Chapter Forty-one

There is something strangely comforting about waking up in a hospital. Knowing that everything possible is being done, and that there is a doctor or nurse close by. Of course, getting one of those nurses to your room at three in the morning is another story.

Kevin struggled against a cloud of drugs, his brain clicking-off the last few days of his life, while the sounds around his bed took on a life of their own, growing shapes, becoming real. Eyes closed against the pain, he knew what to expect when he let the view enter his retinas,. Only police talk like police. He also knew the layout of the room he occupied with the window on the right hand wall bringing no light, and the door for the nurses who working around both sides of his bed, to his left. A chair was close by and Kevin knew it was Karen who had camped there all night.

The voice's worked their way across the room through a vapor of Dilaudid and morphine. Words crashed like loose dishes against his ears. They were friendly, but they were still there. Certainly Karen had told much of the story, but even Paul was waiting for some direct news.

Having finally heard enough, Kevin opened his eyes and turned towards Karen. His perception of the room had been sharp, but about his own body, he had been wrong. His left arm was in an airplane splint, hand pointed at the ceiling. There was no way to roll over, but he could twist his head and glimpse the woman seated beside him.

Her eyes opened the moment he glanced her way. There was no fear trapped inside them, and no resignation, only the remembrance of the day. A smile worked slowly across her lips and she reached out to him. She would have made a fine nurse, Kevin thought.

Two officers drifted past, and out the door. Paul stopped at the foot of the bed.

"This isn't going to get you more than a couple of strokes per nine holes you know."

They chatted briefly, much less than Kevin was expecting. A few questions, a few answers. Then Paul headed home to the wife that always waited. He had to hurry, she had dinner and a good, strong hug waiting for him.

Kevin spent his time taking-in the view of the woman he loved. There were just whispers now between them. She filled him in on his surgery, and let him know that he could probably get out of helping with the dishes for a few weeks. He smiled that crooked smile, and drifted slowly, peacefully.

"You told the police everything?"

"Mostly, but I left out the part about the jewelry store. The hell with the insurance company."

"And Paul, did you tell him I thought he was involved?"

"No," she said, with a quiet tone.

"So it was Toni, and the guys in the Penthouse?"

"So far, yes. Now go back to sleep. There will be plenty of time for stories in the morning."

Kevin leaned his head back and forgot about the events of the past week. The only thing worth remembering now was the woman at his side. With that comfort, it was easy to slip back to sleep, and so he did.

Chapter Forty-two

At the Reno Police Department, Fred Meyer briefed Chief Packard about the shooting. The media knew a kidnapping suspect had been apprehended after a shoot-out in a local casino. They knew one person was dead, another wounded. They knew no officers were involved in the crossfire. That was enough for now.

What Packard wanted to know about was Vellardi. How was it possible for him to get out of the hotel with officers all over the property? How could he just vanish?

"Listen, you guys were a day late, and are now a dollar short. Your explanation doesn't hold water. Vellardi couldn't just walk out. He must have left yesterday, so I want to know who was on the stakeout."

"Cap, we did everything we could here. What we had was some questions at the Royal, but a lot more pressing things going on with Mr. Webb. We found the cabin, and we've dusted everything from here to Tahoe and back, looking for a kidnapper. In Carson City we found their last hideout and there is no question we have the right man from the Lester murder."

"I see in your eyes that you have your *suspect*, but not your killer. What's the theory?"

"Our kidnap victim states she was not forced to accompany Mr. Webb, and she willingly took him to a location in Lake Tahoe, then to Carson City."

"For what reason?"

"She believed his innocence in the Lester murder, and that he was also going to be killed, so she was hiding him."

"Fred, did she say anything in her interview that is verifiable fact, and not based on second-hand horseshit from him?"

"No, but..."

"You've got two officers at the hospital?"

"Yes sir."

"I want you to hold her down here. Either harboring a fugitive, or obstruction of justice, and maybe a gun charge"

"I don't think it's necessary. It wouldn't hold-up, and he's more likely to talk if he thinks we're taking care of her."

Packard was visibly unhappy. "Make sure I see Kozar in the morning, before he starts the interviews at the hospital. And tell me something about Vellardi."

"You mean where he is? Ms. Cannon mentioned Denver, that they might be going to another City Casino property."

"He knows he's safe, the prick."

"Everybody's watching, the FBI, the Justice Department, us, and nobody can do anything, sir."

"Curtis, from Justice wants to see Webb too. Like I said, make sure I see Kozar early in the morning, I want our interviews before Justice takes over."

"Yes, sir."

Packard gave a nod of his head, dismissing Fred Meyer. He walked on to his office with the gears going, his head smoking. He knew Vellardi was involved, and he knew there was money leaving the casino, but nobody had all the pieces yet.

He gave Kozar a call at home. "Make sure you are on time, and don't forget the information on Tolan"

"All right, Fred. By the way, what's your gut say about Kevin?"

"The girl was dirty, and he may have been trying to keep her quiet, or maybe take her job with Vellardi. This Cannon lady may have no idea what she is really involved with. But if he *is* dirty, where's the money, unless he was paid to get rid of Terry King and used the pay-off to erase his debt with Tolan."

"Tolan has been a loan shark for twenty-years here. We've had discussions before, and there's no doubt in my mind that he's telling the truth about getting paid-off. But he say's the money came by messenger, not directly from Kevin, so who knows."

"Don't be late tomorrow!"

"Okay, bye."

Meyer leaned back in his chair and blew an imaginary smoke ring at the ceiling, knowing he wouldn't have jurisdiction over Vellardi. If anything could be tied to him, the case would go to Federal prosecutors and the RPD would play a minor role. Early retirement was looking better and better.

Chapter Forty-three

The roller coaster of nightshift in the hospital rolled on, slow, then busy, slow, then busy. Nurses buzzed, like so many bees, in and out of Kevin's room. Pain shots came every two hours, and the intravenous "drip-system" they attached to him managed to go into alarm mode every time he slipped-off to sleep. Karen was amazingly constant, her bright face alive with a combination of concern and reassurance as Kevin worked his way past the gates of fear and fatigue.

At seven in the morning he tried to rise from his incarceration, but there was not enough strength in his body. Karen had gone for breakfast, and there was no way to avoid calling for a nurse, he was drowning. Squeaking came from around the corner, and a nice lady brought the necessary devices for him to relieve the unwanted sensation. The efforts were exhausting, and a nap was in order. He dozed until he heard his name. The voice was unfamiliar and far away; the news at nine, on channel eight. Soon another voice drifted across the room.

"Good morning Mister Webb, you've awakened just in time. She had a pleasant voice, but was carrying a sharp instrument.

"I feel like a pin cushion, can't I start taking pills?"

"I'll ask the doctor, but you'll need to take this last shot."

"Enjoy it while you can, sweetheart. It could be the last time I ever let you show your butt to another woman."

"Thanks, Karen. All right nurse, do as you must."

He was lanced quickly with her sword, then fastidiously dabbed at the spot of blood on his hip. She smiled as only a nurse can do, then treaded out of the room.

"Karen, could I get a wet towel for this crust on my lip?"

"Careful, you have stitches there."

Kevin had more silk across his body than a good tie, plus staples. The side of his chest and biceps were webbed with the stuff, and the doctors threw in a few for his eyebrow and scalp to get to an even hundred.

"Do I have some of those in my back, or am I sleeping on steel wool?"

"I would imagine you are feeling the drain below your shoulder blade, and the wire around two of your ribs. There was no damage to your lung, but the muscles were shredded."

"Any other good news?"

"You can have morphine, even with the police sitting right outside."

There was a screech of metal on tile, as the officer outside shifted in his chair.

"What's up with that?"

"Would you like the full Fred Meyer or condensed Paul Kozar version?"

"Fred who?"

"Meyer. Paul's boss, nice guy but windy."

"I thought Packard was Paul's boss."

"That would be the Chief of Police. Fred is king of detectives, and he can have me arrested for obstructing justice, and various other sundry items. You are to be considered under arrest, and will be charged soon. He also......"

"Wait, what did Paul say?"

"Paul said he would be here this morning, and I had to promise not to go anywhere but my home and here. Becky says "hi", and get a lawyer."

"A lawyer would probably be good."

"Don't worry, I've got a brilliant attorney on the way."

"Is that an oxymoron?"

"Watch it, or I'll leave you to a public defender."

Jim Kelley was at the door as they were speaking, the officer outside following his orders, but eventually allowing him to enter when the second officer returned from the bathroom. Introductions were made, and Kevin kept his jokes in check.

"Based on what Karen has told me, I've agreed to represent the both of you. You need to start filling me on every detail involving the past two weeks. The list of possible charges is long, and we only have a short time before your interview with RPD will begin. We can't close the door, so first, tell me if you have any guilt or complicity in the deaths of Terry King, Steven Lester, or Theodore Ryan, but keep your voices low."

Kevin did as he was told, and then subjected his new lawyer to a long dissertation on the propensity of the Royal's slot machines to disgorge themselves of cash at an unnatural rate.

"How about your debt to your bookie?"

"Tolan? He's not my bookie, he's a bartender at the Mustang Ranch."

Karen had an exasperated frown on her face, but Kevin tried to explain he only went there to *pay* Tolan.

"You see, his memory goes bad as long as you put a little cash in his jar. If you're a businessman from some bible-belt town, you don't want the folks back home to know you were doing any riding and roping with wild horses. I borrowed $10,000 from his brothel bank a couple years ago."

"And how did he get paid back three days ago?"

Kevin was dumbfounded. He proclaimed his innocence, while Karen sat with her mouth agape.

Their discussion came to a close when Paul arrived. Behind him was Josh Winslow and some other "suit" from the Gaming Control Board. Chairs were scarce, and Jim Kelley asked that only the RPD enter the room.

This time, the door slid shut, and Paul opened his briefcase. It must have taken two trees to produce all of the forms and notes he had lugged over from headquarters.

"Kevin, you are in as deep as Bill Gate's pockets. There is no way around that, but if you are totally innocent, then Karen should be in protective custody. I spent the morning with the Chief of Police, and then my direct boss, Fred Meyer. The police department has an obligation to protect the people of Reno, and the district attorney's office will tell us who they feel they can prosecute successfully. Are you ready to answer some questions?"

Kevin gave a sheepish nod, and his attorney shook his head in the affirmative.

"Kevin, this is what I've got: A guy who owed you money was left spread out along both sides of Virginia Street; a fellow you didn't like tripped over a four-foot wall on a roof you were working on and fell two-hundred feet to the parking lot. You paid off a $20,000 debt to a loan shark with cash, then brutally murdered a woman's boyfriend because you were obsessed with her. She started carrying a gun, then two days later you hunted her down, lodged three bullets in her, and watched her life slip away."

Kevin's mouth was wide enough to park a train in, and Paul continued speaking.

"Here is what you've got: You don't appear to be a kidnapper, and Karen did the actual shooting at the hotel. Do you know Frank Wallace?"

"No, but I know he was registered in the room and had been there before."

"Do you know Vincent Vellardi?"

"No, just know you were working on his case because I overheard you and Packard at the golf course."

"What were you taping above the penthouse?"

"I thought it might be Vellardi in the room, and I wanted to catch something on tape."

"And what did you get, Kevin."

"You tell me, what was on the tape."

"What tape?" Paul asked.

"It was in the pocket of my jacket, a VHS tape."

Kevin looked at Karen, who buried her face in her hands.

"Kevin, we took everything from your pockets in the emergency room. There was no tape."

The questions continued until the weight on Kevin was Nebraska, and Oklahoma. Squeaky shoes arrived and brought lunch for Kevin. The bill of fare was disappointing at best, but it allowed a break in the fun.

Chapter Forty-four

After a lunch barren of taste, Kevin and Karen worked with their lawyer. He assured them that there was a growing swell of interest in their case. The Gaming Control Board was waiting to interview them, and he had just been in touch with the FBI.

Things were muddled and deep, but improving. Vellardi was known to local law enforcement as well as to the Bureau. He had a large cash flow for his businesses, and had been arrested before, but not convicted. If Kevin could provide a little more than what the RPD already knew, the FBI would probably offer immunity should they be able to prosecute Vellardi.

"Right, Jerry, but what could the FBI get him for at this point, not paying his tab at the hotel?" said Kevin.

"What we need," explained Kelley, "is for Gaming Control to come-up with some very convincing numbers from the Royal that show money is being filtered out of there. If they are able to find anything like a specially programmed chip, or somebody caught on tape exchanging chips, then we can drag your boat off the sandbar."

"Kevin, there are still many unanswered questions," Paul allowed, "but the panning has turned up a few nuggets. Both Toni and Terry had enough money squirreled away to retire tomorrow, had they lived. Gaming's investigation is going to drag on, with RPD following the same waltz, and by that time, the FBI will feel left out and want to join-in by picking-up Vellardi. He's got cash, so he'll have the latest incarnation of Clarence Darrow working for him. We'll leave an officer outside your room, but we don't have any charges yet."

"Do you think any charges will get filed?" Karen asked.

"Well, Packard is pissed, but Meyer sniffed this all out two days ago. He's smart enough to know how strong Vellardi is. You are probably safe, this was just sensational enough for him to want to keep you two breathing, and the DA's Office will let the current charges against you sit for a while."

"Comforting," Kevin said while straining to turn and look at Karen.

Paul continued with what he thought might happen, then tried to sum everything up.

"Listen, we're talking six-months down the road before this investigation gets through., maybe longer. The Royal is going to look bad, Gaming Control is going to look bad, Vellardi gets hit with ties to three murders. If you have faith in our court system he goes to jail, maybe he winds up pleading to conspiracy and tax evasion."

"So, all my work will be for nothing?"

"No, you got him out of the state, and out of my hair."

"You owe me a thank-you?"

"I wouldn't go that far, Kevin!"

Karen's soft voice entered their conversation with a simple request to call it a night. They were all tired, and each had earned a rest.

"Kevin, your job right now is recuperating. After that, you can come work at the jewelry shop."

"That's not a bad idea, Kev', I think you can give up on the golf-pro idea now."

"Thanks, Paul, but I have a better idea right now, and it involves getting you out of here so I can enjoy this beautiful young lady and have some dinner."

The officers will be outside, and I'll be back in the morning," Paul said on his way out.

Heels clicked, and they could still hear them echoing outside after the door closed. It was the first time in two days they had been alone together. It felt wonderful.

Chapter Forty-five

After three days of bed arrest, Kevin was able to pad down the hall clutching his IV holder. It had four wheels, at least one of which had been produced by the same people that make shopping carts. He took refuge at a window near the front of St. Mary's hospital, and scrutinized a family in the courtyard. A young mother was in a wheelchair, cradling a speck of a newborn, while its brother and sister played in the sun. He loitered, allowing the comely scene to soak into his pores.

"You done down there?" a gravely voice asked from the hall near Kevin's room.

"Yes," Kevin intoned, "thanks for the break."

The officer sank back down to his chair in the hall as Kevin walked gingerly past. His leg muscles had withered quickly, and his motion was stunted. He avoided the bed and approached the small window overlooking the roof and duct work.

Karen had been allowed to go home for the first time, and Kevin tried to enjoy his seclusion. So far the only charge against them was use of an unlicensed firearm. The District Attorney of Washoe County had told them to expect Kevin to be arrested for his connection with the slaying of Steven Lester, but their attorney Jim Kelley had scoffed at that possible charge.

There was a knock on the doorframe, just a tiny, hollow sound. Kevin swiveled slowly to see Becky at the door. Her blue eyes matched the flowers she held, and as she talked, her nose scrunched-up and those same eyes did a vanishing act.

"Can I come in?" She asked gingerly.

"Sure, where's Karen."

"Down in the gift shop again. She wants something else to bring you for the last day of your stay."

"Last day, are they really going to discharge me?" Kevin's eyes rushed past Becky as though he could see the family outside again.

"That's what Paul thinks." she exclaimed as her eyes disappeared again.

They talked for a few more minutes. Mostly about the food, the color of the room, and what good care he was getting, staying on the surface until Karen joined them. She had changed into a light spring dress which hung loosely on her frame.

Sweeping into the room with more flowers, she glided up to Kevin with an entrancing aura about her. She twirled in front of him, then gave him a lush kiss.

"You, are getting out," she giggled, while Kevin nodded. "In fact, you get to go home with me in the morning." Her smile was luminous.

Kevin reached out his arm and grabbed her waist. The IV went into alarm mode, and a nurse came by to check.

"Just happy, honest," Kevin told her.

The room got quiet again and Becky found a place for the two new floral additions, before taking a seat.

Kevin turned towards the door at the sound of leather soles. It was Paul, and he had conjured-up a pizza from The Max in Sparks. The savory aroma settled into the room. "Does this mean I am a free man?" Kevin asked.

"In the morning we will pull the officer off the door, and you will be allowed to go home if your doctor releases you," Paul stated, while lifting the box lid and allowing the full power of the pizza to escape.

"My home, Paul," Karen said.

"You know, Kevin, you were the perfect fall-guy for what happened the last few weeks, especially with Tolan getting paid-off," Paul stated, his head rattling in disbelief. "You really crawled-out from under."

"No, I *pulled* him out," Karen insisted, "he is only safe with me."

"Well," said Paul. "You are not completely in the clear…like I said, the investigation is going to take a long time. You know, the Royal won't be shutdown by Gaming Control during their investigation. There may be some statistical anomalies, but they aren't rushing to have such events besmirch the entire gaming industry of Nevada. It would help your case a lot if we could find the tape you say you had."

"I don't know, Paul. I would have sworn I still had it in my pocket when we got to the shooting scene. It must have fallen-out somewhere along the way."

"Yeah, we've had officers all along the route you took from the roof. No luck."

Chapter Forty-six

Kevin enjoyed looking into the backyard of Karen's house. It was a pleasure to see trees and the mountains beyond, after being cooped-up in the hospital for the past week, not to mention months upon months in the tiny surveillance room at work.

The right side of his body had healed, the left side was still confined by the airplane-splint. The ache was dull and continuous, he did not care for the pain-killers. It was better to have his mind sharp and put up with the pain than be addled both physically and mentally.

Karen buzzed around the room when she was home, and not on the phone. Becky and Karen were plotting a vacation for the four adults as soon as Paul was able to get away, presuming that all charges were dropped against Kevin.

Kevin found himself alone, again, a week after being released from the hospital. Karen had gone off to work, and when the phone rang, Kevin sprang himself up from the recliner and answered it.

"Hey, this Kevin?"

"Yes."

"Kev', listen, your car is ready. Looks sharp as new. You want I should bring it over to ya?"

"Mickey, that would be great. Shit. I am so sick of being inside. Are you coming right over?"

"Soon as I take my coverall's off."

"Thanks, see you soon."

The world brightened.

"Mickey, you old shit-kicker. Where did you call me from, the corner?"

"No, I was at the shop. I might'ta give her a little kick in the ass, just to clean-out the carb' a little."

"Right. Man, I suddenly feel great."

"Knew you'd feel better with wheels. You should be able to drive her with the top down."

Mickey was right, no problem. Kevin took Mickey back to the Dent-N-Rent shop and found that Karen had already paid the bill. He then drove around town for an hour with no destination, just enjoying the sun. Eventually the newly painted MG found its way to Grayson's, and Kevin walked into the shop.

He waved at the assistant manager and crinkled his brow. A shaking thumb told Kevin that Karen was in back. Walking carefully to avoid banging anything with the crazy splint and his arm sticking forward, Kevin slipped into the back room to surprise Karen.

"No, no, it is not what was expected, but he will stay until he does not stay any longer. She had a shot and missed, this is cleaner anyway. It is was very tough working with her, I really do not think the information was worth the trouble, she…"

Kevin cleared his throat and said, "Hi, Honey".

"Listen, I have got to go. Call me next week."

"Who was that?" Kevin asked.

"Oh, my mom. She is still worried about the charges against you, and me. She will be fine, though."

"Yeah. I got the car back, you didn't have to pay for the damages you know."

"Consider it an early Christmas present. You need to have a spiffy car to drive around in, but since you love that old MG, well…………"

"Hey, that's no way to talk about one of my best friends. That car and I have been through thick and thick together."

"Well, I hope you are happy with the color."

"Looks great. Lunch?"

"I really can't. I will make a nice dinner tonight, though. Paul and Becky are coming over about 7 p.m."

"Sounds great. I'm gon'na head back home and get some rest."

"See you tonight, dear."

She blew him a kiss, but he ducked, then winked. He then caught himself against the door-jam, dizzy.

There was a ticket on his windshield when Kevin got back to the street. Twenty-five bucks for forgetting to drop a dime.

"What the hell, I don't have any money anyway," Kevin said as he slid gingerly back into the car. He waited for the traffic to slow, then eased back onto the road. The trip home became a half-hour drive as the car followed Kevin's thoughts and drifted along.

Once back inside, Kevin went to the closet and looked at the clothes that had been returned by the dry cleaners. There was the pair of pants, and a shirt he had borrowed from Jeri in Carson City. "What the hell am I thinking, the nylon jacket I wore wouldn't be here, Toni blew a hole in it." Kevin shook his head, wondering why he wasn't thinking more clearly.

After getting a glass of water in the kitchen, he rummaged around aimlessly. When he came across his prescriptions from the hospital he read each label carefully. The Percocet he had refused to continue taking was almost gone. The prescription was for 28 capsules, to be taken four-per day. There were only two left in the bottle.

The phone rang and Kevin put the bottle back in the third drawer down to the left of the sink.

"Hello."

"Yeah, don't say anything but yes or no. You know who this is?"

"Yeah."

"Listen, you got some serious problems, man. You realize that?"

"Well, things are looking better."

"No, listen here, Lee Harvey, you better meet me. You remember the last place we talked."

"Uh, well, up on…"

"Shut-up. Food, right?"

"Yeah, I…

"Be there at four and see Tim at the bar." Kevin heard a dial tone and hung-up the phone.

"Well, Tolan is sure being secretive." He busied himself for any hour, then headed to the Italian Restaurant looking over the city. When he arrived and talked to Tim, he was told to wait at the end of the bar. In a few minutes, the phone next to him rang, he looked over at Tim, who nodded.

"Hello?"

"Hey, sorry, but Tim tells me you got a brace on your arm. No way to sneak you out of there."

"Yup, it's a little awkward."

"Well, just listen, then. This phone is safe, but you got police watching you."

"Yeah, it's no big deal."

"Yes, it is. Why didn't you call me?"

"Hey, I figure my phone is probably tapped, and you got paid, so there was no hurry."

"Sure I got paid, aren't you worried about that."

Kevin twisted in his seat and listened for another minute, then put his head in his hands and breathed-in and out as though he had just run a hundred-yard dash.

Chapter Forty-seven

The dinner party at Karen's house was a chore. Kevin was impressed that Paul was willing to be seen with him, but unnerved when Becky stated they had been talking and concluded that maybe it was time for Paul to retire. They had done well in the stock market, and he had a good retirement. Kevin crashed at 8:30 and headed into the bedroom. He could still hear his friend's muffled voices, they laughed a lot.

Kevin felt as though he had slipped back two weeks and had no clue as to what was going on. He tried to listen to the conversation in the living room, but sleep overcame him.

In the morning, once Karen had gone off to work, Kevin haunted the third-drawer down again. There was a new bottle of Percocet. He dumped the pills on the counter and counted, 18.

Kevin placed a call to his father.

"Hello, Son. Are you feeling better?"

"Yes, Dad. I appreciate your calling twice while I was in the hospital. I know that was tough, I know you're disappointed in me."

"Nonsense, you're my son."

"No, really. I know what you think. Listen, I'm disappointed in me. Hey, I'm 38-years old, don't have a family, been married twice, drive a car that's about as old as I am……"

"You feeling sorry for yourself?"

"No, I'm looking at things realistically, I'm at an age where I have to be honest with myself and admit I'm not the brightest guy in the world. I, …I need your help."

"You're the one went off to college, never came back."

"You're the one who told me to make my own way, be a man."

"Never said to forget your heritage, never said to give-up on yourself. I been waitin' almost 40-years for you to ask for my help. Well?"

"I'm a shit, huh?"

"Sometimes, now what'cha want."

The events of the past month spilled-out of Kevin's chest, leaving him space to breath for the first time in what seemed a lifetime. When he got to the part about putting a camera in his neighbor's downstairs apartment he waited for a lecture. It never came.

"My son ain't no patsy, you been set-up, but you ain't taking the fall. You talk to that woman of yours about the pills, and listen closely. See if she gets mad, or is all lovey-dovey about takin' care of you. If she's mad, or gets frustrated with you, well, you're probably safe. If she just turns on the charm, be careful. And don't confront her about the tape that could be hittin' too close to home. And, Son, don't ask her about what the bookie told you, about the accountant in Carson City bein' connected. She hears that and you won't know who to trust, and you won't know who paid-off that bookie, either."

"Thanks, Dad. I'll call you next week. No, I don't need to come down there and stay with you right now, but thanks."

Kevin struggled the twenty-steps to the bed. He lay across the bedspread, not bothering to get under the covers. When Karen came home, she cooked him a steak, and cut the meat for him. By nine that night they were both asleep.

Kevin inhaled the breakfast Karen brought him in the morning, before she headed to work. He fell asleep in the recliner, then awoke, groggy. Blinking, Kevin staggered into the kitchen and hit the third drawer. The cap was secretive, and wouldn't budge, but Kevin put-up a good fight and the lid finally popped-off, the pills scattering across the floor.

Down on his knees, Kevin tried to find all the pills. Surely there were plenty hiding, for he could only find six. He leaned his head against the cool tile, rested, and listened to the waterfall.

"What are you doing, sweetheart?" Karen asked, a disarming smile working across her red lips as she came to Kevin's side, and put an arm around him.

"The pills, I dropped the pills."

"So I see. Let me help you. You should relax, take a nice bath."

The bathwater running could be heard clearly now.

"What's with the pills?" Kevin sighed, I wasn't taking anymore," he said while trying to catch his breath.

"Honey, I've been helping you. They have been in your food. You need to relax. Let me help you up." Karen pulled at Kevin's side, proving to be stronger than he expected.

"No, no more pills." Kevin fought against being picked-up and asked slowly, as though talking through cotton, "Where's the fucking tape?"

"You will not talk to me like that, you need to get in the bathtub, now get-up," Karen insisted.

She twisted at his left arm, pulling the splint towards his chest. The pain seared into Kevin, and he tried to crawl away.

"You are a joke, you can't even stand-up," Karen said in a tone that both mocked and pitied him. Then she kicked him from behind and Kevin was face-down on the hard tile. Stitches popped along his side and bicep as the splint folded in front of him. Blood immediately leaked through his shirt and onto the floor.

"Now I'm going to have to clean that up. You are going to get up this very instant."

Her words were still moving to Kevin's ears as he asked weakly, "Where did you put the tape?"

"I thought your father told you not to ask me about that. You shouldn't have made any phone calls from here, honey. Now, you do not ever need to worry about the *fucking tape*. You are going to take a nice long bath, a forever bath," Karen yelled. She grabbed Kevin's left leg and spun him around the kitchen table, knocking two of the chairs over. His left arm was locked underneath him, his right trying desperately to grab a hold of the floor.

As they came towards the bedroom door, Karen suddenly twisted Kevin's leg, causing him to flip over onto his back. A short shot to his face from her boot snapped his head back. "Now I will have to say you fell into the bath, you didn't just fall asleep and drown," Karen said, while giving him a second kick. "The bruises won't matter, remember, you fell."

Kevin lay still, as though a bear were sniffing him. His breathing was furious, but he shut his eyes and stopped flailing about.

"That's more like it. Pill's finally taking effect, huh?"

She pulled him through the door and across the hardwood floor. The bathwater was already spilling down the overflow drain and Karen slammed his leg down. She walked to the edge of the tub and shoved a washcloth against it to stop the draining, then returned to his motionless body.

"It's all over, honey. Just enjoy the warmth."

Karen got down on her knees and pulled Kevin's shoulders up to get him into a sitting position, then pushed him towards the water. When he was against the tub, she raised up and cradled him in her arms, then pushed upwards with her legs. They were slow dancing.

She moved her left leg into position to drop him into the tub, and as she did, he opened his eyes.

"No bath," Kevin cried, bringing his left arm down over Karen's shoulder. There was a loud snap and Kevin screamed in pain as the splint snapped into a locked position against his body, her arm underneath it.

"I should have let Toni shoot you more than once," Karen hissed into Kevin's ear, while kicking her leg against him.

"Bullshit, you wanted us both dead," Kevin said.

"Right, and it's still going to happen!" Karen yelled, trying to spin out of his grip. Her boots lost the battle with the wet tile and they crashed backwards into the tub. Water drenched them as Kevin kicked at the wall, Karen underneath him. He tried to push himself out of the tub, but a strong arm reached around his neck crushing his windpipe and holding him down. The water was over his head. He swallowed a mouthful and continued kicking.

Karen struggled to rollout from under him, but the tub was small. Kevin jammed a foot under the faucet and pushed backwards, knowing she couldn't last much longer underwater. The next thirty-seconds were literally a lifetime, and when her grip loosened, she was gone.

Wrenching his neck from her right arm, air became the most wonderful thing in Kevin's world. He coughed heavily, water coming from his lungs and out into the bathwater. He shook his head and tried to sit up. The water, continuing to rise, lapped at his chin. The dead weight behind him refused to budge, his body and the splint wedged into the tub.

Writhing in the water, Kevin worked feverishly to get the splint to pop back into the upright position. Wearily, his right arm struggled against the metal. Water traveled up his nose, gagging him. Air rushed out of his lungs and he resisted the urge to gasp, the water now over his eyes. Kevin kicked again at the faucet, trying to twist himself out of the tub, and tasted his blood in the water. His will faded, his strength was gone. He was sleepy, he would dream.

There was a muted "pop" and his left arm was once more pointed upward. There was no pain this time, and Kevin tried to see through bloodied eyes.

"Kevin, keep breathing, keep breathing," an old friend said.

"Get him on the floor and I'll get her out of there," another voice said.

Sounds rushed around Kevin, but he couldn't stay awake.

Minutes later Kevin was able to understand the words spoken to him by Paul Kozar. Beside him was a body bag. It was occupied.

"Kevin, just keep breathing. You're doing fine. You need to have a little work done on your side again. We're taking you back to St. Joseph's hospital." Paul was talking directly and slowly.

"Hell of a month I've had. Funny thing is, she was the best woman I've been with, maybe ever."

"Murder's are usually done out of necessity, like the money she needed," Paul stated.

"Paul? How did you know?" asked Kevin.

"Detective work. That's my job. Plus your father called."

"I'll be dammed," Kevin said solemnly.

"Probably, but for now you've got a few good years left. We knew the accountant was connected, and when we found out the jewelry business she owned had been in serious financial trouble a year ago and was suddenly out of debt, well, we got lucky. I figured I'd just drop by and talk with you. Simpson, here, came along for the ride. You got lucky. I miss a light on the way over and………"

"All right, I owe you a favor. Thank you, very much."

"Just make me a promise, when you go out to look for a job next month, don't apply at the police department. I can't keep showing up to saving your ass, you know."

"Fair enough," Kevin said wearily. "How about if I become a private detective?"

Paul shook his head and told the paramedics, "Go easy on him, he's not a well man."

They put him on a stretcher and wheeled him outside while he faded off to sleep, dreaming about being Robin Hood, and stealing from bandits.